TR...
DEATH IS SWEET.
THE DEAD SHALL RISE,
THE LIVING TO EAT.
BORN IN HELL,
NONE SHALL QUELL
THE EVIL BRED
FOR MAN'S DEATH KNELL.

PRANK NIGHT

Dying is no trick—
or treat.

PRANK NIGHT

DAVID ROBBINS

LEISURE BOOKS NEW YORK CITY

To Judy, Joshua, and Shane.
Also, to Craig and Jeff, two wild and crazy guys.

A LEISURE BOOK®

October 1994

Published by

Dorchester Publishing Co., Inc.
276 Fifth Avenue
New York, NY 10001

Printed in the United States of America.

*The evil that men do lives after them;
the good is oft interred with their bones.*
—William Shakespeare

PRANK NIGHT

Chapter One

The bellow rumbled through the Walker house like an ominous thunderclap. "Johnny, get out here. Now!"

Twelve-year-old Johnny Walker set down the comic book he had been reading and sat up in his bed. A tingle of fear shot down his spine. He knew his father's tone all too well; he was in for it because he had done something wrong. But although he racked his brain, young Johnny couldn't think of what it might be.

"Did you hear me, boy? Haul your skinny ass to the living room before I come back there and drag you out!"

Panic caused Johnny's heart to flutter wildly. He dashed to his door, flung it wide, and hurried down the hallway. If he kept his father waiting, he knew his punishment would only be worse. He had to do exactly as he was told. It was too bad his mother was at work since she often spoke up for him when his father got mad.

The living room reeked of beer and other stale odors. Horace Walker roosted in his frayed easy chair, a can of his favorite brand in his brawny right hand. He lifted his bloodshot eyes as the boy entered, then grinned in smug satisfaction at the terror the boy barely held in check. Long ago Horace had learned that the key to keeping his kid in line was the wide belt around his waist. Ten or 20 licks was all it took, and the boy would behave like a perfect angel for five or six months at a stretch. "Took you long enough," Horace grumbled. "What the hell were you doing?"

"Reading," Johnny answered without thinking. Inwardly, he flinched at his mistake.

"Reading what?" Horace demanded, but went on before his son could answer. "As if I can't guess. It's those stupid comics again, isn't it? The ones about those silly superjerks?"

Despite himself, Johnny said, "Comic's aren't stupid, Dad." Since his eighth birthday, when his uncle had bought him a dozen comic books, Johnny had read every one he could get his hands on. His small collection was his pride and joy. When his parents were going at each other tooth and nail, he'd close himself in his room and lose himself in the adventures of one of his heroes. "Miss Kelton says they're food for the imagination."

"Spare me, boy," Horace said. It galled him to no end that his only son would rather read about goofy-looking men in tights than go out and play football or baseball with friends. "Little Miss Goody-Goody has her head in the clouds. Imagination doesn't put food on the table or clothes on your back. That crap you read has nothing to do with the real world."

"She says—"

"I didn't call you out here to argue about that bimbo," Horace snapped. "She's a teacher, for crying out loud. She doesn't really work for a living, so what would she know?"

He drummed his fingers on the arm of his chair in irritation. It was bad enough his wife stood up for the kid. If not for Mabel, he would have ripped all his son's comics to shreds years ago. But Mabel had warned him to leave the boy be in that regard; she said that every child should have a hobby and comics were Johnny's. Since he and his wife fought about enough as it was, Horace went along with her wishes even though sometimes his son's weird passion sorely tried his patience.

"Why did you want me?" Johnny quickly asked to change the subject.

"Take a look around the room. See if you can guess."

Johnny glanced at the TV, which was tuned to a Seahawks football game; then he looked at the worn furniture and the ratty carpet. None of his clothes nor any of his few toys were lying anywhere. "Everything looks okay to me."

"Look again, dimwit. Over in the corner." Horace jabbed a thick thumb at the one in question.

The door to the wood stove hung partway open and Johnny saw glowing coals inside. He remembered that his parents always insisted on closing the door to prevent smoke from filling the room. "I didn't leave it open like that," he said, protesting his innocence.

"Duh," Horace said with an exaggerated slur. "Where the hell were you when they gave out brains, boy? I opened the damn door so I could put in a few more logs. But I was wasting my time. Can you figure out why?"

The bin to the right of the stove was empty. Johnny nervously licked his lips and said, "I'm sorry. I forgot to bring in more logs this afternoon."

"Seems to me you forget an awful lot," Horace said, then took a sip of beer, "but only when it suits your purpose. You're real good at forgetting chores, but I never see you forget to go to Iguana once a month to buy a miserable comic."

"I'll fill the bin right now," Johnny offered, his fear returning as he noted a flinty cast to his father's features. The last time he'd forgotten to fill the woodbox, his dad had whipped him something terrible.

"You do that," Horace said sarcastically. "And put on a coat, moron. It's cold out."

Scooting to the wooden pegs by the back door, Johnny donned his green coat. A blast of chill wind drew him up short on the large redwood deck and he pulled up his collar to protect his neck. He'd heard the weatherman on television say that cold weather would last another day or two at the most, and he couldn't wait for the warm weather. Not that he minded the cold. It simply meant he would have one less chore to do each day.

Twenty yards from the rear of the house stood the huge pile of logs his father had stockpiled for the winter. An old tarp covered the top of the pile to keep out the rain. Johnny untied one end and began filling his arms. He carried five logs inside and went back out for more. As he reached for the top log, a twig snapped loudly in the forest bordering the Walker yard.

Johnny shifted and stared at the inky wall of trees and dense brush. His friend Freddy had told him that a black bear had been seen recently at the west end of Knob Road. Nervous, he waited and listened, and sure enough, another twig snapped. He backed up a step toward the mobile and heard the *crunch-crunch-crunch* of heavy footsteps.

Pivoting on a heel, Johnny dashed inside. He was in the living room before he quite realized what he was doing. His father glared at him.

"What's the matter with you? You look as if you'd just seen a ghost," Horace said. He shook his head in disgust. The boy was such a baby that Horace found it hard to believe that Johnny came from his loins. Practically everyone in Cemetery Ridge knew that Horace had served in the Marines 20 years earlier. It was a fact Horace mentioned often. He never bothered to elaborate, to point out that he had worked in the mess hall and had seldom carried a weapon, let alone used one.

"I think there's a bear in the woods," Johnny said, hoping his father would allow him to finish filling the bin later. Bears were nothing to sneeze at. His dad had told him so many times.

"Oh, bull," Horace said and grinned. "It's your imagination. It's what happens when you read as much of that science fiction crap as you do."

"I heard footsteps," Johnny said. "In the trees close to the yard."

Horace regarded his son a few moments. As much as he disliked the kid's childish ways, he had to admit that the boy rarely lied, even when lying would spare Johnny a licking. "Maybe it was a stray dog."

"No. It's too big. Come and listen for yourself."

The last thing Horace Walker cared to do was step out into the cold. But since there was a commercial on the tube and he'd polished off the brew and needed to grab another, he sighed and pushed his ponderous bulk erect. "All right, scaredy-cat. But I'm telling you now. If nothing is out there, I'm taking away your comics for a whole month."

Johnny gulped. As much as he feared being whipped, he feared having his comics confiscated even more. He could hardly stand to be

14

without them. Fortunately, his father preferred to beat him. Once, however, about a year ago, his dad had taken his box of comics for a whole week; that week had been the longest of Johnny's life. And when Johnny got back, he'd been appalled to find two of his favorite comics had been ripped in half. An accident, his dad had claimed, but Johnny knew better.

Horace saw the dread his threat inspired and chuckled. Once day, Mabel or no, he was going to take that damned box and burn it to ashes. He'd teach the boy to grow up whether the boy wanted to or not. Kids couldn't be kids forever. They had to learn to face up to life and not escape into idle fantasy worlds.

Stepping to the screen door, Horace peered out into the chill night. He listened for a minute, but the only sound he heard was the wind rustling the trees. "I knew it," he said gruffly. "There's nothing out here."

Just then, as if on cue, a distinct crackling arose in the firs and pines lining their property. Horace started and cocked his head to catch every sound. There was something in the woods, and judging by the racket, it had to be big. He looked at Johnny, who gave him an I-told-you-so smile.

"What do you think it is?" Johnny asked.

Horace had no idea, but it could well be a bear. Knob Road, on which their house was located, ran parallel to an 8,000-acre tract under the supervision of the Bureau of Land Management. Wildlife abounded. There were plenty of black bears but the dumb brutes rarely bothered the local residents. "I think you're right, son."

"I am?" Johnny said, amazed his father would admit as much. "What do we do? Call the police?"

"Don't be ridiculous," Horace said. "I'll chase it off myself."

"You will?"

"Watch and learn." Horace noticed his son's astonishment and grinned slyly. The boy would think he was the bravest man alive, going out into the dark to confront the beast. Johnny didn't know that most black bears were afraid to death of humans. At the sight of people, black bears headed for the hills just as fast as their legs could move.

Horace wasn't about to tell the boy. It wasn't often he could impress Johnny, so he intended to milk the situation for all it was worth. "You just be ready to call Chief Sinclair in case it gets me."

Johnny Walker glanced out the door. As much as he disliked his father, the thought of his dad being ripped to shreds tightened his stomach into a hard knot. They'd shared some happy times, after all, back before the logging business went sour. His father's hadn't always been so mean to him. "Maybe we should just leave it alone. It might wander off all on its own."

"And have it come on back again one day soon when I'm not around to look after you or your mother?" Horace said. "Not on your life. If I chase it off now, it'll know to stay away from our place."

Horace crushed the empty beer can to show his strength, then turned and stepped to a closet. Propped behind a row of coats was his .30-06. He had to rummage around to find the box of shells.

Johnny stepped nearer the door. The sounds had died out, which meant, he hoped, that the bear had already gone elsewhere. He watched his dad load the rifle and wished more than ever that his mother were home. She wouldn't let his dad pull a fool stunt like this. "I think it left," he said.

"You never know with bears," Horace said, trying to sound like an expert. Secretly he had his fingers crossed that the beast had left. Timid as black bears were, they could get nasty when cornered. He took his time inserting the bullets, and when he was done, he aligned the coats and neatly arranged the items he had moved aside while rummaging about, something he would never ordinarily do. Housework was for women—that was his motto. And any man who thought differently wasn't a real man at all.

Horace worked the bolt, injecting a round into the chamber. He saw his son giving him a strange look; worried that Johnny might think he had gotten cold feet, he barreled out the door. Almost immediately he wished he hadn't. The white T-shirt he wore barely fit over his bulging belly and had a hole under his left arm big enough to drop a baseball through.

The breeze bit into him like an invisible icicle, causing goose bumps to break out all over his skin.

Johnny followed his father outdoors. He deliberately let the screen door slam shut behind him so that the bear would hear and perhaps leave if it hadn't already. But his good deed drew a withering look from his dad.

"Make a little more noise, why don't you?" Horace said. "That way the damn bear will be sure to know I'm coming."

"Don't go," Johnny said, bothered by an uneasy feeling. "Stay until Mom gets home."

"I don't need your mother to hold my hand, thank you," Horace said, miffed that his own flesh and blood lacked confidence in him.

Squaring his sloped shoulders, he walked toward the woods. He made sure to hold the rifle level at his waist and to keep his finger on the trigger. A .30-06 could drop any black bear that ever lived, and the knowledge restored some of his flagging courage.

Young Johnny nervously bit his lower lip and raised a hand to call out. But he changed his mind. His dad would only get madder if he interfered again. Besides, he told himself, his father should be all right, carrying that high-powered rifle and all.

It was a very jittery Horace Walker who paused at the tree line to look back at his son. Horace could tell the boy was worried, and it warmed his heart to know that Johnny really cared. Horace almost turned back, almost

18

decided to leave the stupid bear alone. But if he did, he wouldn't be able to hold his head high around his boy. If he gave up without setting foot into the forest, Johnny might think he was a coward.

So, breaking out in a cold sweat, Horace entered the gloomy woods. He took small strides and stopped every few feet to look and listen. The forest had gone deathly quiet; it was as still as a graveyard. Horace halted after going all of eight feet and looked to learn if his son could still see him. If not, he planned to stay right where he was for about two minutes, then stroll on out and announce the bear had gone. To his dismay, he saw that Johnny had advanced halfway across the backyard and was still in plain sight.

"Damn dumb kid," Horace muttered, stepping to the right, where a high bush would hide him. He stood in its black shadow and peeked through the small branches. The boy had stopped and was anxiously scanning the vicinity. This would show him, Horace thought. This would prove there was more to his old man than he ever suspected.

Horace was so tickled at proving his manhood to his son that it took a few seconds for the sounds he was hearing to sink in. Suddenly the muted crackle of brush registered. Stiffening, he gazed into the depths of the woods, his goose bumps seeming to grow to the size of golf balls. The bear had not left. Worse, it appeared to be prowling closer to where he stood.

Twin drums commenced beating in Horace's temples. His breath caught in his throat and his knees buckled. He heard a strange clacking sound, then realized his teeth were chattering. Clamping his mouth shut tightly, he raised the .30-06 to his shoulder. One shot was all it would take, he assured himself. And even if he missed, the blast would drive the bear back into the murky wilderness where it belonged.

The crackling grew steadily louder. Horace took a few deep breaths to steady his nerves. He was embarrassed by his fleeting fear. Here he was, a grown man, a former Marine. What the hell did he have to be afraid of? he asked himself.

As near as Horace could tell, the bear was about 25 yards to the southwest. Crouching down so the animal wouldn't spy him before he spotted it, he waited, tense with anticipation. He had to remember to shoot at the head, not the body. In the dark it would be next to impossible to hit the heart and he had to drop the beast with the very first shot. A wounded bear was highly dangerous; it might rip into him before he brought it down.

The next moment the noise stopped and did not resume.

Horace had a thought that cheered him. Maybe the bear had caught his scent, or maybe it had caught sight of the light above the deck and was slinking off. Bears could move like ghosts when they wanted to. Horace grinned as he glanced at the boy, who appeared ready to keel over from fright at any second.

The truth be known, Johnny Walker was filled with fear for his father, not for himself. He believed his dad to be in great danger. The resentment he always felt, spawned by years of accumulated bitterness, was momentarily gone.

Yes, Horace treated Johnny badly, but Horace was still the boy's father, and that fact counted for more than all the beatings and tongue-lashings. As few good times as there had been, Johnny remembered every one and cherished the memories dearly. They fueled the flickering embers of his love, which no amount of abuse could extinguish.

So now, with his father nowhere in sight and the woods grown eerily silent, Johnny did the one thing that those who knew him best would have thought the very last act he would ever do; he moved toward the trees so he could be close enough to help if his father were attacked. He had gone but half the distance when the strangest sensation he ever felt rooted him in place.

It was as if a bolt of electricity zapped Johnny from clear out of the blue. From head to toe the boy quivered violently. A sharp tingle shot down his spine, not once, but again and again and again. He was jolted to his core and had no idea why.

Confused, Johnny opened his mouth to yell for his dad, but no sound came out. His vocal cords were frozen as surely as if they were encased in ice. And then the strangest thing of all happened. Unbidden and unwanted, chilling words flashed through his mind, words spoken in an alien voice laced with sinister intent.

"The feast! The sweet feast!"

At first Johnny figured that he had imagined the words, but then the same bizarre voice spoke again.

"After all this time! The nectar will be mine!"

Johnny looked all around, thinking that someone must be nearby. It occurred to him that the whole affair might be a practical joke staged by one of his friends. Eddy Webster would be just the type to pull such a bone-headed stunt. But Johnny sincerely hoped not. Given his father's notorious temper, Johnny would be made to pay for their antics. But no one else was there—not Eddy, not Jake, not George, not any of his buddies. And he realized that blaming them was a dumb notion since none of his friends would dare waltz around in the woods after sunset. Yet if they weren't to blame, where had the voice come from?

Horace Walker was asking himself the same question. He still couldn't hear the bear or see anything moving in the undergrowth. But he had heard a threatening voice, speaking, as it were, inside his own head—an experience so utterly unexpected and so startling that Horace had no idea what to make of it. He shrugged the voice off, thinking his imagination had played a trick on him. Then it happened again.

"Such hunger! Such need!"

Those last words seemed to peel in Horace's skull like claps of thunder. He heard nothing other than the breeze, which compounded the mystery and made him wonder if he should cut back on his beer guzzling. Words didn't just pop into a person's head, he reminded himself. There had to be a perfectly logical explanation.

So disturbed was Horace by the shock of having alien thoughts intrude into his brain that for a full five seconds he failed to notice that the crackling had resumed. When he did notice, he half rose, the short hairs at the nape of his neck prickling. The bear was coming straight toward him!

Panic-stricken, Horace backed up. He forgot about the bush behind him and collided with it, his right foot becoming entangled. Anxious to get free, he wrenched hard, but instead of being released, he lost his balance and fell. He threw both hands behind him to cushion the impact. In so doing he accidentally swung the rifle against the bush and lost his grip. The .30-06 clattered beside him as he landed on his backside, hurting nothing except his dignity.

"Damn idiot!" Horace chided himself and reached for the gun.

At that moment, the pines directly across from the bush parted, bending to either side as if pushed by gigantic hands. Something snorted.

Horace Walker looked up and blanched. He had to tilt back to see the awful, grotesque head of the menacing creature looming like a huge grizzly above him. Dazed by the sight, speechless with abject fear, he felt his insides churn and his heart pound like a jackhammer.

The thing moved, striding into the open.

Panic riveted Horace a few seconds more. Then he tried to lunge for the rifle, but his body seemed to be moving of its own accord and, worse, in slow motion, as if he was trying to reach for something while underwater. He almost closed his finger on the stock. Then a searing, brilliant light exploded within his mind and he couldn't move a muscle or do anything at all. Above him, the creature bent down, and for the first time Horace saw its features clearly. For the first time he saw its teeth.

Not far away, Johnny Walker was galvanized into action by the stark shriek of mortal terror that issued from his father's throat. Somehow it broke the paralysis that had rooted Johnny to the ground and he dashed into the forest, shouting, "Dad! Dad! Dad!"

He saw something move and dug in his heels. Then he spotted his father. At the same instant, a great, blinding flash of light flared into his brain, and although he wanted to scream, he couldn't. All he could do was watch in horror.

Chapter Two

Benjamin J. Shields was going home after a nine-year absence and he didn't know whether to be glad or upset. As he cruised at the speed limit down I-5, he turned the dial on the car radio, trying to pick up a Grants Pass station. He'd already passed Roseburg, and in high school, he'd often listened to a rock station that could be heard at least that far away. At the point on the dial where the rock station should be, however, the voice of a popular conservative commentator rumbled out. Heard in stereo, booming from the twin speakers in his van, the voice sounded as if the man were perched in the passenger seat.

"Times change," Ben said wryly to himself and clicked the radio off. He decided his time would be better spent steeling his nerves for the ordeal to come. The thought brought a frown of self-reproach. He had no reason to be so hard on his family. They could have changed. He had, hadn't he? So why did he feel as if he were Daniel being sent to the lions?

The question sparked a smile. It had been a long time since Ben had thought about anything having to do with the Bible, and he wondered if it was coincidence or whether the prospect of seeing his great-aunt again had something to do with it. Aunt Agatha had been strict about Bible studies.

Ben spied a state patrol vehicle parked on the shoulder of the road ahead and automatically glanced at the speedometer to verify he wasn't speeding. Although he had a reputation among his friends for being the slowest driver on the face of the planet, he had a knack for getting speeding tickets. Whenever he lapsed and went more than five miles an hour over the limit, he was sure to get a ticket. It was as if a vengeful genie took perverse delight in making him out to be a dope with a leaden foot when the opposite was the case.

Ben grinned when the trooper aimed a radar detector at him. Go head, he mused. Do your worst. He lowered his hand to his side and happened to brush against the small pile of books nestled next to his leg. They were his masterpieces—four copies each of the two novels he'd had published. He'd promised his mother he would bring them. And while he should be proud, he was filled with worry over how the books would be received.

In due course Ben came over the crest of a mountain and saw Grants Pass unfold before him. The city had grown by leaps and bounds since last he'd been home; the number of new buildings surprised him. He somehow had gotten it into his head that the city would always be as quaint as he so fondly remembered.

"Progress," Ben muttered. He drove past the first exit although he was keenly tempted to take it and go off in search of former pals. But he couldn't. Not this day. His family didn't live there. He had to go on, to the last town on earth he wanted to visit, to the place he had once dubbed the armpit of western civilization.

Cemetery Ridge lay halfway between Grants Pass and the town of Rogue River, on a ridge a mile to the east of the river by that name. It had been built on the site of a battle between the U.S. Army and the Cayuse Indians—a fact that had never failed to amaze Ben. How anyone in his right mind could think of starting a town on a battleground was beyond him.

Even more bewildering, Cemetery Ridge had prospered during its early years. First the town was a mining community, and its coffers had been filled by those who flocked there after gold was found in the creek that wound along its base. Later, after the mine closed down, logging had been the backbone of the community until the spotted-owl controversy turned the loggers themselves into an endangered species.

Ben had left Cemetery Ridge long before the owl flap. But he had been kept informed by his younger brother, who still wrote on occasion. Jeff claimed that the town was deader than ever, which Ben found preposterous. When he'd gone off to make his way in the world, Cemetery Ridge had been, in his opinion, the dullest spot in all creation. It wasn't possible for it to get any worse.

Or so Ben thought until he came to the exit and wheeled to the bottom of the short ramp. Right away he noticed there was hardly any traffic, which was odd in the middle of the afternoon. Turning left, he wound along the pine-lined road until he came to the fork he remembered so well.

The left branch went along the bottom of the ridge, flanking Gardner Creek, named after the grizzled old prospector who found gold there over 100 years earlier. The other fork led up into the heart of Cemetery Ridge. Simmons Boulevard, it was called, after the man who built the trading post that one day blossomed into the town.

Ben turned up the boulevard. The tall firs that he recalled were still there, standing like silent sentinels, guarding the approach to the cultural fortress of solitude above. He passed a few frame homes, a few mobile homes, and an old mansion built back at the turn of the century by a timber king named Victor Richards.

The outskirts of Cemetery Ridge began a few hundred yards farther on. The ridge itself was over two miles long and the town took up most of it. Lining the crest were the squat buildings that made up the business district. Farther along were the dozen or so huge homes belonging to the town's elite. Out beyond them lay the old cemetery.

Ben drove through the center of town for old times' sake. He was surprised at finding so few cars and so few people abroad. Quite a few of the businesses he remembered were closed. One was the corner drugstore, which had been a personal favorite. Many an hour he had whiled away there as a boy, either sipping pops or shakes or feasting his eyes on the latest covers and wishing he had the money to buy every novel there.

Ben was even more shocked when he saw that the bank had gone out of business. If a church was the soul of a community, then the bank was its financial heart. The Ridge Bank had been in operation almost as long as the town had been in existence. To see the shades pulled down and cobwebs in the windows reminded Ben that towns, like people, could indeed die. The sight made his brother's words more real than anything else so far.

Past the bank stood Clane's Market, which was still in business. On an impulse Ben whipped into the lot and parked. He strolled into the cool interior and was pleased to find everything exactly as it had been. Apparently some things never changed, he observed with satisfaction. Finding the candy counter proved easy, and he took two chocolate bars to the register.

Ben didn't pay much attention to the woman ringing up the merchandise until he was in line. At the sight of her face, he did a double take and almost blurted out her name. He waited nervously for the customer in front to finish, then stepped forward and set his candy down. "It's been a long time, Nadine."

The pert redhead glanced up sharply. Her green eyes widened, and the hand she had started to reach out faltered. "Ben! My goodness! I didn't know you were back in town."

"Just got in. Visiting my family," Ben said lamely. A dozen questions sprang to mind but he felt too awkward to ask any of them, especially with another customer waiting behind him.

Had Ben only known it, an equal number of questions were on the tongue of Nadine Somersby. She slowly rang up the price of the candy while trying to think of the right words to say. Finally, as she stuffed the bars into a small bag, she said, as if to make small talk, "If you just got in, then I guess you haven't heard that I'm divorced."

Ben swore his heart missed a beat. "News to me," he admitted. He had rarely heard sweeter news. He wanted to say more but couldn't muster the courage.

To his relief, she said what was uppermost on his mind. "Maybe we can get together and shoot the breeze about old times before you leave?"

"That would be nice," Ben said, his voice unaccountably hoarse.

"I'm in the phone book," Nadine said. She feared he would leave town without seeing her and wanted to make it as easy for him as she could. She recalled all too well that Ben Shields had never been the bravest of souls where women were concerned. She watched him leave and was delighted when he paused to look back and wave. Smiling, she waved in return, suddenly feeling happier than she had in months.

That smile puzzled Ben Shields. He walked to his van, slid in behind the wheel, and inserted the key into the ignition. But he couldn't bring himself to turn the engine over. Not yet. He sat and stared at the shimmering plate-glass window covering the front of the market, seeking a glimpse of the woman he had once longed to wed. It seemed like ages ago, but it had only been ten years.

A horn blared out on Simmons Boulevard, drawing Ben's attention. A small boy on a bike had tried to cut across the street without looking and had nearly been run over by a shiny hearse. The driver had leaned on the horn, scaring the boy so badly he lost control and smacked into a street-light. A police car pulled out of line at the end of the short procession and pulled up beside the boy. An enormous officer whose ample girth gave him the aspect of a human blimp eased from the vehicle and bent to help the child.

David Robbins

Ben watched the policeman dust the boy off and hand over the bike. He couldn't hear the officer's words, but the big man's stern expression and jabbing thumb left little to the imagination. Grinning, Ben started the van and wheeled out to the boulevard in time to join the funeral procession as it crawled on past the last of the businesses and homes.

Funerals had been the next best thing to parades when Ben was a kid. He recollected many a time his friends and he had chased after Ira Gravelman's long hearse, shadowing it all the way to the graveyard and then hiding in the bushes to watch the burials.

It had been exciting, Ben remembered, one of the biggest thrills of their young lives. Death had seemed so foreign to them, something he and his friends wouldn't experience for many, many years, if ever, and they could never quite understand why others had to die. They had wondered about the deceased, imagining victims of the gruesome monsters that they all knew lived along Gardner Creek or perhaps poor souls rubbed out by the trigger-happy gangsters that his buddy Horace Walker claimed ran things in Grants Pass.

"Those were the days," Ben said, smiling. With a start he realized he had developed the silly habit of talking to himself, and he chuckled. Being eccentric was the earmark of a professional writer, so he was making progress.

The wrought-iron gate that permitted entry into the cemetery hung wide open. Old Man

Stoner stood to one side, his leathery face as wrinkled as ever, his clothes the grimy rags they had always been. He glared at the hearse, as he always had, because it meant more work for him and he despised work. Stoner would rather spend all his time snug in his small shack, a bottle glued to his lips.

Ben had his window down, so he smiled at the old man and gave a short wave. Stoner didn't appear to notice. The gravedigger's lips worked soundlessly, as they always had, and his left eye jerked open and shut, a nervous tic the man had had even when Ben was still a boy.

The hearse wound along past the mausoleums of the former rich and powerful, past the neat rows of the former middle class, and on to the scattered plots lining the north boundary of the cemetery. Rejects Row, the locals called it, the place where the poor and the socially unfit were consigned to their final rewards.

Ben pulled off and parked. He didn't want to intrude on the private grief of people he might not know. Because he had been on the road for over five hours since leaving Portland early that morning, he opted to get out and stretch his legs. A cool breeze stirred his long brown hair as he emerged.

A freak late-October heat wave had Oregon in its grip, but even so, the temperature at the north end of the ridge was a few degrees cooler than it had been in town. Ben figured it had to do with all the asphalt and the stone and brick buildings retaining more of the heat. When he had been a boy he'd often traipsed with his buddies to the cemetery on hot days to sit in the shade of one of the many fine trees.

Ben thought of those carefree days as he stretched and stared off at a former favorite spot. He was so engrossed in his bittersweet memories that he jumped and cried out when a hand abruptly landed on his shoulder.

"I don't like vagrants in my town, buddy. Maybe I ought to kick your sorry ass clear back to the interstate."

Turning, Ben gazed into the hard eyes of Cemetery Ridge's chief of police. The heavyset man held that challenging look a moment longer, then broke into a broad grin as Ben did the same.

"Travis, you ornery son of a bitch," Ben said good-naturedly, cuffing the officer on the arm.

Travis Sinclair chuckled and enfolded Ben in a great bear hug of an embrace. "It's good to see you again, buddy."

Ben was surprised by the unexpected show of affection. He patted the big man on the back while inhaling the scent of the cheap cologne his old friend had always preferred. "You haven't changed much," he said.

Travis stepped back and regarded Ben as if he were crazy. "Who are you trying to kid? I've put on about a hundred-and-fifty pounds since you saw me last." He laid a fleshy hand on his bulging middle. "It's all the damn sitting I have to do. Desk work will be the death of me yet."

"Either that or sneaking up behind people all the time," Ben said. "You haven't lost your touch there."

The statement took Ben back in time again to his boyhood days. There had been five of them then, inseparable, the very best of friends. They had done everything together, from dogging the funerals to swimming buck naked in Gardner Creek to swiping candy from the five-and-ten.

"I expect you would have heard me if you weren't so deep in thought," Travis said. "That's where you haven't changed, I see. You still spend more time inside your head than you do outside of it. Must have something to do with why you became a writer."

"You've heard?"

"Who hasn't?" Travis said. "Your mother must have told every soul in town. She did everything but take out an ad in the Grants Pass paper to announce the fact." He hooked his pudgy thumbs in his belt, his brown eyes twinkling. "I can't believe I'm talking to a famous person."

"Oh, hell!" Ben said and laughed. "Having two measly books published hardly makes a person famous."

"You must be doing all right by yourself," Travis said with a nod at the van. "New wheels and all."

"If you must know, I used the advance on my second book for the down payment on this buggy," Ben said, "and I've been struggling to keep up the payments ever since."

He didn't care to talk about his so-called literary career, so he looked past his friend at the handful of black-garbed citizens standing near the open grave. "Anyone I know?"

The lawman's features clouded. "As a matter of fact, yes. That's old Horace they're planting."

Ben was shocked. Horace Walker had been one of the inseparable five, a gangster nut who had plastered pictures of Al Capone and Elliot Ness all over his bedroom walls. Ben tried to recall the last time he had seen Horace, but couldn't. He and his friends had strayed apart after high school.

"How did he die? A truck hit him?" he asked, since Horace had always had the constitution of an ox and Ben had never heard of him being sick a day in his life.

"No," Travis said, the corners of his mouth pinching together. "It was a bear. At least, that's the official version."

"A bear?" Ben asked, not quite sure if he had heard correctly. He half thought it was a poor joke on the lawman's part but Sinclair was deathly serious. "No one has been attacked by a bear in this part of the country since the turn of the century."

"Until now," Travis said, his shoulders drooping. He stared off toward the mourners. "I liked old Horace. We hadn't seen much of each other since he tied the knot with Mabel,

but every now and then we'd get together at Spider Pete's and share a brew. Talk
about our wives, our kids, that sort of thing.
That boy of his, Johnny, was Horace's pride
and joy. Now the kid is damn near a veg-
etable."

Ben looked and saw a boy of 12 or so standing beside a woman wearing a black veil. "He
looks all right to me."

"Appearances can be deceiving," Travis said.
Then he tried to make light of the tragedy by
adding, "At least, that's what they tell us when
we go through the police academy. Yeah, the
boy seems fine, but he hasn't spoken a word
since the night his dad was killed. He's crawled
into a mental shell, the doc says, and no amount
of coaxing has brought him out. He sits and
stares at walls for hours on end. It's downright
spooky."

"Did you nail the bear?" Ben asked for lack
of anything better to say, and he was perplexed
by the peculiar look his friend gave him.

"Not yet," Travis said. "We tried using dogs
but they wouldn't track. Do you remember
Metz?"

"The old hermit who lives down by the
creek?"

Travis nodded. "He's still there, and he still
owns the best pair of bloodhounds in all of
Jackson County. They've trailed mountain lions,
bobcats, bears, you name it. But when Metz
brought them around to the Walker place, they
acted as if they were scared to death. Walked

around with their tails tucked between their legs and wouldn't take to the trail for love or money."

"Strange," Ben said. He remembered hearing that old Metz had once bagged the biggest black bear ever caught in southwest Oregon.

"Buddy, you don't know the half of it," Travis said. He gestured at the funeral party. "I'd better be going. Mabel can use some looking after. Maybe you'd like to get together before you go back to the big city? Have a drink or two? We can talk over old times or"—he stopped talking, and his pause was pregnant with hidden meaning—"or about what happened to poor Horace. I don't mind admitting I could use some professional advice."

Ben was about to ask what possible use he could be when Travis pivoted and hurried off, moving with surprising speed and grace for a man of his bulk. "I'll give you a ring," Ben said, thinking that he had two calls to make already and he hadn't been home an hour.

A footstep suddenly crunched on the gravel drive.

Ben swung around, not knowing who it would be. It turned out to be the aged cemetery caretaker, who had a wild look in his eyes. "Isaiah," Ben said politely. "I don't suppose you remember me. Ben Shields?"

"I remember you, all right," Old Man Stoner said, his voice as flinty as quartz. He wagged a gnarled finger. "And I heard the chief. You be smart. Leave well enough alone."

"What are you talking about?" Ben asked, holding back a laugh. It amused him that the caretaker was as looney as ever. Candy aisles and crackpots had more in common than was apparent.

"Never you mind," Stoner said. He walked off in the direction of his humble shack, wagging his finger until a tree hid him from view.

"Old coot," Ben muttered. Unlike Metz, the other town oddball, Stoner never had a pleasant word for anyone and wanted nothing to do with others. When Ben had been younger, he'd always been somewhat afraid of Stoner. Ben had often fantasized that the caretaker murdered small boys in their sleep and buried them under his run-down shack. Unfortunately, there had never been any reports of missing boys to prove Ben's hunch.

Another puff of breeze brought a chill to Ben's spine. He climbed into the van and drove to the huge gate. Stoner was way off by the west fence, watching him leave. "Good riddance," Ben said softly.

Pulling out onto Simmons, he drove at a leisurely pace back into Cemetery Ridge. He slowed going past the market, longing for another glimpse of Nadine, but she didn't appear.

Another tour of the main drag turned up no old friends. Ben finally broke down and turned onto Edison Street. He couldn't put off the inevitable any longer. His mother was supposed to be expecting him.

The street had changed little. An ancient oak tree that once stood at the intersection of Edison and Carson had been uprooted by a storm, but otherwise the old neighborhood was almost exactly as Ben remembered. It cheered him, flooding him with delicious memories of bygone times.

Frequently of late Ben had reflected that childhood was the best time of life. A child had few cares, few woes. To a youngster, life was stimulating, filled with adventure and promise. How sad that later life dashed a child's budding hopes on the hard rocks of reality.

One of Ben's personal mottoes hit the nail on the head: nothing ever turned out the way it should. He'd learned that painful lesson during his teen years when an uncle he had loved as the father he'd never had was killed in a car wreck.

His own father—the thought brought a scowl to Ben's face. Ben had been but a baby when his father died and his mother had drowned herself in a bottle. In all the years since, he still hadn't gotten over being raised by an alcoholic. For his mother's sake he had to try. Just once he would like to sit down and chat with her without fighting over the same subject.

Ahead appeared the familiar white frame house. Ben Shields squared his shoulders and turned into the driveway. He toyed with the idea of slamming the van into reverse and leaving before he was noticed, but a few seconds later it proved too late. A shadowy shape filled the doorway and a voice he knew as well as his own hailed him.

"Well, well, well. As I live and breathe, the prodigal returns. This must be my lucky day."

Chapter Three

Chief of Police Travis Sinclar watched with regret as the green van left the cemetery. He wanted very much to talk to Shields, and not for the simple purpose of slinging bull about the good old days. The real reason had to do with the recent string of bizarre killings that had taken place in the area. Unknown to anyone in town except the officer, Horace Walker had been the third victim.

Sinclar was an extremely worried man. As he stood with head bowed and hat in hand listening to Mabel Walker weep, he wished he'd had the good sense to leave Cemetery Ridge after high school, as Ben had done, instead of winding up stuck in a dead-end job that would probably put him in an early grave.

While the minister uttered a few final words

for the dearly departed, Travis scratched his ample midsection and mentally compared his build to that of Ben Shields. It was like comparing Abbott and Costello or Laurel and Hardy. He wondered for the millionth time how he could have let himself go to pot the way he had done, and he wanted to kick himself for being the laziest jackass west of the Mississippi.

Suddenly, Travis became aware that the minister had fallen silent and was looking at him. Coughing to cover his embarrassment, Travis donned his hat and stepped to Mabel's side. She was a skinny woman who had been born as thin as a rail and never gained an ounce thereafter. She was also one of the most humorless people Travis had ever met. He never understood what his old buddy Horace had seen in her.

"Are you ready to leave, ma'am?" he asked politely.

Mabel sniffled, then nodded once.

Little Johnny Walker gazed as blankly as ever off into the distance. He offered no resistance as Travis took him by the elbow and steered him toward the cars. Behind the trio were Mabel's parents. No one else had attended. Horace's folks had died years earlier, and of the old crowd, Travis was the only one who had seen fit to come.

A yellow butterfly flitted past the mourners, and it nearly brushed Johnny's nose. Travis thought the boy showed a bit of a reaction. Not much, just a crinkling of the mouth as

43

if the youngster had been about to smile. But the moment passed and the boy was his stone-faced self.

It was all too depressing for words, Travis mused. One of his few friends had met a grisly end, the friend's son had turned into a clam, and another old friend had come back to remind Travis of how far he had sunk since the good old days.

The lawman sighed wearily. If he was ever offered a job elsewhere, he'd leave Cemetery Ridge in a minute. He'd go off and make something of himself, as Ben had done. He'd break free of the web of lethargy in which Cemetery Ridge had him ensnared and prove to himself and everyone else that there was more to him than a ton of lard.

Or was that wishful thinking? Travis asked himself. How many times in the past had he been fired up with the same resolve, only to lose it the next day while seated over at the cafe, stuffing his mouth with Gertie's doughnuts? Police work was all he knew. If he went somewhere else he'd likely have to start at the bottom and work his way up. And he was sort of used to being the top badge.

Not that the position of being chief in Cemetery Ridge was anything to brag about. There were only two other officers, both part-timers—one a retired Medford patrolman who liked to keep his hand in and the other a wet-nosed kid who had watched too many *Kojak* reruns and couldn't wait to bring organized crime crashing to its knees. The idiot had a lot to learn.

Travis started to chuckle at the thought and heard a sharp gasp behind him. He turned the chuckle into another cough but was certain he had fooled no one. Luckily for him they were near the cars; he quickly opened the passenger door and guided Johnny into the Walker station wagon.

Mabel Walker stopped beside the rear fender. "I want to thank you for attending, Chief Sinclair. My Horace always thought kindly of you. Many times he told me that you were one of the best friends he ever had."

"He was right, ma'am," Travis answered. Once upon a time, he wanted to say, but didn't.

"I hope you won't be a stranger now that he's gone," Mabel said. "Johnny could use a man's help to snap him out of his shock. The doctor told me so himself."

"I'll swing by some time," Travis said, knowing full well he never would and feeling guilty for lying. He hadn't spoken more than six words to the boy in Johnny's entire life, and he certainly felt no obligation to Horace despite their childhood friendship. Those were the old days.

"Please do," Mabel said. She offered a fleeting smile and flitted around the vehicle like a timid sparrow bolting from a hungry wolf.

In moments the mourners were gone and Travis was left standing under the hot sun, his balding head exposed to the scorching rays. He put on his hat and lumbered to the patrol car. Climbing in, he groped in his pocket for his keys. His gaze strayed to the dilapidated shack that served as the caretaker's home. It reminded Travis of a task he had been shirking, and while he would rather be back in his air-conditioned office sipping a cold pop, he squeezed out of the car again and headed for the west fence.

How Old Man Stoner lived in that shack, Travis would never know. There were inch-wide cracks in the walls that allowed blustery north winds to rip right through the building in the winter; holes in the roof let in the rain during the Oregon Monsoon, as some called the rainy season. The shack wasn't fit for habitation, and if not for the fact that Stoner was a war vet who never bothered anyone even when soused, Travis would have long ago forced the old man to find lodgings elsewhere.

Travis spotted Stoner seated on a stump near the shack door. The old-timer had his big folding knife in hand and was whittling, the only pastime Stoner enjoyed besides drinking. Travis touched his hat brim and brought up the topic he had in mind indirectly.

"Shouldn't you be filling Walker's grave?" he asked with a friendly smile.

"What's the rush?" Stoner said. "He ain't going anywhere in the shape he's in."

"That's no way to speak of the dead," Travis said, coming to his former friend's defense.

Isaiah Stoner snickered and took a whack at the piece of wood between his knees. "Hell, Sinclair. The dead don't much care how you talk about them. I should know. I'm surrounded by the dead day and night. I eat next to them, water their flowers when my bladder is full, and talk to them when I'm so drunk I see them rising out of their graves. No one knows the dead the way I do."

"Maybe so," Travis said. He was about to go on to the other topic when something the old man had said gave his hackles a rise. "Wait a minute. You pee on the graves? I ever catch you, Stoner, you'll stay in jail until you're ready to be planted yourself."

"When a man has to go, he has to go," the caretaker said, unruffled. He dug the tip of his knife into the wood. "There ain't no facilities out here, Officer. Hell, the way I see it, I'm doing these poor stiffs a favor."

"How do you figure?"

"I keep their flowers fresher a little longer, don't I?"

Travis glanced eastward, where his father was buried, and scrunched up his face in disgust. "I'm serious, Isaiah. I won't stand for it. Besides, urinating on graves is illegal."

"Figured it would be. Practically everything else is nowadays," Stoner said and sighed. He arched an eyebrow at the lawman. "What are you doing here bothering me anyway? Did you just want to ruin my creative inspiration?"

"Creative inspiration?" Travis said incredulously. "No, I wanted to ask you a few questions about the other night."

"Took you long enough," Stoner said.

"What do you mean?"

"I was expecting you to stop by a lot sooner than this," Stoner said, smirking. "I would have, if the badge was on my shirt."

The insult was the last straw. Travis was not in the best of moods anyway, and to have the town drunk criticize his work performance was more than he would tolerate. He marched up to Stoner, who recoiled as if in fear of being struck, and said, "All right, mister. If you want to do this the hard way, that's fine with me. I'll haul you down to the station and let everyone in town see you in the backseat of my cruiser. That should give the gossips something to spread around. And I imagine that once Victor Richards hears, he'll want to have a little talk with you."

The threat had a remarkable effect. Isaiah Stoner smiled broadly, showing gaps where teeth had been and black teeth on the verge of leaving more gaps. "Now hold on, Chief. I didn't mean to get you upset. I'm just too cranky for my own good sometimes."

"Uh-huh," Travis said, refusing to give an inch.

He knew full well why the caretaker was bending over backward all of a sudden. The mention of Victor Richards had done the trick. Richards was the richest man in Cemetery Ridge, perhaps in all of southwest Oregon. He was also the meanest son of a bitch on earth. And he owned the cemetery. It was no secret Richards despised Stoner and only kept the old man on because Richards's father had liked the irascible recluse. That had always mystified Travis until he heard a rumor that the two had served together in the war.

"Ask me anything," Stoner said. "Go ahead. I'll answer you straight and true."

Travis had his doubts, but he posed his first question anyway. "Where were you the other night when Horace Walker was killed?"

"Right here, where I always am," Stoner said and patted the stump. "Just me and a bottle. Most every night you'll find me here, staring at the stars, waiting for the Lord to claim me."

"I didn't know you were religious," Travis said, suspecting the caretaker of putting him on.

"Where there's smoke, there's fire," Stoner stated, his tone implying it explained everything.

"What's smoke have to do with the Almighty?"

Stoner snorted. "Don't you know anything? I mean, like I was saying, where there's smoke, there's fire. So where there's evil, there must be good. Follow me?"

"You lost me out of the starting gate. And frankly, I don't give a damn about your half-baked ideas of heaven and hell. I'm only interested in hearing about the other night." Travis pointed toward the north end of the cemetery. "Knob Road is just over the end of the ridge

49

there. You can probably see the Walker place if you climb the fence high enough. It's so close, you must have heard Walker's screams. Some of his neighbors did, and they live farther away than the cemetery."

Stoner developed an interest in the piece of wood. "Sorry, Chief. I didn't hear a thing. The state I was in, I doubt I'd have heard the end of the world."

"Have you seen a bear prowling around the cemetery recently?" Travis asked.

"Can't say as I have," Stoner said. "Coyotes, yes. Lots and lots of coyotes. They like to sit on the west side of the ridge and yip at the moon." The caretaker nodded at the high fence. "They're the reason Victor Richards put that up. Coyotes have a nasty habit of digging up graves and eating the dear departed." Stoner paused. "The third Richards, that is, not the pup who ain't fit to fill his ancestors' shoes."

"I know who had the fence erected," Travis said. He was disappointed that the caretaker didn't know more and he had a nagging suspicion that Stoner was holding something back. "Are you sure you can't tell me anything else? Anything at all?"

Stoner raised his head and looked the lawman right in the eyes. "I haven't seen a bear around here for a year or two. And it's not a bear you're after anyway."

"What?" Travis tensed. "What makes you say that?"

The caretaker smiled slyly. "You can't hide secrets from Old Man Stoner. I know all there is to know."

"I'm not in the mood for games," Travis said. "If you know what killed Walker, tell me."

"I wish I did," Stoner said, sounding sincere. "One of these nights it might come after me."

Travis wasn't satisfied. He intended to grill the caretaker, but at that moment his watch chirped, reminding him of the hour. "Damn. I have an appointment. But don't think you're off the hook. I'll be back."

"Just don't come after dark," Stoner said. "The bogeything will be on the prowl."

"That's bogeyman," Travis corrected him and hurried off. He rated their chat as a total waste of his time, but made a mental note to quiz the caretaker again later on.

Once in the patrol car, Travis drove directly to a brick building located across the street from the bank. On his way up the sidewalk he passed a sign that read:

CEMETERY RIDGE HEALTH CLINIC
DR. JAMES RUTLEDGE

TUES. & THURS. 10AM to 4PM

He barged through the glass door and over to the receptionist's cubicle. "Is he done for the day yet?"

Gloria Jenkins, who had worked in the clinic more years than most of the patients had lived, squinted at him and adjusted her bifocals. "My goodness, Chief. You look a little peaked. Are you feeling okay?"

"It's the heat," Travis said. "Let the doc know I'm here, will you? I'm anxious to see him."

"Are you sick?" Gloria asked, ignoring Travis's lie. "If so, you have to come back during regular business hours. We don't make exceptions for anyone, not even the chief of police. If it's an emergency, you'll have to go to the emergency clinic in Grants Pass. You know the federal guidelines as well as I do."

"What's this world coming to when the federal government decides how sick a person has to be before he can see a doctor?" Travis said and shook his head. "Thomas Jefferson would roll over in his grave. No, I'm not here about me. This is official business, Gloria. So get cracking."

The receptionist clearly didn't believe him. She lifted the phone with all the dispatch of a petrified snail and spoke softly into the receiver. "Very well, Chief," Gloria said after a minute. "The doctor will see you. He's in his office."

Travis barely nodded to the nurse as he hastened down the hall and knocked. On being told to enter, he made sure the door was shut tight behind him before he uttered a word. "Well, Doc, what's the verdict? I've been on pins and needles all day waiting for your report."

James Rutledge wore a white smock and a dignified air that matched his clipped gray hair. He leaned back in his chair, motioned for the lawman to take a seat, and folded his hands behind his neck. "I'm afraid you got your hopes up over nothing, Travis. The report from the lab doesn't give us much to go on."

"Let me see it," Travis said, and Rutledge handed him an envelope containing two copies of the lab's test results. He scanned the long list in the far left columns and frowned. "It's all Greek to me. What does it say?"

Rutledge leaned across the desk and plucked the sheets from the chief. "The glucose level was normal. The sodium, potassium, and chloride levels were all well within the normal range for a man Walker's age. Same with his albumin, globulin, and A/G ratio. His cholesterol was way too high, but only because the man's idea of a strenuous workout was to go bowling twice a month. His platelet count was normal." The physician paused and waved the papers at Sinclair. "I could go on and on and on, but I think you get the picture. There was only one abnormal result, which in and of itself makes no sense whatsoever and doesn't help at all in determining the reason Walker's face was the way it was."

Travis held a wave of disappointment in check and clutched at the lone straw. "What abnormal result?"

Rutledge touched his finger to one of the sheets. "It says right here that the lab couldn't find any protein in Horace Walker's blood. The usual range is anywhere from six to eight and a half. Horace had zip."

"Is that possible?"

"Anything is possible," Rutledge said dryly. "But if you're asking me if human beings can walk around without a trace of protein in their bodies, the answer is an unequivocal no. Protein is essential to human life as we know it."

"Then why didn't Horace have any in his bloodstream at the time of his death?"

"I have no idea," Rutledge said. Dropping the report onto his desk, he indicated a shelf of medical books. "Nothing in any of those accounts for it, nor does anything in my previous experience. I'm at a complete loss."

"Terrific," Travis mumbled.

"I warned you about rushing things," Rutledge said. "I advised you against allowing the family to have him buried until after we sent the body over to be examined by the county coroner. I'm not equipped for that sort of extensive testing, nor can I simply farm the work out." The doctor laid a hand on the report. "At least we had the blood work done. It's a start. I can send the results to the county—"

"And have them stick their big noses into our affairs?" Travis said. "No, sir. We'll handle this ourselves."

Rutledge stared quizzically at the lawman for a few seconds. "I don't understand you, Travis. What difference does it make if they're involved or not?"

"You certified the cause of death as a bear attack, didn't you?"

"Yes, but—"

"Then that's all anyone else needs to know for the time being," Travis said, rising. "Besides, as you pointed out, we have nothing at all to go on except a blood test that makes no damn sense. So the county coroner would be just as stumped by it as we are. Let's leave well enough alone."

Rutledge gnawed on his lower lip and folded his hands. "I don't like this one bit. I'm putting my neck out on a limb for you and I don't have any idea why. There's more to this than you're telling me. Hell, there's more to Walker's death than a simple bear attack. Black bears have claws big enough to cut a person up the same way Walker was cut up, but bears don't do the other things that were done to him."

"Maybe this was a once-in-a-lifetime thing," Travis said, his tone showing that he didn't believe the explanation himself. "Whatever the case, I intend to get to the bottom of it without the help of the Jackson County Sheriff's Department."

"Suit yourself," Rutledge said, "but it's only fair that I serve notice. I played along this time. I won't play along again. If this bear, or whatever it is that killed Horace, attacks anyone else, then I'll be obligated to report it through proper channels. Do I make myself clear?"

"Perfectly." Travis took the physician's hand and shook warmly. "Thanks, Doc. You won't regret cooperating."

"See that I don't."

Once out in the bright sunlight, Travis breathed a sigh of relief and absently hitched at his belt as he walked toward his patrol car. He had bought himself more time, but he shuddered to think of the consequences if his gamble failed to pay off. He glanced back at the clinic, then faced front and nearly collided with a passerby.

"Excuse me," he said, embarrassed until he recognized the man. "Oh, it's you."

"What does that mean?" snapped Fred Larkin, a skinny man who wore a greasy flannel shirt, torn jeans, and a baseball cap that had seen its prime when Babe Ruth still played ball. "Don't I have rights like everybody else? I guess you think you can walk right over me and not give a damn."

"Simmer down," Travis said.

Next to Isaiah Stoner, Fred Larkin qualified as one of Travis's least favorite people. In his opinion the man was a walking affront to humanity. For one thing, Fred Larkin never bathed. And Larkin never washed his clothes. The result was a rancid smell reputed to be strong enough to wither roses at 50 feet. For another thing, everyone in Cemetery Ridge knew that Larkin made his living by poaching, and everyone also knew that Travis had been trying to put Larkin out of business for years without any success. So to say that Larkin rankled Travis was the understatement of the century.

"I'll simmer down when I feel like it," Larkin said. "It's a hell of a note when a fine, upstanding, law-abiding citizen like me can't walk down the street in broad daylight without being trampled by the local law."

"Don't push it," Travis said harshly. He knew his dislike of the man was reciprocated. The two of them had been at each other's throats since Travis had pinned on the badge, and they would likely go on bickering until Larkin was behind bars, where he belonged. "You're about as law-abiding as Jesse James."

Travis pushed past the poacher and slipped into his cruiser. Larkin's laughter followed him down the street, and above the purr of the car engine he heard a mocking shout.

"At least Jesse James could climb onto a horse without breaking its back! But don't you worry none, Chief! I promise to stay home tonight watching TV like every other law-abiding zombie in this dying town!"

Heads turned. Tongues wagged. Travis Sinclair gripped the steering wheel so hard his knuckles hurt.

"You'll get yours, you bastard," he said under his breath. "And so will whatever killed my old buddy Horace. Mark my words."

Chapter Four

Fred Larkin had lied to Travis. The sun had hardly been down an hour when he stepped from his single-wide mobile home located northeast of Cemetery Ridge, on the very edge of BLM land. Around his waist was strapped a .44 Magnum. On his left hip rode a bowie knife in a beaded sheath he had made himself. Slung across his thin chest was a bandolier of cartridges for the .45-70 he carried in his left hand.

Larkin walked to a nearby shed and took out a jar. He held it up to inspect the contents in the feeble light and grinned.

"This will do the job," he said to the thin air.

Tucking the jar under one arm, Larkin stepped to the woods. He halted and surveyed the dirt road that meandered along for over a mile and eventually came out at the very end of Knob Road. No vehicles were in sight. Lifting his gaze, he studied the ridge in the distance. Occasionally Chief Sinclair had spied on him from there with binoculars. Seeing no telltale glint, he chuckled and glided into the vegetation as silently as the animal he was after.

Fred Larkin planned to bag the bear that had killed Horace Walker. The hide would fetch a fine price from one of the sportsmen in Grants Pass or Medford who liked to do their hunting from an armchair. The meat would be sold under the table to a butcher who in turn would sell it under the table to select customers. And the claws would be sold on the sly to an Indian who specialized in Native American artifacts.

Larkin stood to make a bundle, and he couldn't believe his stroke of luck. It had been more years than anyone except the hermit Metz could remember since a big black bear had wandered so close to the town, and Larkin wasn't about to let the opportunity go by. Usually he had to trek 20 miles or better into BLM territory to find a halfway decent bear. Yet here was a giant, if the rumors were true, handed to him on a silver platter.

Larkin snickered at the fickle turn of fate. It was doubly delicious because he would kill the bear right under the nose of the pompous chief of police. If he could think of a way of rubbing it in without getting himself arrested, that would be the icing on the cake.

A faint breeze fanned the tops of the trees. Thanks to the pines and the spruce, the air was as fragrant as a flower shop. Larkin inhaled deeply, relishing the night as he might a lover. The night was his element, had been ever since he turned ten and his pa had made him go out to kill small game for the supper pot or go hungry. Since then he had earned his keep by hunting. It had given him the mobile home and built a little nest egg under his mattress. Hunting was his life, his passion. And even Jacob Metz had to admit that Larkin was the best hunter in the state. Maybe the best hunter who ever lived.

Larkin had a secret for his success—a simple secret that had enabled him to bag more game in his 31 years than 1,000 ordinary men brought down in a lifetime. His skill was based on his intimate knowledge of the creatures he hunted. From childhood he had made it a point to learn all he could about every animal in Oregon and northern California: their habits, their diets, their mating cycles, their cries. Anything and everything that pertained to wildlife, he memorized. It was safe to say that no biologist anywhere in Oregon nor any Fish and Game Department personnel knew more about the animals under their care than Fred Larkin knew about the animals he slew.

Bears were a specialty of Larkin's, which was understandable since they brought him more money than any other beast. A single bear was worth ten deer, five elk, and any two mountain lions. For a short while a small group with a vested interest had paid him handsomely to wipe out spotted owls, but that had been a short-term arrangement that had petered out once the court battle began. No, bears were his bread and butter, and he would rather hunt one than he would anything else.

Larkin liked the challenge. Deer and elk and small game were too predictable. All he had to do to slay them was find where they liked to water and then to lie in wait until a suitable animal showed up. Mountain lions were cagier, but they seldom put up a fight unless cornered. Even then the stupid cats would rather climb a convenient tree than turn and fight their pursuer. Dropping one from a high branch was as easy as picking an apple.

Bears, however, were in a class by themselves. They never used the same route twice, and they drank infrequently. Great roamers, they might travel 15 miles in a single night. Although they were heavy enough to leave deep prints, they had a knack for taking to the roughest of country, which made tracking them an arduous chore. And when cornered, they fought with a ferocity unmatched by any other wild beasts.

Fred Larkin could hardly wait to tangle with the one responsible for Walker's death. Through the grapevine he'd heard it was huge, perhaps the biggest damn bear ever to stalk the local area. That fact alone made that night's hunt the greatest challenge of Larkin's life, one that would never come again. He literally tingled with excitement as he crept through the forest bordering Knob Road.

When the Walker residence came into sight, Larkin advanced to the edge of the road, checked both ways, and darted across. He circled around and came up on the house from the rear, which faced due east. His moccasins, crafted from buckskin, made no noise on the carpet of pine needles.

Larkin would have liked to have examined the site before dark, but he hadn't dared risk being detected. All Chief Sinclair had to hear was that he had been snooping around the Walker place and the lawman would run him in so fast he'd be dizzy. Larkin was too smart to make such a boneheaded blunder, too smart for any police officer who lived. His wits had kept his record stainless and he intended it to stay that way.

Finding the exact spot where Horace Walker had been attacked turned out to be less of a chore than Larkin figured. He noticed a pair of oddly bent trees that a closer examination showed had been partially cracked by something massive moving between them. The discovery set his mouth to watering.

A few feet from the trees the ground had been torn up. A bush had been uprooted; a sapling cracked in half. Larkin bent low, his nose to the ground, sniffing like one of Metz's bloodhounds. Bears had distinct scents; every creature did, but bears were more distinct than most. He was mildly surprised to find no bear odor, but blamed the lack of scent on all the people who had tramped around the site since Walker's death.

Larkin reached into a pants pocket and pulled out a pencil-thin flashlight of the type used by professional burglars and teenagers parked on lovers' lanes. He rotated the tiny tip until the slender beam played over the dirt. Human tracks were everywhere.

Moving in a widening circle, Larkin sought prints that had been left by the bear. Past the cracked trees he found several, clearly imbedded in soft soil where the beast had stood for a short while, perhaps watching Walker. Larkin looked and blinked. He dropped to one knee and thrust his face close to the soil.

"This can't be," Larkin whispered to himself.

He knew bear feet as well as he did his own. There were five toes on the front, five on the back; all were capped with long claws. The pad on the front was much smaller than that on the back, and sometimes, when the two overlapped while the animal was in motion, the combined prints were mistaken for those of larger bears by those who didn't know any better.

Larkin knew better. In fact, he knew bear tracks better than almost any man alive. And the prints in front of him were definitely not bear. As to the identity of the creature that had made them, the poacher, for the first time in his life, was baffled.

Sitting, Larkin lightly ran a hand over one of the footprints, noting its characteristics. There were three toes, not five, each as long as his middle finger, each ending in a claw that would have done justice to a dinosaur. In a fashion, the tracks reminded him of lizard prints, but they were the biggest lizard prints Larkin had ever seen.

Oregon teemed with lizards. Alligator lizards of both the Northern and Southern variety called the state home, and in some areas they were as common as rabbits. Larkin had hunted them as a boy and roasted the bigger ones over an open fire. So their tracks were familiar to him.

Now, staring down at lizard prints six inches longer than his own footprints, Fred Larkin whistled softly and leaned back to ponder. He wondered why Sinclair hadn't found them, then smirked. The answer was obvious. Sinclair couldn't track a bull elephant through deep mud. But what about Metz? he asked himself. He'd heard that the chief had brought the old man and the bloodhounds to the Walkers' for the express purpose of tracking the bear down, but the dogs wouldn't take the scent. Still, a man as skilled at wood lore as Metz, who was one of the few human beings Larkin credited with any wilderness savvy, had to have spotted the strange prints. What had Metz made of them?

The prints raised intriguing questions, questions Larkin would very much like to answer. If the creature was an oversize lizard, it was of a species he had never encountered before— a brand-new creature to study, to hunt down, and kill. Best of all, it was a new, fascinating challenge, the likes of which he hadn't had since he'd gone after his first black bear years earlier. It made him feel like a kid again.

But Larkin wanted to know where had it come from. Giant lizards didn't just pop out of nowhere, science-fiction movies notwithstanding. Had it been in Oregon all along, maybe living somewhere deep in the mountains? In the Rogue Umpqua Divide Wilderness Area or perhaps over in the Kalmiopsis Wilderness Area—two of the more remote regions left? No, he decided, because he had poached both areas many times and never seen any sign of a creature like that one.

Larkin rose and tracked the prints, trying to assess the beast's size and gait and other habits. He was startled to find the length of its stride was longer than his own by over two-and-a-half feet, which meant that the creature had to be nine feet tall, possibly taller. And judging by the depth of the prints, the thing weighed in the neighborhood of 800 to 1,000 pounds.

Larkin sought evidence of a tail; lizards had tails, so an oversize lizard should have a whopper. But there were no drag marks. After covering a quarter of a mile, he came on a boggy area at the base of the ridge, just below the cemetery, and there found a whole row of tracks that conclusively proved that the creature didn't have one. Those tracks also revealed something that shocked Larkin badly: The creature had walked erect on two legs.

He sat on a log to mull the implications of his discovery. An uneasy feeling crept over the poacher as he stared at the bizarre prints. In all his years of roving the woods, he had never seen the like. The creature matched no known beast. It was as if an alien monster had been snatched off another planet and dropped in Oregon.

Larkin shook his head in disbelief. It was downright spooky. But it also made him more excited than he had been in a coon's age—and for a reason that no one else would ever suspect.

Fred Larkin had a secret passion that he had never revealed to a soul. It had started when he was a boy and his father had allowed him to watch a half hour of television a night, provided his schoolwork was done. One of the first shows Larkin picked was *The Twilight Zone*. From the very first episode he saw, Larkin had been hooked.

As a boy, Larkin had never been given to flights of fancy, but *The Twilight Zone* changed that. It lifted his mind from the world he knew to the unknown realms of outer space. Many a summer's night he had lain in his hammock staring at the myriad of stars and imagining what it would be like to hunt down some outlandish beast on a different world. He still watched the reruns when his pitiful excuse for an antenna worked properly.

And there, inches from Larkin's moccasins, was the imprint of a creature very much like those the poacher had dreamed about as a boy. Something new, something weird, something deadly. It was all he could ever ask for in a beast, more than he had ever hoped to find. And bringing it to bay would be the sort of challenge he thrived on.

Larkin beamed as he rose and worked his way around the bog to the ridge. He found the trail readily enough, but the tracks led up the sheer bluff, which was too steep and treacherous for him to try climbing in the dark.

Bearing to the west, Larkin searched for a trail to the top. He had rarely ventured this close to the cemetery before. The only game worth taking were coyotes and rabbits and he could find those practically anywhere.

As if to accent the point, a lonesome wail rang out in the night, arising from a rocky point that overlooked the entire countryside from high on the ridge. Larkin spied the silhouette of a lone coyote on its haunches, its head thrown back as it cried mournfully. The coyote was looking for a mate, Larkin figured.

The coyote went on howling as Larkin continued along the bottom of the slope. In due course he passed below the animal and hiked on. The coyote paid Larkin no mind since the man was too far below to pose a danger.

Soon Larkin came to a game trail that angled on high. He paused to study the course it took and heard the coyote launch into another wail that was abruptly choked off. Curious, he glanced up and felt an icy spear rip through his chest.

Something else stood on the rocky point, something huge and massive and sinister. Silhouetted against the night sky, it reared into the heavens like some sort of primeval nightmare. The creature had broad shoulders, thick thighs, and a huge head. The thing held the limp coyote in one great hand and seemed to be examining the dead animal.

Larkin scarcely breathed. He automatically lifted the .45-70, but lowered it again since the range was much too far. To his astonishment, his movement drew the creature's attention. Its head swung in his direction and the inky figure stooped, as if peering at him intently. But that couldn't be, Larkin assured himself. His dark clothes should blend into the background. Dropping the coyote, the creature straightened up and moved onto the slope with amazing speed, and Larkin knew that as surely as he lived and breathed the beast was coming after him.

Grinning with excitement, Larkin stepped to a fir tree and took up a position behind the wide trunk. He tucked the .45-70 to his shoulder, pulled back the hammer, and waited for the beast to appear. One shot was all it would take and he'd have a trophy the likes of which no man had ever had before.

From high on the slope came loud snapping and crackling as the creature plowed through everything in its path. Larkin nervously shifted from one foot to the other. Normal predators liked to stalk prey stealthily. He didn't like the way this beast was making a beeline for him, heedless of the noise that announced its presence.

Tense seconds went by. The thing drew steadily closer. Larkin fingered the .45-70, longing for a clear shot. Suddenly his skin prickled as if from an electric shock, and the sensation triggered a reaction deep inside of him. With hardly any conscious thought on his part, he whirled and ran, fleeing westward as fast as his legs would take him, swept along by instinctive fear so intense and powerful it was impossible to resist.

Larkin didn't try. His instincts told him to get out of there, to run for his life or he'd never live to see the light of day. In a blind panic he crashed through brush and snapped off low limbs. He traveled 50 yards, violating every unwritten law of wilderness survival he had ever learned, and only stopped because his foot hit an exposed root and he toppled.

The shock of hitting the ground snapped Larkin out of his terror. He pushed into a crouch and froze, listening. He could barely hear above the pounding of his own heart, but it was evident that the forest had gone quiet. Either the creature had lost track of him or it was out there somewhere watching him as it must have watched Horace Walker before pouncing.

Larkin carefully scoured the woods, alert for any motion, however slight. Minutes elapsed and nothing happened. He began to think that he had stopped in time, that the thing had indeed lost him in the maze of undergrowth and trees. Then, at the limits of the poacher's vision, something moved.

Larkin knew not to fire at shadows but his unreasoning fear goaded him into whipping the .45-70 up and snapping off a shot. The heavy-caliber rifle boomed, kicking hard against his shoulder. Larkin worked the lever, ejecting the spent shell and injecting a new cartridge. He was set to fire again when he experienced a feeling he never had before. Three words popped into his head as if out of thin air, words that echoed within his skull like a shout in a vast cave. Only these were hissed rather than spoken, reminding him of a nest of snakes.

"Sweet feast again!"

The shadow Larkin had fired at detached itself from a madrona and bore down on him. Larkin didn't waste more ammo. He spun and fled, certain the creature would catch him, dreading the burning feel of razor-sharp claws as they shredded his back. He skirted a thicket, rounded a cedar, and drew up short in surprise.

In front of him gurgled Gardner Creek. Less than ten feet wide and rarely deeper than four feet, it usually posed no obstacle to anyone desiring to cross.

But Larkin hesitated. In the creek he would be exposed, his reflexes dampened by the waist-high water. The footing would be slippery. A single misstep and he would fall, giving the creature pursuing him the opening it needed.

Without warning, the creature was there, rearing up out of the brush so close to Larkin that he could see its scaly reptilian skin. He hadn't heard it, smelled it, or sensed it. Frantically he shifted to bring the .45-70 to bear, but he was still raising the rifle when an incredibly bright blast of white light exploded in his head and paralyzed him from head to toe. As the bullet head of the creature lowered toward his own, Larkin saw a pair of three-fingered hands tipped with wicked-looking claws closing in on his face.

Larkin was a dead man and he knew it. But just as the creature was about to seize him, fickle fate intervened. Larkin had been frozen in place in the act of turning, his entire weight balanced on the heel of his right foot, which was on the brink of the slippery bank. Suddenly his foot gave way, throwing him into Gardner Creek. For some reason, striking the cold water broke the spell that had turned him into a statue and he rose to the surface, sputtering and gasping.

The unworldly beast was gone.

Larkin shook water from his eyes while turning to the right and left. Somehow he had kept his grip on the rifle and he trained it on the west bank while edging to the middle of the creek. He couldn't understand why the creature had backed off when it had him at its mercy. Was it toying with him? he wondered. Or was it waiting for him to turn his back?

Complete silence gripped the forest. Larkin could hear his lungs pumping and the water dripping from his soaked clothes. He realized that he had lost the jar of honey somewhere along the line, but he didn't care. His life was more important. Besides which, he sincerely doubted the creature had a sweet tooth.

Larkin sidled to the south, staying smack in the center of the water. Eventually he would reach scattered houses and could seek help. He guessed he was half a mile from the nearest place. With the living nightmare dogging his steps, half a mile might as well be half a light-year.

The suspense jangled Larkin's nerves. Five minutes without an attack gave him cause to hope the beast had gone. He spotted a bend ahead and slowed in case the creature had plotted an ambush. As he did, his mind was once again invaded by a thought not his own.

"The nectar will be mine!"

The staggering force of the intruding thought was enough to make Larkin wince. He pivoted, seeking the creature without success. A gut instinct told him it was waiting at the bend. But since he wasn't about to go back and he couldn't stay there in the creek the rest of his life, he advanced with the rifle leveled.

Larkin took each step with exquisite care. He tried not to blink in order to take in the entire scene in front of him at all times. That way, the slightest movement would be obvious. A few yards shy of the turn he made a discovery that caused him to gnash his teeth in frustration.

Erosion had carved out a deep pool. Exactly how deep was hard to tell, but Larkin guessed that the water would rise to his chest, if not higher. To cross, he would have to hold the rifle above his shoulders. He might even have to swim a few yards.

Fighting a renewed tide of panic, Larkin inched along close to the right bank. He believed the creature was still on the left side, so he nearly lost his life when it materialized within a few feet of his back and swiped at him with an arm the size of a log. Searing fire ripped into Larkin's right shoulder blade. He twisted and aimed, but the creature tore the rifle from his grasp as easily as it might yank a lollipop from a baby.

Larkin clawed at the Magnum while desperately backpedaling. The creature stepped to the water's edge and leaned far out to swing again. It missed and the blow fanned air on Larkin's face. He managed to get a grip on the .44 Magnum and began to draw a bead on the creature. At the same instant his left foot stepped into a hole. and the mysterious beast swung a third time.

Water closed over Larkin's head as he went under. Above him, the grotesque hand brushed the surface. Larkin thought there was an explosion of some kind, an incredible blast of light and sparks, and his body convulsed as if from a vicious jolt. Then the fireworks, the creek, the stars, and everything else faded. The last sensation Larkin had was of sinking slowly to the bottom of Gardner's Creek.

Chapter Five

"That was tasty chicken," Ben Shields said, complimenting his mother. "You could give Col. Sanders a run for his money."

Elizabeth Shields smiled proudly and fussed with her napkin. "A son always thinks his mom is the best cook who ever lived. It comes from eating her cooking from the day he's old enough to digest solids."

"Same old Mom," Ben chuckled. "You always have to rationalize everything."

"Is there something wrong with that?" Elizabeth asked a tad defensively. "You never objected to the way I talked when you were younger."

This made the third time since Shields's arrival that his mother had taken an innocent remark as a direct assault on her integrity.

The first had been when he mentioned she had hardly gained a pound in ten years and she had insisted on knowing exactly how many pounds he thought she had gained. The second time had been sparked by his comment that she kept the house as spotless as a museum. Now this.

"Are you mad at me?" Ben asked.

"Goodness, no." Elizabeth appeared shocked. "Why would I be?"

"I don't know. But every time I open my mouth, I seem to upset you."

"You have it backward, son," Elizabeth said. She extended her hand, placed it over his, and squeezed gently. "I'm the one who has to tread on eggshells."

"What are you talking about?" Shields asked.

His visit so far had been pleasant, but all too vivid in his memory were the many bitter arguments his mother and he had fought before he'd left home to seek his fame and fortune. To hear her say she was afraid of upsetting him was such a novelty he couldn't quite accept the reality of her claim, especially since she had been the one who started 99 percent of the fights they had.

"Do you honestly think I don't know the reason you haven't been back to Cemetery Ridge in so long?" Elizabeth said. Straightening, she smoothed her freshly ironed blouse and fiddled with a pink button. "It's all my fault, for the horrible way I treated you, isn't it? For taking out my grief on you all those years instead of finding another way to let it out."

Ben wanted to pinch himself, but resisted the urge. All the way down from Portland he had worried that he'd blunder and accidentally bring up the old days. He'd promised himself that the subject would be taboo, that this time, at least, they would get along without squabbling. Yet here was his mother not only mentioning yesterday's wounds, but apologizing for her part in the rift that had driven him from home. It had to be a dream, he reflected.

"I know this is a terrible time to bring it up, but if I don't do it now, I may not have the courage to later on," Elizabeth said, going on in a rush. "When I lost your father, I went all to pieces. I didn't know how I was going to make ends meet, how I would keep, clothe, and feed you, Jeff, and Susan. I was scared to death, son. And I coped the only way I knew how."

"By drowning yourself in a bottle?" Ben said before he could stop himself.

"It was the only way I knew," Elizabeth said and took a breath. "Looking back, I can see I was wrong. But hindsight is always twenty-twenty, isn't it? A lot has happened since you lived here, Ben. I'll bet you didn't know that I started attending AA meetings about five years ago."

Ben could have been floored with a feather. It was as if the church had just announced his mother had qualified for sainthood. Never in his wildest dreams would he have thought her capable of taking such a big step. "No one told me."

"I asked Jeff and Susan not to say a word. I was afraid I wouldn't see it all the way through and you would think less of me for failing. But I haven't touched a drop in four years."

Rising, Ben walked around the end of the table and hugged his mother as she stood. No words were necessary. Years of conflict were being put to rest, and at that moment in time he was the happiest man alive. A lump formed in his throat, making it hard for him to swallow.

Unexpectedly, there was a light rap at the front door.

Ben stepped back. "Did you invite someone over?"

"No. Your brother and sister are supposed to stop by tomorrow afternoon, but they're the only ones I know of. And Halloween isn't for two days yet." When Elizabeth admitted their guest, she said graciously, "My goodness! Look who it is."

Nadine Somersby stood on the porch. She smiled and started to enter, but hesitated in the doorway, sensing by the expressions of mother and son that she had interrupted something. "I'm sorry. I didn't think. The two of you must have a lot of catching up to do. Maybe it would be best if I came back another time."

Ben was torn by conflicting emotions. He wanted to talk some more with his mother, to share the feelings he had long held in. By the same token, he also wanted to see Nadine, to talk about old times and learn the details of her divorce. To his relief, his mother solved his dilemma by speaking first.

"Nonsense, my dear. I'll have Ben all to myself tomorrow. There will be plenty of time for us to catch up. Come on in." Elizabeth took the younger woman's elbow and escorted the redhead into the comfortably furnished living room. "Have a seat," she said, nodding at the sofa. "I'll bring you a drink. What will it be? Tea? Pop?"

"Nothing, thank you. I'm fine."

Ben couldn't take his eyes off her. It had been years, yet she was as lovely as ever. Oh, there were a few more facial lines than he recalled, but she was the same woman he had once loved with all his heart. Seeing her again, he wondered if perhaps he still did.

Unknown to Ben, Nadine Somersby held similar feelings. She found his rugged good looks every bit as stimulating as she had in high school, and she found herself marveling that she had ever been foolish enough to let him slip through her fingers.

"So how is the job at the market going?" Elizabeth asked, launching them on a round of small talk that lasted for over an hour. Finally the mother excused herself to tend to the dishes.

Nadine indicated the small pile of books on the end table. "I have both of them. Bought them as soon as they came out."

"You did?" Ben said, secretly delighted beyond measure. "If I'd known you were interested, I would have sent you autographed copies."

"Why wouldn't I be interested?" Nadine said. "We've always been the best of friends, haven't we?"

"Yes, but—" Ben said and clammed up before he upset her.

"But what?" Nadine asked. "But I dumped you? But I went and stupidly married Victor instead, thinking his money would buy me all the happiness I ever needed?" She became downcast, but rallied right away. "People make mistakes, Ben. And we learn from our mistakes, too."

Ben knew for sure that he must be dreaming. First his mother had apologized for the heartbreak she had caused him over the years because of her drinking, and then the woman he had once thought would be his wife implied that she regretted having ever turned her back on him.

"Maybe it's the water," he said, without thinking.

"I beg your pardon?"

"Nothing," Ben said.

Nadine glanced toward the kitchen, then at the front door. "Say, it's a bit stuffy in here. How would you like to go for a walk and get some fresh air?"

"Fine by me," Ben said, surprised by the request. "Let me get my coat."

A chill wind shook the trees of Cemetery Ridge and rattled the bushes lining the front porch. Nadine pulled her own coat tighter around her body and grinned. "The last few days we've had a heat wave. In a few more days we might get snow. That's Oregon weather for you."

Ben stepped to the rail and leaned on it. He recalled a comment his mother had made. "In two days it's Halloween. Remember the fun we used to have? The tons of candy we used to get?"

"It's a miracle any of us still have teeth," Nadine said, moving over next to him.

"I doubt I've given Halloween a second thought since I left town," Ben said wistfully. "It's a holiday only kids really enjoy."

Nadine laughed gaily. "You sound as if you're an old man. But neither of us are over thirty yet. Maybe we should get dressed up and go around collecting treats."

Ben looked at her to see if she was serious. "You always did come up with the craziest ideas," he said, complimenting her. "There was never a dull moment when we were together."

"No, there wasn't, was there?" Nadine said and placed a hand on his shoulder. She thought of all the grand times they had shared as teenagers and longed to live those bygone days over again.

"You said something about a walk?" Ben said. Taking her hand, he went down the steps and out to the street. He turned to the right and strolled slowly, savoring the scent of her hair and the warmth of her palm. It was like old times, and he feared his heart would break from aching.

"There's something I'd like to say and I would be grateful if you didn't interrupt," Nadine said.

Seeing him that afternoon had rekindled the flame that once burned in her breast. For hours she had wrestled with her feelings, trying to decide whether to brazenly visit him or to wait for him to call her. Now that she was with him, she was unsure of herself. For all she knew, he had a sweetheart somewhere. Maybe he was even engaged, although his mother had never mentioned as much during her weekly trips to the market.

Nadine looked at Ben out of the corner of her eye and decided to come right out with how she felt. She might never get another chance. He was leaving in a few days, his mother had said, and Nadine didn't have much time.

"I've missed you, Ben. I've thought about you a lot since the divorce. Heck, before the divorce, too. My relationship with Victor had gone sour a long time before we called it quits."

Ben didn't know what to say, so he made no comment, as Nadine had requested.

"Oh, the first few years were all right," Nadine said. "We traveled to Europe and South America. Victor was always buying me things. A new car one day, a new boat the next, a new wardrobe the day after. You have no idea how many ways the filthy rich have to spend their money."

"Maybe I'll win the lottery one day and find out," Ben said.

"Or write a bestseller," Nadine said and gripped his hand tighter. "But we're straying off the track and I want to clear the air before I lose my nerve. Marrying Victor was the biggest mistake of my life. But what did I know back then? I was young, barely out of high school. I was impressed by his good looks and his money—especially his money. I was a greedy little bitch who couldn't see the forest for the trees."

"You're being too hard on yourself," Ben said.

"Like hell. If anything, I'm being too soft." Nadine stopped walking and faced him. "I want you to know I've learned my lesson the hard way. There are more important things in life than money and wild parties and good times. Money can't love." She paused, then cut to the heart of the matter, to that which bothered her conscience the most. "I hurt you worse than I have ever hurt anyone. Can you find it in your heart to forgive me?"

Ben clasped Nadine's other hand. "I forgave you a long time ago, Nadine. But why are you telling me all this? I can tell it's upsetting you."

"Can't you guess?"

Ben looked into her eyes and his pulse quickened. For a few seconds the world seemed to spin and he was catapulted back in time. He was 18 again, not 28, and he was walking her home from high school, not around the block. Old feelings flooded through him, and they were too strong to resist. Before he quite realized what he was doing, he leaned forward and kissed her lightly on the mouth.

"So you do still care?" Nadine said breathlessly.

"I never stopped caring." Ben had dated quite a few women since leaving Cemetery Ridge; he'd even lived with one of them for over a year. But none had ever had Nadine's special magic.

She bent toward him, her lips parted enticingly, and he bent to meet her halfway. The next instant there was a scraping sound, a rush of wind, a grunt, and Ben was struck so hard in the shoulder that he flew a half-dozen feet and landed with jarring impact on his side in the gutter. Stunned, lanced with pain, he heard someone snicker and strong hands gripped his arm.

"Jeez, mister! I'm so sorry. I didn't see you standing there. Are you all right?"

Ben shook his head to clear it. He was being helped to his feet by a brawny teenager who looked big enough to be a linebacker for the L.A. Rams. The boy acted as if he was concerned, but the corners of his mouth curled upward.

"What the hell did you do?" Ben demanded angrily. "Run into me?"

"Not run, dude." The teen lifted a leg and tapped a roller blade. "My fault, man. I had a full head of steam and wasn't watching where I was going."

Other teens skated up. Ben counted three boys and two girls. The pain in his side was already going away and he could find no other damage. "No harm done, I guess," he said.

"Like hell!" Nadine snapped, stepping forward and giving the husky teen a shove that nearly knocked him over. "You did that on purpose, Paxton!"

"Hey, chill, Aunt Nadine," the teen protested, holding up his hands as if to ward off blows. "Why would I do such a lame thing?"

"Yeah, why?" asked a brunette whose chest resembled a pair of watermelons. "You've got no call to be dissing Pax."

Ben thought for a second that Nadine was going to lay into the brunette. He had never seen her so mad. "Hold on here," he said, moving between them. "Did I miss something? What is this all about?"

"I'll tell you," Nadine said and poked the big teen in the chest. "Ben Shields, permit me to introduce Paxton Booth."

"You sound as if I should know him," Ben said.

"This is Victor's nephew. He's been staying at the manor since September and going to school in Rogue River." Nadine's loathing was thick enough to be sliced with a knife. "Seems young Pax here got into so much trouble with the police in Denver his mother had to ship him here."

Only then did Ben recall that Victor had an older sister, 12 or 15 years his senior, who had already been married and living in the Rockies when Ben and he were in high school together.

"Vic is Paxton's idol," Nadine said with biting sarcasm. "Which explains a lot, doesn't it?"

The teen had taken her abuse in stride, but now he glowered and said, "Whoa, Auntie. Don't be joanin' me about Uncle Vic. He's done right by me." Paxton put his hands on his hips. "And you won't catch me turning my back on him like a certain bitch I could mention."

Ben almost grabbed the boy by the front of the shirt to give him a shaking. Instead, he reined in his temper and said coldly, "That will be enough out of you. Just go on about your business and leave us alone."

Paxton snorted. "Or what, old man? You figure you're man enough to make me move on if I don't want to?"

Suddenly Ben became aware that the other teens had hemmed Nadine and him in. Two of the other boys were husky types like Paxton, and the girl with the huge boobs had a mean look about her, as if she was spoiling for a fight. He knew that if he lifted a finger against Booth, the rest would swarm all over him—and Nadine.

"We don't want any trouble," he said calmly.

"Is that a fact?" Paxton retorted. "Well, maybe—"

The third boy, a skinny kid who wore glasses and had stringy hair the color of straw, urgently cleared his throat and broke in with, "Ix-nay, Pax. Check it out, man. The street."

All the teens turned and saw a police car rolling slowly toward them. Paxton hissed like a viper, then growled, "Every time we turn around! A guy can't spit in this stinking town without the local law sticking his big nose in. Come on, people. We'll get our kicks somewhere else."

He gestured and skated toward Simmons Boulevard, his faithful pack trailing. A short way off he yelled over a shoulder, "Don't think you've seen the last of me, Shields. And I'll be sure to tell my uncle you sent your regards."

"The little weasel," Nadine said.

"Little gorilla is more like it," Ben said. "Do you really think he slammed into me on purpose?"

"I know he did," Nadine said. "You saw how he is. He's got the same wild streak Victor had at his age; only he's ten times worse."

"But why would he ram into me like that for no reason?" Ben said. "It doesn't make sense."

"Probably because he knows that Victor wants me back," Nadine said and promptly fell silent because the police car had braked a few feet away. She wanted to explain, to detail how Victor had been badgering her to get together again, but she wasn't about to do it in front of Travis Sinclair.

David Robbins

The hulking bear of a lawman climbed from the vehicle and stood watching the teens race into the night. "What was that all about? I came around the corner back there and it looked as if the bunch of you were about to come to blows."

"Then you didn't see Paxton bowl Ben over?" Nadine asked.

"What? No," Travis said. He looked at his friend. "Was it deliberate? I'll gladly throw him in a cell if you'll press charges. That spoiled brat has been nothing but trouble since he showed up."

"I don't think I care to file a complaint." Ben saw that both of them were disappointed. In his estimation they were blowing the incident all out of proportion. To change the subject and get himself off the hook, he said, "Were you on patrol in the area, Travis, and just happened by?"

"No," Travis said. "I was on my way over to see you."

He didn't add that it was about Horace Walker's death, not with Nadine standing right there. He would much rather talk to Ben in private.

"What about?" Ben asked.

Travis had come prepared. He reached into the patrol car, then held out a copy of *The Were-Beast*. "Your latest, I believe. Just bought it at the store and thought you might sign your John Hancock for me. You never know. One day you might become famous and your autograph will be worth thousands."

"I wish," Ben said.

He accepted the book and patted his pockets in search of a pen. Despite having had two novels published, he couldn't get accustomed to the idea of people treating him as if he were a celebrity. The truth was quite the contrary. Few people realized that there were over 35,000 fiction writers in the country, some with hundreds of books to their credit. Compared to those writers he was small potatoes, as the saying went. Compared to the greats, like Poe and London and Burroughs, his work amounted to mere scribbling.

Travis saw Ben trying to find something to write with and produced his own pen. "Here. You'd think a writer would be prepared to sign his own books, for crying out loud."

"At a book signing, yes," Ben said. "In the middle of my neighborhood after dark, no." Still, he obliged his friend by scribbling a few words and signing his name.

"To the next head of the F.B.I.?" Travis read and chortled. "Brother, you do have an imagination. I'll be lucky if I hold onto this job until retirement the way things are going."

"What do you mean?" Ben asked.

"Oh, just a figure of speech," Travis said, evading the question. He glanced at Nadine, wishing she would go elsewhere, but since she showed no sign of wanting to leave, he sighed and turned to his cruiser. "Well, guess I'll be going. Maybe we can talk tomorrow if you're free."

"Whenever you want," Ben said. "I should be home all day."

Just as Travis went to enter the car, his radio squawked. He hopped in and pulled the door shut.

"I guess that's our cue to go?" Nadine said, eager to have Ben all to herself. She looped her arm in his and they resumed their walk.

"Something is bothering Travis," Ben said. "I can see it on his face."

"He's a big boy. He can take care of himself," Nadine said and grinned. "Now what were we discussing before we were so rudely interrupted? Oh, yes. Us. I'd like to finish that chat, if you don't mind."

Before Ben could reply, the patrol car lurched forward and slammed to a stop next to them. Travis poked his head out the window and addressed Ben.

"Someone else has been attacked by the same thing that killed Horace. How would you like to come along?"

It was an opportunity Ben could hardly afford to pass up. For a writer to visit a crime scene was a form of on-the-job training. And he had one other reason for going. "I'd be happy to. But there's something you should know, Travis."

"What's that?"

"I write books in my spare time. It's not how I make my living, because if it was, I'd starve. I earn my bread and butter doing something else."

"Which is?"

"I'm a reporter for *The Portland Star*. I'll go with you, but if there's a story here, I'm warning you in advance that I'll phone it in to the paper. I can't afford to pass up a scoop."

Travis hid his alarm and beckoned. "Come on, then. It's a code three. I have to roll."

Ben gripped Nadine's wrists. "You don't mind, do you? I'll call you just as soon as I get back."

"Go," Nadine said halfheartedly. "I've waited this long. I can wait a while longer."

"Thanks," Ben said. He dashed around the front of the patrol car and climbed in. It wasn't until Travis had the pedal floored and they were wailing toward the boulevard that he wondered what she had meant.

Chapter Six

"Now where do you suppose the fuzz is off to in such a rush?" Cindy Drew asked as she watched the cruiser speed down Simmons Boulevard with its lights flashing and siren shrieking.

"Who the hell cares?" Paxton Booth said, glaring at the vehicle's taillights. He was in such a foul frame of mind that he looked around for something to throw at the police car, but it was out of range in moments.

"What has you so bent out of shape, Pax?" skinny Jimmy Howell asked as he adjusted his glasses on his nose. "That Somersby babe?"

Paxton whirled on his smaller companion. "What business is it of yours, jerk face?"

"I only asked," Jimmy said.

"Anyone ever tell you that you flap your gums too damn much?" Pax said. "One of these days

I might take it into my head to sew your lips shut so you won't bug anyone ever again."

"Calm down, will you, Pax?" Cindy said. "Jimbo only has your best interests at heart. He warned you about the law, didn't he?"

"Big freaking deal." Paxton shouldered past them and bladed northward at a brisk pace. He didn't give a damn whether the others kept up or not. They were as lame an outfit as he had ever seen. It was just his rotten luck that he had been banished to the outer limits of civilization and had to hang out with first-class dweebs.

Paxton blamed his mother. She had no business sending him to live with Victor. As much as he liked his uncle, he liked Denver more. It was his turf, where he belonged. His best buddies were there; his girlfriends were there. But, no! He had to wind up stuck in a town straight from the fifties, with a gumby, a glitterbag, two zoids and a swivel neck. It was enough to make a guy puke.

Pax swirled to a stop at a corner to wait for the light to change. The others were still behind him, dogging his heels like a bunch of mindless puppies. He shot across the crosswalk a few seconds before the light was due to switch in the hope he would lose them, but the dexters kept up.

What was a fella to do? Paxton asked himself. He was at the end of his rope, more bored than he had ever been, spending his days in a dead zone of a school and his nights roaming the town that time forgot. There had to be some way of putting a little excitement into his life.

Pax passed a store window decorated for Halloween. He didn't think much of it until he looked back and read the big trick-or-treat sign. A germ of an idea took root and he smiled. At the end of the next block he bladed in a tight circle and leaned against a streetlight as his pack of punies joined him.

"So what's it to be tonight, big guy?" asked Jess Weaver, who was once voted the dumbest kid in his class by his homeroom peers. He looked on Paxton as the coolest kid who ever drew breath, and he considered himself lucky to be among Paxton's inner circle.

"Yeah," said Bill Paine, the only teen in the entire history of the Rogue River High School to be kicked off the football team for biting the nose off of an opposing player. "Let's have some fun. Throw rocks at dogs maybe. Or swipe a few mailboxes."

"Listen to you, airhead! You call that having a good time?" He gazed up and down the main street, his features lit by a smile that would have done justice to Jack the Ripper. "There are better ways."

"Like what?" Jimmy asked, hoping he didn't sound as nervous as he felt. He didn't like the look on the bigger teen's face. Nor did he much like associating with Booth. But the girl of his dreams, Manda Joyce, was the sixth and last member of their gang.

Manda Joyce happened to be Cindy Drew's best friend, so where Cindy went, Manda went. And since Cindy all but worshiped Booth and glued herself to him day in and day out, Manda tagged along. As a result, Jimmy had no choice but to do the same. In truth, he would rather be home watching television or reading a good book.

"Did you see that sign back there?" Pax asked.

"Which one?" Jimmy asked.

"The one about Halloween, dork," Pax said. "It's the day after tomorrow."

"So?" Bill asked. "We're a little old to be dressing up in costumes and going door to door, aren't we?"

"I don't know," Jess said. "It would be neat to have a bag of candy to scarf down."

"Neat? Spare me, Beaver. I have an idea that will rock your socks." Paxton glided to the edge of the sidewalk and surveyed the quiet town. "Forget candy, boys and girls. Forget mailboxes and stinking bowwows. Think big. Think as big as you can."

"What are you on about, handsome?" Cindy said.

"Trick or treat, babe," Paxton said. "Mainly the trick, with a capital T."

"I don't follow you," Manda said.

"It's simple. The whole idea behind Halloween is the trick-or-treat thing, right? A person either forks over some sweets or their windows get soaped." Paxton sneered at the buildings lining the street. "Well, I say we give this town tricks the likes of which it's never seen and never will again. I'm talking prank city."

"I still don't see," Manda said.

Jimmy saw the big teen lift a hand as if to slap Manda for being so dense and he tensed to leap to her defense. But Paxton merely waved his hand in contempt.

"Think, bimbo," Paxton said. "Use that tired excuse for a brain. Halloween is the one night of the year kids can play all kinds of pranks and get away with it. So let's prank to the max, prank until we drop, prank until this town begs us to stop."

Cindy giggled. "Oh, lover! You have me interested. What kind of pranks do you have in mind?"

"I don't know yet," Pax said, "but we have two days to come up with a few brilliant ideas. Or maybe one whopper that will blow everyone away."

"Sounds nifty," Jess said.

Paxton fluttered his lips in contempt. "Nifty? God Almighty. You hayseeds are enough to drive a guy nuts."

Pivoting, he bladed across the street, passing so close to an elderly couple that they stepped back in fear of being hit. Laughing, he pushed on, feeling as restless as a caged bird. He traveled two blocks before he again stopped.

The others caught up one by one. Jimmy, the poorest roller blader of them all, was last to arrive. He made a show of examining his watch.

"It's getting sort of late. Maybe we should call it quits for the night."

"You can if you want," Paxton said. "I'm just getting warmed up. How about the rest of you?"

To Jimmy's dismay, the rest agreed to hang out longer, even Manda.

Paxton stared across the boulevard at Clane's Market and debated whether to go grab some eats. He glanced to the right to check oncoming traffic and suddenly remembered what lay at the extreme north end of the ridge. "Son of a bitch!"

"What is it?" Cindy said.

"I just had an idea to end all ideas," Paxton said. "Of course! Why didn't I think of it sooner!"

"What? What?" Manda asked.

"Back in Denver about two years ago, a couple of friends and I went on a tear one night," Pax said. "We were so stoned we didn't know if we were coming or going."

The remembrance made him giddy with glee. Those were the good old days, when he could do as he damn well pleased, and no matter how much trouble he got into with the law, his folks always bailed him out. Then his mother had put her foot down, stranding him in Nowhere, U.S.A.

"So what happened already?" Bill asked.

Paxton was about to relate his adventure that night, but changed his mind. Knowing the other kids as well as he did, he figured, they might turn chicken on him if they knew his scheme in advance. None of them would show up on Halloween. "You'll find out in two nights."

"Ahhh, tell us," Cindy said.

She loved to listen to her hunk talk, although at times she had to admit he talked a little too much. Her mother claimed Paxton Booth was in love with the sound of his own voice. Cindy didn't much care. She was in love with his bitchin' bod.

"On Halloween," Pax said to Cindy.

In the meantime, he reflected, it wouldn't hurt to check out the area and make note of the nearest homes and the best escape routes. He'd only been by there two or three times and never paid much attention. "Follow me," he said, pushing off on his roller blades.

The rest meekly complied. Bringing up the rear was Jimmy Howell, and of them all, he was the only one worried. He wouldn't put it past Paxton to pull a stunt that put them all behind bars. For a few weeks he had been thinking about quitting the gang, Manda or no Manda. The time might be ripe.

Jimmy was amazed that his other friends let themselves be bossed around by the new teen without complaint. He'd always thought Bill Paine was the toughest kid in school until Paxton had showed up and wrapped the burly bad boy around his little finger without half trying. And Jess Weaver, while being as dense as a brick, had never been anyone's fool until now.

Jimmy was smart enough to know he was being a hypocrite when he criticized the others for running with Paxton since he did the same. But they had no excuse for letting themselves be used. He did, in the alluring form of Manda Joyce.

No one else at Rogue River High thought Manda was anything special. Her sandy hair was dull, her features plain, her figure the opposite of Cindy Drew's. Jimmy suspected that Manda hung out with Cindy just to get Cindy's leftovers. But he could be wrong. It was rumored in the boy's locker room that Manda was easy. All a guy had to do was date her and he would have her clothes off before the night was done. Jimmy rated the rumor false. He'd dated Manda several times and the most he had gotten out of her were several halfhearted kisses. But then, he hadn't tried to get much else. He was too shy.

Passing the last streetlight brought Jimmy out of his reverie. He glanced around, mildly upset they were leaving the town. Long, dark stretches of road loomed ahead, broken only by the porch lights of the some of the ritziest homes in Cemetery Ridge—homes usually set so far back from the curb that the lights failed to relieve the gloom. Soon they had passed most of the houses, too, and it was only then that Jimmy guessed their destination.

"Damn. No," he said to himself.

There were no lights at the cemetery, no forewarning they had arrived until the huge wrought-iron gate abruptly towered above them. Paxton coasted to a stop in front of the bars and peered at the rows of headstones inside. He tested the gate and found it locked.

"What are we doing here, handsome?" Cindy asked.

"I don't like it," Manda said. "Graveyards give me goose bumps."

Paxton ignored them and moved to the right. The fence stood only six feet high. He gripped it and shook, testing to gauge its sturdiness. "Take off your blades. We're going up and over."

"We're what?" Cindy said. "We could get in trouble if we're caught messing around in there!"

"Who's going to catch us, airhead?" Paxton said. "The top badge is off on a call. You saw him go roaring off yourself. And we all know there's only one cop on duty at a time." Sitting, he began tugging at his laces. "So let's go, girls."

Jimmy gazed at the mausoleums. Was it his imagination or did something move back in there? "You're forgetting one fact, Pax," he said, trying hard to keep the dislike out of his voice.

"What's that, Dexter?"

"Old Man Stoner, the caretaker," Jimmy said. "He's a mean son of a bitch, and they say he carries a big knife."

"That's right!" Jess said. "My dad told me about him. Stoner was in a war once, and he killed a lot of men. Ever since then, he's lived out here all by himself and doesn't want anything to do with anybody. It's his job to drive trespassers off."

"If the old man tries driving us off, I'll take that big knife of his and shove it where the sun doesn't shine," Paxton said. He removed one roller blade and applied himself to the second. "Move your butts. I don't intend to stay here all night."

Because everyone else obeyed, Jimmy did likewise. He glanced again and again into the cemetery, seeking signs of Old Man Stoner. His stomach twisted into knots when Paxton scaled the fence with ease and his friends imitated their leader's example. Jimmy stepped to the bars, jumped straight up as high as he could, and caught hold of the top. He tried pulling himself up and over, but lacked the strength.

"Come on, weakling," Paxton taunted and ran off. He was eager to learn the layout of the graveyard and pick likely targets for Halloween night.

Jimmy saw the others vanishing into the darkness. Fear at being left alone stabbed through him, lending him the extra boost he needed to hook a leg over the fence. In short order he alighted on the other side and raced after the vague figures of the others.

The skinny teenager would rather had been anywhere than where he was. Every tombstone hid a phantom; every noise was made by a lurking nightmare. He hoped he and the others would get the hell out of there before something dreadful happened.

The gang had stopped next to a mausoleum. Jimmy caught up with them and relaxed a little. He saw Paxton running a hand over the smooth marble.

"This is the Richards tomb," Paxton said and swept all the others with a hostile look. "A lot of my ancestors were laid to rest in here. This is one we don't touch no matter what."

"Touch how?" Cindy asked.

"You'll find out on prank night," Paxton said. Moving on, he jogged from mausoleum to mausoleum. On some were ornate carvings of gargoyles and other outlandish beasts. None of the mausoleums, he noticed with satisfaction, were bigger or more ornate than the Richards tomb.

"How much longer are we going to run around like this?" Cindy said when they stopped beside a row of small headstones. "I'm hungry. Let's go back to town and grab a burger."

"Be patient, babe," Paxton said. He walked northward, delighted by the number of graves. "Say, Jess?"

"Yo, Pax," the class dullard said.

"Didn't you tell me once that your old man runs a construction company?"

"Not exactly," Weaver said. "He owns a rental company in Grants Pass. You name it, my old man will rent it to you. Everything from power tools to backhoes. He makes me work there twice a week and on Saturday. What a drag."

"Perfect." Paxton was overjoyed. He slapped a thigh and laughed. "We'll make headlines all over the state. Hell, all across the country. We'll probably be on CNN. I bet my mom will see it on the news and have a heart attack right there on the couch! It would serve her right!"

"What are you going on about?" Cindy asked. "What will be on the news?"

"You'll see."

On an impulse he swept Cindy into his arms and gave her a passionate kiss. Then, to everyone's surprise, he did the same to Manda.

Jimmy felt himself flush with anger and was glad the night hid his reaction. He wanted to pound Paxton for daring to lay a finger on his girl. Manda, he noticed, didn't resist. She kissed Booth with more ardor than she had ever shown kissing him. Jimmy had to turn away before he did something he would regret, and so it was that he glimpsed a fleeting flash of light 30 yards away to the west near a stand of trees.

"What was that?" he asked.

"You saw something?" Bill asked.

Again a pale bluish-green glow lit a small area; only this time it occurred a good ten feet closer. To Jimmy it appeared as if a miniature lightning bolt had cleaved the air from a spot ten feet above the ground. He heard a distinct but faint crackle that reminded him of static electricity.

"There!" he said and pointed. "What do you make of it?"

"Jesus!" Cindy said, taking a few steps toward the gate. "Let's get out of here."

"Hold your horses," Paxton said, intrigued. He had never seen anything like the flash, but he wasn't about to run from a harmless light. He had his reputation to think of.

"Could it be a ghost?" Jess asked apprehensively.

"Ghost my ass," Paxton said. "I saw a TV show on this once. Scientists call it ball lighting."

While the others argued, Jimmy studied the phenomena. It became apparent that the light was moving toward the mausoleums, not toward them. The tiny bolt flared at ten-second intervals, and each time it flashed it was several feet closer to the tombs. The glow was slightly dimmer in each instance. Although Jimmy earned high marks in science, he had no idea what the thing could be. He was fairly certain it wasn't ball lightning, if for no other reason than he didn't see a ball.

"Let's get closer," Paxton said.

"Let's not and pretend we did," Cindy said.

The light reached the mausoleums and moved among them, blinking on and off at regular intervals. Then, near the center of the tract reserved for the stone and marble structures, it blazed twice in succession, illuminating a wider area than before. In the brief, fiery radiance of the second flash, a blurred form solidified for the span of several heartbeats, an enormous form that appeared to writhe as if in pain.

Jimmy saw it or thought he did. But it was gone so fast he couldn't be positive. After the nimbus faded there were no more brilliant displays. He had been enthralled by the dazzling show but he was grateful it had ended. "I vote with Cindy. Let's book while we still can."

"Wimp," Paxton said and turned to go deeper into the cemetery. He drew up in midstride on seeing a scarecrow of an old man weaving toward them, the blade of a large knife glistening dully in the apparition's right hand. "What the hell!"

Cindy let out a shriek of terror. Manda backpedaled, then spun and fled, sparking a general rush for the gate. Everyone took off except Paxton, who refused to tarnish his image by fleeing like a scared rabbit. He retreated slowly, never taking his eyes off of the shuffling caretaker.

"Run, you fool!" Old Man Stoner roared. "Get the hell out of here before it gets you!"

Paxton saw the caretaker stumble and realized the old man was drunk, not merely trying to scare the daylights out of them. He took a few strides toward Stoner, intending to wrest the knife from the old buzzard so he could teach the caretaker not to hassle them, but the man regained his feet too fast.

"Didn't you hear me, idiot?" Stoner railed at Paxton. "Move your ass or you'll never get out of the cemetery alive."

"You don't frighten me, old-timer!" Paxton said. "I'm not a wuss like those countrified losers!"

"Paxton!"

Cindy's high-pitched scream made Paxton look around. For a few moments he saw nothing to justify her warning. Then, among the mausoleums, at about the same spot where the light display had last flashed, something moved. He couldn't see it clearly in the sepulchral shadows, but the little he did see was sufficient to lend wings to his feet. The creature was gigantic. It walked on two legs. And it was after him.

Belatedly, Paxton remembered Horace Walker. The newspaper had reported a bear was to blame, and it dawned on Paxton that the same bear was going to tear him to shreds unless he reached the fence first.

"Bear! Bear!" he shouted, then poured on the speed.

Manda took up the refrain, screeching a demented mantra in stark horror while blubbering hysterically. Jimmy veered to her side and helped her when she flagged.

Paxton glanced over his shoulder to learn if the black bear had gained. A stray kernel of knowledge he had gleaned in school to the effect that bears were faster than humans was spurring him to his utmost, but he didn't know if that would be good enough. The bear, thank goodness, was still upright and lumbering sluggishly in their wake.

Jess and Bill gained the fence first. They clawed to the other side, then stood there staring fearfully as a frantic Cindy tried to join them. She slipped and cried out as she fell onto her backside. Manda and Jimmy caught up with her and Jimmy gave both girls a boost.

Paxton came to the fence just as Jimmy swung over. He looked back again and was stupefied to see Old Man Stoner between him and the bear. The caretaker was waving his knife and shouting at the beast to go away.

"The stupid bastard," Paxton said.

It took him two seconds to scale the fence. The others had grabbed their roller blades and fled in their stocking feet. Since he didn't care to be left behind, Paxton did so, too. The night closed around him like a black shroud. He soon spied a house light ahead and felt safe enough to slow down. It was about that time that the muted screams began—ghastly shrill yelps of mortal anguish. They lasted a minute or two; then there was silence.

Paxton never once thought about going to the caretaker's aid. He never once thought about running to that first house and phoning for help. He sprinted toward Cemetery Ridge, content that his own hide was safe. And that was all that mattered.

Chapter Seven

Ben had not been along the road that parallleled Gardner Creek since his late teens. He'd forgotten how high the trees reared, how the clinging moss and ferns and dense brush painted the area in moody, somber strokes. Roaring along at 60 miles an hour with the police car's siren caterwauling like a wildcat, he recalled his last visit to the area, to a quaint pond bordered by a small park where locals sometimes went to park and neck. He'd brought Nadine there to propose. Instead, she had revealed she planned to date Victor Richards.

Travis took a turn too fast and had to fight to keep the vehicle under control. He zoomed along the next straightaway, then slowed so as not to repeat the mistake at the bend beyond.

Travis wanted to bring up the subject that

had been bothering him all day. He finally had his friend alone, but he couldn't bring himself to do it; he couldn't find the right words. And unless he pitched his case just right, Ben was liable to brand him as unduly selfish and think unkindly of him. Ben might even contact the Jackson County Sheriff's Office, and Travis dared not let that happen.

The whole point became moot when the narrow track that led to Jacob Metz's cabin appeared on the right. Travis braked, fought the rear end as it tried to skid, and raced down the weed-choked excuse for a drive at three times the safe speed. Another turn brought him to the spacious clearing in which the rustic cabin stood. He brought the squad car to a sliding halt, almost colliding with Metz's clunker of a pickup.

The cabin door opened as the two men rushed forward. Jacob Metz, ramrod stiff as ever, his rail of a body topped by a shaggy mane of white hair, stood framed in the doorway. He wore the same baggy canvas coat Ben remembered seeing on him ten years earlier. In his hand was a pipe, which he tapped against the jamb while regarding them with amusement.

"Lordie, boys. Where's the war? I haven't seen anyone in such a hurry since the time Billy Williams ate a gallon of canned prunes at one sitting."

Travis had his hand on his service revolver. "Where's the thing that nailed Horace? Dispatch said you saw it from your cabin." He swiveled to scour the clearing. "And where is the person who was attacked?"

"Goodness, calm yourself before you have a hernia, Chief," Metz said in his gravely voice. "That dispatch lady must have misunderstood. I didn't see the thing at all. I heard Larkin shooting."

"Fred Larkin?" Travis said, flabbergasted. "He's the one who was attacked?"

"One and the same," Metz said, removing a tobacco pouch from his coat. "I didn't think anything could get the better of that boy in the woods, but I guess I was wrong. When I found him he was about half dead. Come on in and see for yourselves."

Ben went up the rickety steps last. The interior smelled of wood smoke and tobacco. Dishes were stacked high on a tarnished sink. He took a few steps, then halted on hearing a low bark. Turning, he saw the biggest pair of bloodhounds he had ever laid eyes on resting on tattered blankets in a front corner. One rumbled deep in its chest and started to rise.

"Be still, Achilles," Metz commanded. "These are guests. I can't have you eating the chief of police or they'll haul you away to the pound and put to you sleep." To Ben, Metz said, "Pay them no mind, mister. I spoiled them when they were pups. Now they think any stranger is fair game."

Being called a stranger reminded Ben of his social lapse. "I forgot to introduce myself. Ben Shields. I'm a reporter."

"No need to advertise a character flaw, son," Metz said, shaking hands heartily. "Me, I've always been a hunter and trapper. Not like Larkin, though. I always do mine legally."

Travis waited a few feet away. "Where is Larkin?" he asked. "I can't wait to question him."

"You might have to," Metz said.

The reason why became obvious when the venerable hunter parted a blanket partition and they saw Larkin lying unconscious on a cot. His clothes were drenched, his shirt torn, his back laced by claw marks. Oddly, his skin appeared scorched in spots.

"What the hell?" Travis said.

"I was out front enjoying a smoke when I heard that cannon of his go off," Metz said. "Knew right away it had to be him. No one else I know of uses a .45-70." He indicated a rifle propped near the cot.

"Do you think he shot it?" Travis asked while picking up the gun. He worked the lever and a shiny cartridge sailed out of the chamber. It clattered on the floor, rolling to a stop at Ben's feet.

"He might have," Metz said, "but I didn't see no blood." He wagged a thumb at the .45-70. "Turn it over."

Travis did and felt his skin crawl. Deeply etched in the stock and receiver were three grooves, each over an inch long. They looked for all the world just like claw marks. "These can't be what I think they are."

111

"I'd say so," Metz said.

"But bears can't cut through solid metal," Travis said and wanted to bite his tongue when Ben scrutinized him. To divert his friend's attention from the rifle, he stepped to the cot and said, "I don't get this, either. How can the man be burnt and soaking wet at the same time?"

"Beats me," Metz said. "I found him in the creek, pretty near drowned. Had to pump his chest a spell before he sputtered up enough water to suck air into his lungs."

Travis gripped the older man's arm. "You didn't even get a glimpse of it, Jacob? Not a single glimpse?"

"No, son. I didn't. And I sorely wanted to. I can't begin to imagine what kind of creature can scare my dogs so badly they won't track it. Why, they'd go into a grizzly's den without batting an eye. But this thing has them spooked."

Ben had heard enough. He cleared his throat and said, "It doesn't take a genius to figure out that something out of the ordinary is going on here. Travis, it just hit me that you keep calling the animal that did this a thing. And, Jacob, you've hunted this region all your life, yet you give me the impression we're up against something the likes of which you've never encountered before. What the hell is going on?"

"A regular chatterbox, aren't you?" Metz said, grinning. "But you've hit the nail on the head, Mr. Shields. Judging by the tracks alone, this creature can't be from around these parts."

"Tracks? You never mentioned anything to

me about any tracks. Where did you find them?"

Metz fiddled with his pipe, as if to delay answering. "At the Walker place," he said at length.

"And you never said a word to me?" Travis snapped.

"I didn't want to get you all bothered until I had a few more answers," Metz said.

"Damn it!" Travis said, shoving the rifle at him. "How do you expect me to do my job properly when I don't have all the facts?"

At that moment Fred Larkin groaned and his eyes fluttered open. He slowly rolled onto his side, then saw the three of them. "Where?" he asked, appearing confused.

"You're at my place, Fred," Metz said. "I fished you out of Gardner Creek after you tangled with whatever is running around loose out in the woods."

Larkin's confusion was instantly replaced by unbridled terror. He sat bolt upright and clasped his hands to his temples. Vivid in his mind were images of being jumped at the bend, of the sting of the creature's claws as they ripped into his back and the strange blast of sparks and light.

Ben put a hand on the man's ankle. "It's all right. The animal that attacked you is long gone."

Travis was stunned by the poacher's behavior. As much as he despised Larkin, he had to admit that the man was braver than most. Few had the courage to go traipsing through the forest at night. Fewer still had the guts to confront bears and mountain lions in their own element and on their own terms. Travis stared out a window at the black night. The thought that he had to hunt down whatever had terrified Larkin so badly was enough to make him wish he had become a librarian instead of a law officer.

"Care for some whiskey, Fred?" Metz asked. "A good jolt might do you some good."

"Thanks," Larkin said. He slowly lowered his hands, ashamed of how he had acted. A man in his line of work didn't dare give in to fear or he was ruined. And until his run-in with the thing in the woods, Larkin had never known a moment of genuine cowardice in his entire life. It was a bitter, humiliating pill to swallow.

"I need to know what happened to you," Travis said. "I won't ask what you were doing in the woods after dark. I don't care. All I'm interested in is nailing the thing that killed Horace Walker." He leaned on the cot and his voice quavered with emotion when he said, "Did you see the creature, Larkin? Do you know what we're dealing with?"

"I saw it," Larkin said softly. "But I have no idea what it is."

Travis was so excited to have an eyewitness that he grabbed the poacher's wrist without thinking. "What did you see? Describe it to me."

Ordinarily Larkin would have jerked away

when the lawman, or anyone else, touched him. But he was still dazed from his ordeal, so, in a low croak, he answered, "I'm not sure, Sinclair. It was big. Damn big. And faster than anything I've ever seen. God. So fast!"

"But what was it?" Travis asked. "I have to know. What could do that to a man? It wasn't a bear, right?"

"No," Larkin said and laughed sourly at the notion. "No bear. Like nothing on this earth."

The last words came out in a horse whisper. Ben wasn't certain if he had heard properly. The idea was so preposterous that he grinned and said, "What, then? Did you meet up with a Martian?"

The sarcasm stung Larkin like a whip and sobered him as little else could have. "You think this is funny, mister? A game I'm playing?" Twisting, he wagged a finger at his fresh wounds. "Think I did this to myself?"

"No, of course not," Ben said, seeing he had angered the man. "I just meant—"

"I know damn well what you meant," Larkin said, sliding off the cot. Girding his legs, he rose unsteadily and swayed.

Metz returned, a shot glass in his hand. "You're in no shape to go anywhere, Fred. Why don't you lie back down? If you want, you can spend the night here. The hounds and me won't mind."

"Thanks, but no thanks." Larkin swallowed the whiskey in a single gulp and trembled as the burning liquid scorched his throat. "I have

115

a lot of thinking to do, plans to make. I need to go home."

"Plans?" Travis said. "Do you intend to go after the thing again after it nearly killed you?"

"My pa always said that the quickest way to get over being thrown from a horse is to climb right back up in the saddle." Larkin gave Metz the glass, retrieved his .45-70, and headed for the front door.

Despite himself, Travis was impressed. He tagged along, saying, "If that's the case, then we should work together. I have to stop this thing before anyone else dies. Maybe the two of us can get the job done."

"I'll give it some thought," Larkin said, but his tone lacked conviction.

"I'm serious, damn it," Travis said. "For once in your life work on the same side as the law instead of breaking it. Help me stamp out this menace and I'll be forever grateful."

"Now that's what I call incentive," Larkin said. He was tired of hearing the lawman chatter like a chipmunk. Pausing, he glared at the chief and said, "All these years, all this time, and you've never asked for my help before. Why now? What's so special about this creature? Why are you so afraid?"

"Me? Afraid?" Travis laughed. "You're way off base. I'm worried about more people losing their lives. That's all. Remember the motto on my patrol car: to serve and protect?"

Larkin walked on. "Don't call me, Chief. I'll call you." He went out without another word.

Ben had witnessed the exchange with interest. He, too, sensed desperation in his old friend, an insight confirmed when Travis turned haunted eyes on him. "What will you do now?" Ben asked.

At that moment, from outside, came an electronic squawk punctuated by the metallic rattle of a woman speaking urgently into a microphone.

"My radio," Travis said, hurrying to the door. "I'll be right back."

Metz clucked like a hen while setting the glass on the kitchen counter. "That man won't live past fifty, the way he runs himself ragged." He nodded at a rocking chair. "There's the secret to long life, you know. Take each day as easy as you can."

"A nice philosophy, but hardly practical in this day and age," Ben said. "Rush, rush, rush. That's all any of us does anymore. Relaxation is a dying art."

"Then I'm thankful I learned how before it died out," Metz said, seating himself. His wise old eyes narrowed. "So tell me, reporter. What do you make of all this?"

"I was about to ask you the same thing."

"Were you now?" Metz asked and grinned. "Well, I can't say as how I have any answers, but I might have a clue you could use to root out more information. If you care to, that is."

"Of course, I'm interested. This could turn out to be the story of the year. What clue do you have?"

"Old age."

"Pardon?"

"The years I've lived, the events I remember," Metz said, once again producing his pipe. "For instance, when I was about eight or nine, I seem to recall there being a slew of killings. An animal was blamed even though the deaths were all mighty peculiar."

"Peculiar how?" Ben asked.

"That's all I remember. And the only reason I do is because the chief of police back then, a man named Talbot, came to my pa for help since he was the best damned hunter in these parts." Metz pursed his lips. "They never did find the thing."

"Are you saying that the animal blamed for those deaths when you were a boy is the same one responsible for killing Horace Walker?" Ben asked skeptically.

"No, I wouldn't go that far," Metz said. "Maybe the one that ripped up all those folks back then was the pappy of this one. I don't know." He twirled the stem of his pipe. "I'm seventy-nine. So you shouldn't have to search back more than seventy years or so."

"Is that all?" Ben said, holding in a laugh. It was doubtful any records existed after seven decades. Trying to track the lead down might be a monumental waste of his time.

"Seems to me it would be worth pursuing," Metz said, as if reading Ben's mind. "Before more folks die."

"Do you think the thing will strike again?"

"I know it will."

"Why?"

Metz commenced rocking slowly. "If you'd seen Walker, you wouldn't need to ask. Whatever got ahold of him enjoyed sucking the life from his body."

"Being a little melodramatic, aren't you?" Ben said. "Animals don't kill for thrills. They kill to fill their bellies."

"A wildlife expert, are you?" Metz asked, smirking.

"Well, no, but—"

"Then I wouldn't be so quick to render judgment if I were you," Metz said. "Have you ever seen a sheep pen after a cougar has had a killing frenzy?"

"Can't say as I have, no," Ben said.

"There are dead sheep everywhere, all bitten and slashed and torn to ribbons. Might be twenty, thirty head or more piled in bloody heaps." Metz stuck the pipe in his mouth. "And the odd part is, only one or two will be even partially eaten. The cougar doesn't kill all those sheep because it's hungry. It slaughters them for the sheer hell of it."

"What's the connection to our mystery beast? Do you think that it goes into a feeding frenzy of some kind?"

"You haven't been listening," Metz said, "and you're putting words in my mouth. All I'm saying is that this thing, whatever it is, acts like a kid in a candy shop where people are concerned. We're nothing more than lollipops to this monster."

Ben found the comparison too silly to merit a reply. He was spared from having to say anything by Travis, who poked his head in the door.

"We have to roll. There's been a disturbance at the cemetery." The chief nodded at Metz. "Thanks for calling me about Larkin. Can I count on your help if the thing strikes again?"

"I'll be glad to lend a hand," Metz said. "But I doubt that I can be of much help without the dogs. I'm a fair tracker at best. Larkin's the one who can track a flea across solid rock."

Ben had no desire to ride out to the cemetery. He almost asked to be dropped off at his mother's so he could give Nadine a call while it was still early. But as the cruiser pulled out of Metz's driveway, Travis posed a question that so intrigued him, he forgot all about going to his mother's.

"Do you believe in vampires, werewolves, and stuff like that?" When Ben looked at him, he laid a hand on the novel Ben had autographed. "I'm not pulling your leg. I'd like to know. Both of your books deal with the supernatural, don't they? You must have done a lot of research on the subject before you wrote them. Do such creatures really exist?"

"Do you have a flask hidden in this car somewhere?" Ben asked and chuckled. "I can't believe you're asking me that with a straight face. No, werewolves and vampires don't exist.

They're figments of the imagination, just like fairies and leprechauns and demons."

"The creature that killed Horace isn't a figment of anyone's imagination," Travis said and bobbed his chin at the forest. "And it's out there somewhere, hunting more prey." He pushed his hat back on his head and wearily rubbed his forehead. "I was hoping it had wandered off into the deep woods after it attacked him, but no such luck."

"You've been losing a lot of sleep over this, haven't you?"

"Can you blame me?" Travis said. "If I don't find it soon, another person will die. I can't stand the thought of having another death on my conscience."

Ben put a hand on the other man's shoulder. "If you ask me, you're taking this way too personally."

"Brother, you don't know the half of it."

Few pedestrians were abroad in Cemetery Ridge. Travis went down Simmons Boulevard at the speed limit, but once past the last business he floored the accelerator. "The Danbridge family called in the disturbance," he said. "I don't think they lived here when you did. Their house is closest to the cemetery."

"What was the nature of the disturbance?" Ben asked.

"They told the dispatcher that they heard a lot of shouts and screams," Travis said. "Mr. Danbridge wanted to investigate but his wife wouldn't let him. She made him call it in."

He flicked on the overheads, but not the siren, then grinned. "There's nothing quite like flashing lights to convince the good people of our fair town that their chief of police is busting his chops on their behalf."

Travis slowed and turned on the spotlight mounted on the top of the patrol car. By twisting a control stick inside, he directed the beam at the side of the road. When they had passed the last house, he aimed the spotlight directly ahead and illuminated the wrought-iron gate. "Bingo."

Ben leaned forward for a better look. He knew he was being silly, but all the talk of savage wild beasts and bloodthirsty monsters had his nerves on edge. Thankfully, the graveyard was as quiet as it should be. "I don't see anyone."

"Me neither," Travis said. "But we'll have to go on in and look around, just the same." He brought the squad car to a stop and swiveled the spotlight so the beam played over the tombs and headstones. "Maybe Old Man Stoner will spot the light and come to the gate. If he does, I'll have him do the searching. It's his job, after all."

No one appeared. Travis sighed and got out, his hand resting on his revolver. "Stoner!"

There was no answer. Somewhere an owl hooted. Ben listened to the wind and glanced with envy at the lawman's gun. "I guess we go in then."

Nodding, Travis walked to the gate and gave the middle bars a shove. The gate creaked, but wouldn't open. "Just great. It's locked." He pressed his face to a gap and scanned the west side of the cemetery. "And there's still no sign of Stoner. He's probably passed out, drunk." Travis glanced at the top of the fence. "Now what do I do? I sure as hell can't climb that."

"I could," Ben said without considering the consequences. He wanted to beat his head against the gate when the lawman agreed.

"Would you? I'll give you my flashlight and you can go over to Stoner's shack and get the keys from him."

Ben could think of a few others things he would much rather do, such as running barefoot across broken glass or dousing himself with gasoline and setting himself on fire. But he didn't care to give the impression he was having seconds thoughts, so he agreed. Moments later he had the flashlight. Switching it on, he went up and over the fence and dropped lightly to the grass on the other side.

In the distance something howled.

Chapter Eight

Nadine Somersby was restless. She paced the floor of her living room, her mind awhirl with images of Ben, her soul burning with frustration. There was so much she wanted to say to him, and she would have, too, if not for Travis Sinclair's pathetic sense of timing.

The human heart was a contrary thing, Nadine reflected. It never seemed to know exactly what it wanted except on a few rare occasions, and then it usually turned out that the object of the heart's desire brought nothing but heartache.

Her choice between Victor Richards and Ben Shields was a case in point. In high school she had been attracted to them both, even loved them both. Her heart had been torn between the two, but finally swayed to Victor because she felt his easygoing attitude would bring her greater happiness. Victor had been flashier, more fun to be around. Ben had been too serious all the time, too wrapped up in life and in her.

Appearances, as the old saying went, could be deceiving, and Nadine's heart had been royally deceived. Now, gazing back over the span of years, with the benefit of all she had learned in the interim, she wondered how she could have missed seeing the truth about Victor. Any man who had a casual attitude toward life would have the same attitude toward love. Victor had claimed he reciprocated her love, and perhaps in his own way he did. But he didn't love her enough not to fool around with other women.

The hurt tore at her insides like a red-hot knife. Nadine felt moisture rim her eyes and fought back the tears. She had already cried enough to fill Crater Lake. There would be no more wallowing in sorrow. She had made a mistake and paid the price. Now she had to get on with her life.

Seeing Ben again had sparked hope in her breast. He still cared for her, she could tell. And even though he still took life much more seriously than life warranted being taken, she saw that as a plus, not an evil. Ben Shields was the kind of man who would never take her love for granted. He would honor and respect her all the days they were together. She would never have to worry about coming home early from a meeting and finding Ben in bed with another woman.

Nadine stopped pacing and glanced at the wall clock. Over two hours had gone by since Ben had left with Travis. Her tummy rumbled, reminding her she had neglected to eat supper. Throwing on her coat, she went out and locked the front door behind her.

A breeze had picked up. She pulled the collar of her coat higher and headed for the market. A container of raspberry sherbet would be just the thing to satisfy her hunger and take her mind off Ben for a while.

Nadine's brick house was located three blocks from Clane's Market. She liked the convenience of being able to walk to work, but she couldn't say much about the hourly wage she was paid. If not for the alimony Victor reluctantly forked over, she would barely be able to make ends meet. Many times she had considered leaving Cemetery Ridge and going off to Medford or perhaps even Portland, where there was a better chance of securing a higher-paying job, but she never had. Something had held her there, a vague feeling that she shouldn't leave just yet.

Now Nadine believed she knew why. Subconsciously she had hoped to see Ben again, hoped that if she hung around long enough she would hear he was back in town and could go see him. Deep in her heart of hearts, she had always had a special regard for the man she had so stupidly cast aside.

Nadine smiled as she strolled, thinking of the next day when she would see Ben again. Maybe she could prevail on him to come to her place, where there would be no interruptions, nothing to keep them from letting their true feelings out. The prospect filled her with excitement.

At this hour there were few cars in the parking lot of the market. Nadine swung around the south corner into the glare of harsh light. She had taken only a few strides when she heard a familiar scraping sound and whirled around.

"Well, if it isn't Auntie Nadine," Paxton said, bringing his roller blades to a halt inches away. He wore a mocking leer as he leaned down. "Don't you know it's not safe to be wandering the streets at night?"

"Not with Neanderthals like you roaming around." Nadine glanced behind him, but saw no sign of his five shadows.

"They had to go beddy-bye," Paxton said, having guessed her reason for looking. He snorted in disgust. "Those hicks are too lame for words."

"I'm one of those hicks, remember?" Nadine said. "And you know what you can do with your superior airs."

"My, my," Paxton said and smirked. "You're a regular tigress. No wonder Uncle Vic took a liking to you." He lowered his face until his mouth was so close to her that his warm breath fanned her lips. "And I have to admit, you do

127

have one def body. What say you and me go find us some hooch and party down until the sun comes up?"

"In your dreams," Nadine said and turned to go, but Paxton grabbed her arm, holding her in place.

"Not so fast, Auntie. I can't say as I like your attitude. Maybe I should drag you out behind this store and have some fun whether you're willing or not."

Nadine stiffened. "They call that rape."

"Like I care," Paxton said. He shifted and started to pull her toward the corner.

Angered beyond words, Nadine jerked backward with such force that she tore loose from Paxton's grasp and he lost his balance. Cursing, he clutched at the wall for support, but his roller blades swept out from under him and he fell onto the curb.

"Damn you!" Paxton said, putting his palms flat to push erect. "I'll fix you but good, bitch!"

Suddenly a figure stepped between them. For a moment Nadine thought it was Ben and her heart leaped in pure joy. Then she saw the man's long black hair and recognized the expensive trench coat he was partial to and a chill settled over her.

"Who—" Paxton said. His rage dissolved, wiped out by surprise and not a little fear. "Uncle Vic! What are you doing here?"

Victor Richards was a big man, bigger than Ben and far bigger than his nephew. Almost nonchalantly he reached out, seized the front of Paxton's shirt, and hauled the teen to his feet with a brusque motion that cracked Paxton's teeth. "You're in a world of trouble, Pax, my friend."

"Why?" Paxton said and gestured at Nadine. "You mean her? I can explain. I was just—

Victor shook Paxton as a terrier might shake a rat. "Save your lies for later. Right now I want you to head on home. I'll be along shortly, and if you're not there I'm going to phone your mother and suggest that you be sent to a military academy in Salem. That will keep you out of my hair and hers."

"A what?" Paxton said, aghast. "Man, you've got to be jiving me, right? I mean, you couldn't be so cruel, could you? Not to your favorite nephew."

"You're my only nephew, so you earn the title by default," Victor said, releasing Booth. "But one more incident like this and I'm washing my hands of you. There's only so much even I will tolerate. Now go before I lose my temper."

Scowling, Paxton skated off across the lot, slowing as he neared the street to glare over a shoulder at Nadine. In a juvenile burst of temper he poured on the speed and shot across the intersection. He failed to look both ways and was almost hit by a car, whose driver leaned on the horn. Paxton, true to form, stabbed his middle finger at the driver.

"That boy will never learn," Victor Richards said and chuckled.

"Maybe that's part of his problem," Nadine said.

Victor faced her, his handsome features curled in roguish glee. "You've lost me."

"Treating him like a boy when he should be treated like a man," Nadine said. "Every time he does something wrong, you give him a slap on the wrist. His mother does the same. What he really needs is to be busted in the chops so hard he'll remember the lesson the rest of his life." She rubbed her wrist where Paxton had squeezed it. "I've half a mind to report him to the police for what he did."

"Oh, come now," Victor said in the condescending fashion he had perfected to a fine art. "You're the one acting childish. The boy was only having a little fun."

"He was going to try to rape me."

"Ridiculous!" Victor said. "All I saw was him pulling on your arm." He showed his pearly teeth. "But then, the two of you never did get along."

"Can you blame me? The first time I met your innocent nephew, he tried to stick his hand down my skirt." Nadine ruefully shook her head. "Mark my words. He'll bring you to grief if you don't get rid of him. Send him to that academy. It would help set him straight and make him realize that he can't go through life being so selfish and crude."

"I was bluffing about military school to put a scare into him," Victor said, grinning. "I'd never banish the poor kid to a prison like that."

"Same old Victor," Nadine said.

"Now don't start in on me. This is the first time we've chatted in days. The least you can do is be pleasant." Victor slid his hands into the pockets of his coat and leaned against the wall. "I hear he's back."

"Who?"

"Don't play the innocent, my dear. I happen to know that you saw him."

Suspicion flared in Nadine's mind. She knew Paxton hadn't been home to inform on her, and none of her other acquaintances were aware yet that Ben had returned, so far as she knew. "Have you been spying on me?"

Victor laughed. "Please. Give me more credit. Once you turned your back on me and walked out the door, you were free to do as you pleased."

"Oh? Then why do you keep insisting that we should get back together?" Nadine asked.

"You're straying off the subject. I was talking about my former best friend, the man who almost stole you from me in high school."

"You've got it backward," Nadine said. "You stole me away from him."

"Whatever. How is bashful Ben doing these days?"

"Why don't you ask him yourself?" Nadine said. There had been a time when she had thought Victor's devilish outlook to be irresistibly attractive. Now she merely found it annoying, and she was anxious to go on about her own business.

"Maybe I will. Maybe I'll hold a party in his honor and invite everyone who has read his books." Victor's eyes lit up. "There must be two or three people who have."

"I'm going," Nadine said and went to do just that.

Her ex-husband gripped her fingers lightly. "Aren't you the touchy one. I was only making a joke. Don't run off on me."

Nadine shook his hand off. "Like nephew, like uncle." She walked to the pneumatic door, which hissed open, and said in parting, "I might as well tell you now. I intend to see a lot more of Ben Shields. A lot more."

The richest man in Cemetery Ridge watched the redhead go into the store. Then he wheeled on a heel and stalked to his sports car. He gunned the engine, cut the steering wheel, and sped out onto the street. The light turned red before he reached the intersection, but he flashed on through anyway since no cars were coming.

"Ben Shields!" Victor snarled under his breath. He was so mad he wanted to punch something. Blocks later he spied his nephew roller blading south and screeched to the side of the rode. He threw open the passenger door. "Get the hell in!"

Paxton obeyed. He had never seen his uncle mad and didn't know how Victor would react if he balked. His mother claimed that her brother had a fierce temper and was prone to acts of violence when provoked, which Paxton had

132

always thought was her not-so-subtle way of trying to scare him into behaving himself. Until now. "You okay, dude?"

Victor seized the teen's shirt and yanked him roughly over the console. "I should break your neck, you little weasel. She told me that you were going to rape her."

Paxton tried to pry himself lose but the bigger man had a grasp of steel. "Hey, man, chill out. I never tried any such thing. She was trying to get a rise out of you. You said yourself that she likes to make your life miserable."

Slowly Victor cooled down. He shoved the teen back into the seat and accelerated, shifting smoothly. "That she does, boy. I've tried everything I could think of to win her back. I send flowers, but she refuses them. I send candy, but she sends it back unopened. For her last birthday I wanted to buy her a car, but she wouldn't let me spend a penny. All she'll take is a little alimony."

"I don't get it," Paxton said. "A cool dude like you could have his pick of any woman in this state. Why do you beat your brains out over the Somersby babe? What does she have that makes her so special?"

"She was my wife."

"Yeah. So? How does that make her different from all your girlfriends?"

"I doubt you'd understand," Victor said. In truth, he didn't know how to explain. Nadine had always been unique, in his opinion, because she had accepted him as he was and never tried to mold him into the ideal husband. They had meshed really well together for most of their marriage. Theirs had been a perfect match until she had let her old-fashioned sense of morality ruin it.

The thought caused Victor to pound the steering wheel in irritation. He became even madder thinking about Ben Shields. Since the day Nadine left him, he'd held out hope they would get back together. He'd figured it would only be a matter of time. Eventually he'd wear down her defenses and she would be his again. But now Ben had come home after so many years, kindling whatever sparks burned in Nadine's heart. "Damn him," he growled.

"Who?" Paxton asked, then in a burst of insight said, "Oh. Him. That writer fella. He's not much competition, if you ask me."

"I didn't" Victor said in a flinty tone.

"I know. I know. Don't go stratospheric on me, Unc. I'm just saying that if you wanted to, you could stomp that wimp into the dirt without half trying."

"Idiot," Victor said. "Nadine would never look at me again if I hurt him."

"So come up with another way to convince him to take a hike," Paxton said. "Hell, you've got all the money in the world. That should give you some leverage."

"Surely you're not suggesting I buy Shields off?" Victor said. "Even you couldn't be that asinine."

He shook his head and took a curve as if he was driving in the Indy 500, his tires screeching shrilly, his nephew's words echoing in his mind. Maybe the kid had the right idea, he mused. Maybe there was some way he could eliminate Shields from the picture. But how?

"Oh, before I forget," Paxton said casually, "the day after tomorrow is Halloween. I know you want me home by midnight on school nights, but I'd like to stay out later just this once." He winked at his uncle. "It would make up for me having to go home early tonight."

"Don't push your luck."

"I'm asking nicely, aren't I?" Paxton said. "It's not like I'm trying to do it behind your back or anything."

Victor had to concede the teen's point. "Why do you want to stay out so late?"

"So my friends and I can soap up a lot of windows," Paxton said. "We aim to give this town a prank night no one will ever forget."

"Just so you don't get me involved," Victor said. "If I get a call to come bail you out of jail, I'll tell Sinclair to keep you there until Easter."

"You would, wouldn't you?" Paxton said, laughing. "And that fat pig would probably do it. Hell, it would make his day, since he's a good buddy of that writer and all."

"What?"

"Didn't you know? Chief Sinclair and Shields went off somewhere earlier tonight," Paxton said. "You should have seen that cop go flying down the street like a bat out of hell."

"Where did they go?" Victor asked, intensely curious.

"How should I know? The writer and Aunt Nadine were taking a little stroll when the chief showed up. It looked to me like Auntie and Shields were being real friendly, if you get my drift."

Victor flushed with fury at the mental picture of his ex-wife kissing another man. He'd been keeping close tabs on her since the divorce and knew she hadn't gone out with anyone, which was just as well for her since he wouldn't sit still for her going to bed with someone else. For him to play around was one thing. It was expected of men. But for her to do it was an insult he wouldn't abide.

Acting on the spur of the moment, Victor wheeled to the curb. "Hop out and blade the rest of the way. I'll be home shortly."

"Where are you going?" Paxton asked.

"To pick up the things I went to the market to get but forgot all about when I saw Nadine and you," Victor said. He drummed his fingers on the dash while his nephew slid out, then executed a tight U-turn and roared north up Simmons. Actually, he couldn't care less about the wine and munchies. He was more interested in finding out if Nadine would be meeting Ben later.

Two blocks shy of Clane's Victor turned left, drove a block, then turned right. In this way he came up on the market from the rear. Pulling into the shadow of another building, he switched off the motor and consulted his watch. About five minutes had gone by since he'd left Nadine. He debated whether to sneak over and see if she was inside, but figured he would give her another five minutes or so.

Hardly had Victor made the decision when Nadine and another woman appeared at the corner of the market. He remembered seeing the other one around town, a mousy blonde named Priscilla who had a hubby and three rug rats. If his memory served, she had been a grade behind Nadine and him in school.

The women talked for the longest while. Twice Nadine's gaze roved over the shadow shrouding Victor's car, but she failed to spy the vehicle, or if she did, she failed to realize it was his. He sat hunched low in the seat, only the top of his head above the dash. Part of him felt stupid for acting so childish. But he had spied on her so many times since the divorce that it was old hat to him.

At last Nadine and the woman clasped hands; then Nadine swung homeward, a small sack cradled in her left elbow. She hurried and kept glancing into the bag. Once she touched its bottom and wiped her fingers on her pants.

Victor trailed her on foot. He had on soft-soled shoes, so she never heard him. And by sticking to the darker patches, he followed her all the way without being spotted. When she went indoors, he crossed the street and hid in the shrubbery beside her house. From there he could see into her kitchen.

Nadine removed a container of sherbet and scooped herself a heaping bowl. She placed the rest in the freezer atop her fridge. Taking a seat at the kitchen table, she propped her feet on another chair and ate slowly. Her expression showed she was deep in thought.

Victor knew she was thinking about Ben Shields. He had always had a jealous nature, but the surge of raw jealousy that tore through him at that moment was so powerful he clenched his fists until his nails bit into his flesh. His vision blurred for a few seconds. When it cleared, she was gone.

While creeping through the shrubbery to a different vantage point, Victor saw Nadine take a seat in front of her television. She didn't act as if she were about to go out again or have a visitor, but he stayed there anyway, savoring the sight of her shapely legs and the swell of her sweater.

It struck Victor as a cruel stroke of fate that he should want her so much now when he had hardly given her presence a second thought during their marriage. She had always been there, like a painting on a wall that one passed every day without really noticing. Then one day she was gone, leaving a blank spot in his being, much like a missing painting would leave on the wall where it had hung so long.

Victor would get her back again. Of that he was confident. But first he had to come up with a way of eliminating the competition, as his idiot nephew had pointed out. He thought back to the old days, to when Ben had been his best friend, and he tried to recall any weaknesses Ben had that he could exploit.

Inside, the phone rang. Nadine dashed to answer it, but frowned when she had the receiver pressed to her ear. Clearly she had hoped it would be someone else, probably Ben. She hung up after a short while and resumed watching the tube.

Victor had seen enough. He melted into the night and hastened to his car. By the time he slid in behind the wheel, he was smiling. He had cooked up a scheme to eliminate Ben as a rival without Nadine being any the wiser. He laughed at his brilliance as he peeled out. Sometimes, he reflected, life was too grand for words.

Chapter Nine

An unnerving silence gripped the cemetery after the lingering echoes of the howl drifted away on the wind. Ben paused a dozen feet from the gate and began to sweep the area in front of him with the flashlight. To his annoyance the beam dimmed. He gave the flashlight a vigorous shake and the light flared to full strength, revealing the tombs nearest the front fence.

"Just head west," Travis called out. "You can't miss the shack."

Ben went on but he was far from pleased. By rights Travis should be the one going to find the caretaker; he was the lawman, after all. Granted, Travis was too overweight to scale the fence, but Ben felt there was more to the situation than that. His friend could have backed the patrol car up, climbed onto it, and climbed from the roof to the fence and over. But no. Travis let him go.

It reminded Ben of a fact he had nearly forgotten after being away from Cemetery Ridge for so long, a fact he had known all to well in high school. Travis Sinclair was the laziest person alive. In the past, Travis had been notorious for never doing a task he could get others to do. He had paid other students to do his homework, farmed out his chores for a share of his allowance, and avoided getting a job until his father had threatened to cut off his meals unless he secured work.

Now that Ben thought about it, he remembered that Travis had been accepted as a part-time policeman by kindly old Chief Boggs, who'd had one of the softest hearts in town and had no doubt taken pity on the boy. Ben wondered what had happened to Boggs, and he made a mental note to find out. He suspected that the old chief had died and Travis had been picked by the town council to fill his shoes since Travis was already on the force and knew all the ins and outs of the position.

Suddenly the flashlight started to die again. Ben gave it another shake and the beam brightened once more. He feared the batteries were on the verge of failing, so he doubled his pace. Being alone in the dark in a cemetery was not high on his list of favorite pastimes. Especially not with a savage beast roaming the countryside.

141

It didn't occur to Ben until that moment that the beast might be in the graveyard. He stopped dead in his tracks to listen more intently. A jittery sensation came over him, as if unseen eyes were on him. Ben grinned and shrugged the feeling off. So what if it was night and he was in a cemetery? He was a grown man, not a kid. He had to get a grip on himself.

"Is something the matter?" Travis yelled.

"No," Ben said testily. Firming his grip on the flashlight, he pushed deeper in among the mausoleums. The feeling of being watched returned, and it was so potent it took all of his willpower not to turn tail and flee. He passed one of the bigger tombs and shivered as a wave of cold air washed over him. Convinced it was all in his mind, Ben hastened on.

Once past the mausoleums Ben no longer felt as if he were being watched. Out in the open among the headstones, all his anxiety evaporated. He saw his fear for the sham it had been and was upset with himself for behaving childishly.

The shack stood out like the proverbial sore thumb, a squat wood affair that didn't look fit for human habitation. Ben was within a stone's throw of the structure when he saw the door had been left hanging wide open. Recalling how disagreeable Old Man Stoner could be, he stopped and said, "Stoner! It's Ben Shields. I'm here with Chief Sinclair. He wants you to unlock the gate."

No response came from the bleak dwelling.

"Isaiah? Do you hear me?" Ben said, advancing warily. He didn't care to have the caretaker rush out in a drunken rage and try to stick him with the big knife he carried. "The chief of police wants to see you."

Ben halted a few feet from the door. Bending at the waist, he peeked inside. A rank odor assailed his nose. He covered his nostrils and mouth with one hand and stepped into the doorway. "Stoner?"

The one-room dwelling was unoccupied. Ben saw a rickety table, a chair, a bookshelf, and a large cooler in a corner. That was it, except for some clothes on a short rack.

Ben would never understand the caretaker. It made no sense whatsoever for the man to live in a hovel when there were nice rooms for rent at low rates in Cemetery Ridge. Ben backed on out and made for the gate, winding among the headstones at a different angle from before. Instead of going through the middle of the mausoleums he planned to avoid most of them by swinging wide to the right.

Ben was no more than halfway there when the flashlight flickered twice, then went completely out. He tried his trick of shaking it but this time the batteries were totally drained. Now he had a choice to make. Should he bypass the tombs, which would take him 40 yards out of his way? Or should he cut straight across to the gate and save himself a minute of walking? He chose the latter since it meant spending less time among the morbid reminders of human mortality.

"Ben, everything okay?" Travis asked.

"Just fine," Ben grumbled. "I couldn't find Stoner."

He was soon among the stone and marble tombs, and almost immediately he had that troubling feeling of being observed. It was ridiculous, he knew, but he felt it just the same. Glancing right and left, he broke into a run, eager to put the sepulchers behind him.

Ben covered 20 yards. He had passed the largest tomb and was skirting another when his feet collided with an obstacle in his path. He threw his arms out in an attempt to regain his balance but gravity wasn't to be denied. His elbows and knees took the brunt of his fall, lancing his limbs with pain.

"Ben?" Travis said.

About to answer, Ben reached out to gain purchase for his left hand and his palm made contact with something lying there in the shadows, something soft and yielding. He plucked at it, ran his hand over it, and recoiled in horror upon identifying the obstacle.

"Dear God!" he breathed, leaping erect. Then, much louder, he said, "Travis! Get in here! There's a body!"

"What? Are you sure?"

Ben lost his last shred of patience. "Damn it, I know a corpse when I touch one! It's a dead man, I tell you!"

Over by the gate, Travis gulped and ran as fast as his bulk allowed to the patrol car. He hoped against hope that Ben was wrong, that he had merely stumbled on Stoner, who could have passed out from drinking too much alcohol. Revving the engine, he put the car into reverse and backed up over 60 feet.

Travis knew that Victor Richards would be upset, but he had to get into the cemetery quickly and there was only one way to do it. Jamming his foot onto the gas pedal, he roared toward the gate. The speedometer peaked at 50 miles an hour a few seconds before impact.

A crash shattered the night. The cruiser struck the gate squarely in the center, breaking the lock and bending several of the wrought-iron bars. The two halves of the gate were flung wide as the patrol car, its fender crumpled, its grill smashed, sloughed onto the grass and shot toward the tombs.

In the blazing glare of the headlights Travis saw Ben—and the body. His stomach churned as his worst fear came true. He slammed on the brakes almost as an afterthought and came close to running Ben over. In moments Travis stood beside Ben, staring in helpless horror, seeing in that grisly corpse the end of his law-enforcement career.

Ben was equally horrified, but for a different reason. He had seen Stoner earlier that day and knew the body was the caretaker's by the clothes the man had on. But how Stoner had changed!

"What could have done this?" he breathlessly asked the lawman.

Isaiah Stoner lay on his back, his arms out

145

flung, his mouth locked in the scream he had been voicing when he met his end. From the neck down he appeared normal, although his torso bore deep gashes. From the neck up he was a ghastly mockery of his former self. His skin lay shriveled on his skull, his eyes were sunken pits, his nose a flat flap, his ears drooping as if made of melted wax. His whole head was unnaturally white, as if bleached. Even Stoner's grizzled hair had turned the color of wintry frost. In the middle of his forehead a neat, round hole the size of a golf ball oozed a trickle of gore. The wound penetrated clear into the brain, which appeared shriveled and dehydrated and was as starkly white as Stoner's skin and hair.

"This is impossible!" Ben said, resisting an urge to bring his supper up. "Look at his face! It's as if he's had all the life sucked out of him."

"This is how Horace looked," Travis said, too stunned to think straight. "And those others."

Ben glanced at the chief. "What others?"

"The two tramps I found out by the interstate," Travis said without realizing what he was doing. Uppermost on his mind were the consequences he must face when Dr. Rutledge reported Stoner's death to the county coroner.

"I never heard anything about them," Ben said.

"That's because—" Travis began and then awakened to the blunder he had made. He'd be in enough hot water over Horace. If word got out about the hobos, he'd be crucified. Recovering his wits, he said quickly, "I have to call this in."

Travis headed for the cruiser, but stopped as a brainstorm hit him. He might be able to hold onto his job if he could keep word of the tramps' deaths from getting out. Since the only one who knew was Ben, he figured that shouldn't be too hard. "It looks as if I'll be out here all damn night, but there's no need for you to stick around. I can have the dispatcher call your mother, if you want."

"She goes to bed early," Ben said, reluctant to disturb her even though he didn't see that he had any choice. Then he thought of one other person whom he could impose on. "Have the dispatcher phone Nadine Somersby and ask Nadine if she'll run out to pick me up."

"Will do," Travis said.

Inwardly elated by his cleverness, he slid in and raised Hazel, the dispatcher. While he waited for her to call back, he took stock of the situation and realized it wasn't the tragedy he had made it out to be. He had a logical excuse to explain his lapse with Horace. And so far as everyone else knew, Stoner was only the second death attributable to the thing in the woods. He might be able to salvage his job yet, with no one the wiser about the secret he harbored.

Nadine had dozed off while watching the tube. The jangle of her phone snapped her awake and she was on her feet before the first

147

ring faded. Snatching the receiver to her ear, she mumbled, "Hello?"

"Ms. Somersby?"

"Yes." Nadine didn't know the voice.

"This is the Jackson County dispatcher calling at the request of Chief Travis Sinclair. He would like to know if you can drive out to the cemetery to bring Ben Shields back to town."

"Ben?" Nadine said, puzzled by the request. What were they doing out there? she wondered. And why hadn't Travis brought Ben back himself? She gave her head a toss, dispelling lingering tendrils of sleep, and said, "I'll be glad to. Tell him I'll be there in ten minutes."

After hanging up, Nadine stood staring into the wall mirror. It was her wish come true, a chance to finish the talk she'd had with Ben, to find out if she had a prayer of reclaiming his affection. Glancing upward, she mouthed the words, "Thank you." Then she saw that her clothes were rumpled and her hair was a mess. She ran to the bathroom, applied a brush to her red mane, and tucked in her blouse.

It took her a full minute to find her keys. She dashed out the door without bothering to lock it and in moments backed her car onto the street and raced toward the boulevard. Just as she went to turn onto Simmons an ambulance zoomed by with its lights flashing. She pulled in behind it and followed it all the way to the north end of the ridge.

Ben waited near the shattered gate. He waved

to her, then watched the ambulance pull into the graveyard. He wore a pinched expression as he opened the door and settled himself.

"What's going on?" Nadine asked. "Are you all right?" Through the fence she could see Travis directing the ambulance toward a certain spot. She gasped when she saw a body covered by a blanket. "Oh, my!"

"Old Man Stoner," Ben said. "The thing that killed Horace Walker nailed him, too."

"The bear, you mean?"

"That's the story," Ben said bitterly. The events of the evening had left him drained and weary. He leaned his head on the top of the seat and closed his eyes.

"Something's wrong, isn't there?" Nadine said as she slowly drove in a loop that brought her onto the road. Another vehicle with flashing lights was approaching from town—a county sheriff's car.

Ben didn't answer right away. He was torn in two directions. On the one hand he wanted to forget all about that awful night, to blot everything from his mind. But by the same token his journalist's instincts had been kindled and he was intensely curious to learn the answers to a number of burning questions.

"Are you sure you're okay?" Nadine asked. Ben appeared haggard and seemed to have aged ten years since she'd seen him last.

"Fine," Ben said. Taking a deep breath, he opened his eyes and sat up. "How well do you know Travis?"

"Not very well, I'm afraid," Nadine said. "He keeps pretty much to himself. What little free time he has, he spends with his family. Or so I've heard. Why?"

"I thought I knew him, but I'm beginning to wonder," Ben said and let the subject go at that. He couldn't get Travis's comment about the two tramps out of his mind, nor the evasive manner in which his friend had acted. It was as if the lawman had something to hide, and if that was the case, whatever Travis wanted to conceal had to be potentially embarrassing— and newsworthy. So what should Ben do? Go after the story and possibly cause his friend some grief? Or leave well enough alone and let Travis slide?

"If you don't mind my saying so," Nadine said, "you look terrible. How about coming over to my place for a nightcap and then I'll take you home?"

"Fine," Ben said, lost in thought.

Nadine wriggled with excitement. If not for Ben's somber air, she would have been positively ecstatic. At last she would have him all to herself. Now if only she could make him forget about whatever was bothering him for just a while.

Ben looked at her. Nadine seemed so eager to help him that he debated revealing the information he'd learned. She might know something he didn't. "Have you heard about anyone else being killed by this so-called bear?"

"Besides Stoner? Just Horace, like you said."

Nadine had to negotiate a turn, then she gave him a quizzical look. "Wait a minute. Are you telling me it wasn't a bear?"

"Not unless the bear came from another planet."

Nadine didn't know whether to take him seriously. "What are you saying? How exactly was Stoner killed?"

"It had to be seen to be believed. It was as if something drained him dry," Ben said, using the same words he had with Travis. "As if it sucked the life right out of him."

Suddenly Ben was back in Metz's cabin, listening to the old hunter say, "Whatever got ahold of him enjoyed sucking the life from his body. We're nothing more than lollipops to this monster."

Nadine heard a sharp intake of breath and saw Ben clutch the dash. "What's the matter? Are you going to be sick?"

"No," Ben said softly, staggered by the connection. Metz had been right all along. It made Ben wonder how much Metz wasn't telling. And it reminded him of Metz's claim that the same thing had happened years earlier. Could it be true, too? Ben abruptly realized Nadine was addressing him.

"Earth to Shields. Come in, Shields. Are you ignoring me on purpose?"

"I'm sorry," Ben said. "What did you say?"

"I asked if you wanted me to stop and pick up a TV dinner at the market? It's late or I'd cook you a full meal."

"No, thank you. I'm not hungry." Ben stared out the window at the indistinct black shapes flitting past. He speculated on where the creature might be at that very moment, on whether it was feasting on another poor victim somewhere in Cemetery Ridge. He remembered the hole bored through Stoner's forehead, right through the thick skull bone itself. Did the thing feast on human brains? Was that the key?

Beside Ben, Nadine didn't know what to do. She wanted to take his mind off Stoner's death and bring the conversation around to the two of them, but she was afraid of seeming shallow and selfish. He shifted toward her and she was shocked by the intensity his features radiated.

"I can use your help," Ben said.

"How?"

"There's more going on here than we know about and I intend to get to the bottom of it before I go back to Portland."

"What help can I be?" Nadine asked uncertainly. She was overjoyed that he wanted her assistance, but doubted her ability to be of any use. She knew next to nothing about being a reporter and even less about how to conduct investigations.

"I've been away too long. You know more people in town than I do. You might be of help with contacts. You can help me do research." Ben noted her worry and smiled to reassure her. "And it gives me an excuse to have the pleasure of your company."

Nadine had the opening she needed. She

grinned self-consciously and said, "You don't need an excuse."

"Then you have no reason to refuse," Ben said.

"No, I don't. And I'll tell you what. Since we haven't seen each other in so long, I'll call in sick and spend the entire day with you. How would that be?"

"Nothing would please me more," Ben said frankly.

A warm flush crept up Nadine's cheeks. She wanted to squeeze herself to see if she was dreaming. Fate had given her a golden opportunity and she wasn't about to waste it.

"There's one thing, though," Ben said.

Nadine tensed. She should have known it was too good to be true. "What?"

"It could be dangerous," Ben said. "I have no idea what we're getting into."

"But you do this sort of thing all the time, don't you?"

"I cover fires and car wrecks and occasionally a murder," Ben said, "but always after the fact. I leave police work for the police."

"Then why don't you let Travis handle this?"

Ben hesitated. The moment of truth had arrived. Should he lie to protect his former pal? Or did he trust his former sweetheart enough to share the truth? His heart wrestled with his conscience and his heart won.

"I honestly don't know if I can trust him. I suspect he's hiding something."

"What?"

"That's for us to find out."

Flattered by his confiding in her, Nadine impulsively reached out and squeezed his hand. "Thanks for telling me. I can't wait to start."

"You won't get into trouble taking the day off, will you?"

"Hardly. I haven't been sick once since I started working at Clane's. If the old fart raises a stink, I might just up and quit on him." Nadine grinned, then dangled some bait. "Maybe I'll move to Portland to be near my favorite writer."

Ben felt his skin grow warm. He squeezed her hand in return and leaned back, relaxing fully for the first time in hours. Her offer of a nightcap held more promise than he had foreseen, a prospect that stirred his loins. Then he gazed out the window again and thought he saw something big move along the side of the road. Twisting, he realized it had been an illusion created by an oddly formed tree reflected on the car's window. Yet it made him see that he was making a grave mistake. "I've changed my mind about the nightcap."

"Oh?" Nadine said, unable to hide her disappointment.

"I'd like you to come to my mother's instead and stay the night."

Nadine thought he was making a feeble joke. He had to be joking. She said as much.

"I've never been more serious," Ben said.

"Give me one good reason why I should."

"Because I don't want anything to happen to

you." Ben slid closer and pecked her on the cheek. "Whatever killed Stoner tonight is still out there. For all I know, it might be prowling the streets of Cemetery Ridge right this minute. I'd feel better if you were with us."

"But it hasn't broken into any homes that we know of," Nadine said. "Besides, what would your mother think?"

"She'd be glad to have you. There are two empty bedrooms upstairs. You're welcome to either one." Ben could tell she was going to politely refuse, so he put a hand on her arm. "Please. For my sake. Humor me."

Nadine's better judgment told her to turn him down. She'd feel silly if word ever got out that she had spent the night at the Shields' house because Ben was afraid she'd be devoured by some stupid monster. But she would be close to him, at least, and close was better than no contact at all.

"I must be crazy. All right. I'll do it."

Ben was thrilled. "I always knew you had a good head on your shoulders."

"Darn. I was hoping you'd noticed my assets lower down," Nadine said brazenly.

"Don't think I haven't."

Moments later the car swerved wildly as Ben leaned over and kissed Nadine full on the mouth.

Chapter Ten

It was the last hour before dawn when the huge pseudo-reptilian shape moved down a quiet side street in Cemetery Ridge. Its head swayed from side to side with each long stride. Now and again it would lift its nostrils on high, as if trying to catch an elusive scent.

All along Lincoln Street, dogs began whining or pacing back and forth, many with their hackles raised. A stocky Doberman emerged from a doghouse at the rear of a residence at the end of the block; it padded to the front corner of the dwelling, body slung low, growling deep in its chest.

The creature came to the curb and turned toward the house. In the same manner as a homing pigeon heading for its loft, the beast zeroed in on a second-story window and advanced.

Venting a fierce snarl, the Doberman charged from around the corner, lips drawn back to expose its tapered teeth. When still six feet from the alien intruder the dog sprang, mouth wide to rip and tear. A normal prowler would have been bowled over by the hurtling 50-pound fury. But not this time.

With an almost casual sweep of one rippling arm, the creature struck. The Doberman yelped as it was knocked flat and nearly senseless. It was barely aware there were three bloody slits that extended from behind its ear to its hindquarters. But it did know when the creature reared over it and felt the vise that clamped on its neck.

The Doberman yelped a second and final time when the towering terror lifted it into the air. The creature turned the dog from side to side as if examining the canine; then its three digits squeezed tightly, its claws shearing through muscle and bone, as if they were so much paper. There was a thud when the Doberman's head hit the ground.

Inside the house, in a bedroom on the second floor, Jimmy Howell stirred, then raised his head. He thought that he had heard his dog Boomer cry out but he couldn't be sure if it had really happened or if he had been dreaming. Drowsily he reached for his glasses, which were lying on the nightstand, and put them on. He intended to get out of bed but he was so sleepy his head plunked back onto the pillow and he closed his eyes.

David Robbins

Moments later Jimmy heard a muted thump from below his window. He sat up, perplexed, and heard it again, only louder this time. It was such an odd sound that he couldn't for the life of him figure out what it might be. Another thump brought him to his feet. Jimmy yawned and stepped to the window in his bear feet, the cool floorboards making him break out in goose bumps.

The sky had turned pale to the east, a harbinger of the new day. In the yard below lay a contorted black shape. Near it lay a large black ball. Between the two was a spreading red pool.

It took Jimmy's sleep-drugged senses half a minute to make sense of the scene. On realizing he was staring at the remains of his dog, he pressed his hands and face to the window.

"Boomer?"

A slight movement drew Jimmy's gaze below the window. He saw a strange shadow, or at least he assumed it was a shadow until it moved again and he realized it had substance and a definite shape. Raw terror coursed through him as he comprehended that the shape was alive, and it was clinging to the side of the house.

Jimmy could only gawk as the thing drew back a long arm and rammed its hand into the wall, imbedding curved claws into the metal siding. Then it slowly pulled itself higher, closer to his window.

Bone-numbing fear riveted Jimmy in place. His body was frozen but his mind raced. He had to be having a nightmare, he reasoned. Simple logic told him this couldn't be happening. But he could plainly see Boomer's lifeblood pumping onto the dew-covered grass. And he could see the creature, with its scaly skin, ungodly big head, and otherworldly eyes that were fastened greedily on Jimmy.

"The nectar! Must have more nectar!"

The words exploded inside Jimmy's head of their own accord. He rocked on his heels, feeling dizzy, disoriented. The creature rammed its other hand into the siding and Jimmy opened his mouth to shout for his parents.

In a twinkling a dazzling-white blaze of light burst inside Jimmy's head, paralyzing him and rendering him incapable of speech. He didn't know what was happening; he was so frightened he thought he would wet himself if his bladder were not frozen, too.

The beast clinging to the outside wall climbed nearer, its head still partially hidden in blackest shadow. One of its arms extended and claws that glittered like indigo pearls tapped the glass as if testing the pane's consistency. The arm was flung back for a blow that would drive those claws through the glass and into Jimmy.

At that instant two things happened simultaneously. From the far end of the house came a bellow, courtesy of Jimmy's father. "Jimmy? What the hell is all that pounding about?" And on the eastern horizon a shaft of golden light rent the sky.

159

Jimmy saw the creature jerk its head around. The thing stared at the brightening skyline a few seconds; then it abruptly released its hold on the siding and plummeted to the ground. With lizardlike speed it sped across the lawn, heading northward. Jimmy suddenly found he could move again and he stepped to the window.

The creature was two yards away, almost to the property of Jeremiah Sachs. It started across the lush lawn and then recoiled in surprise when the sprinkler system sprang to life. Sachs had installed an underground system several years ago that came on twice each day, morning and evening. He was supposed to turn it off before winter set in, but it was a standing joke among the neighbors that he never remembered until the first cold snap froze the system solid.

Now Jimmy stared in amazement as the creature spun and darted toward the street, weaving madly. He didn't understand why until it vaulted clear over a jet of water. It was trying to avoid getting wet, he realized, although why something so powerful would be afraid of a little moisture was hard to fathom.

The creature was only a few feet from the curb when a spray hit it squarely in the side. There was a crackling flash and it clutched at itself, then arched its spine as if in agony. In two incredible bounds it gained the safety of the asphalt and without hesitation flew northward, sprinting so fast its limbs were a blur.

Jimmy stared until it was gone. He touched his cheek to reassure himself that he was actually standing there. In the hallway heavy footsteps showed his father was on the way. Jimmy sagged against the wall, trying to sort out his thoughts, wondering what he should say. He didn't think anyone would believe the truth. But they had to, didn't they? He had proof.

Jimmy glanced out at Boomer and his tears came in a torrent.

Victor Richards awakened that morning in fine spirits. He had a scheme worked out and was eager to put the first stage into operation. For breakfast he polished off six scrambled eggs, as many strips of crispy bacon, two biscuits, and three cups of black coffee. His nephew straggled down to the kitchen as the maid was whisking Victor's plate and silverware off.

"Here comes Mr. Bright-Eyed-And-Bushy-Tailed!" Victor said. "You'd probably find the kitchen that much sooner if you would open your eyes when you climb out of bed."

Paxton sank into a chair and groaned. He never had liked rolling out of the sack before noon. In his estimation, having to get up at seven in order to be at school by eight was downright obscene.

"What's got you in such a good mood?" Paxton asked. "I haven't seen you this happy since that night you came home with a fox on each arm."

Victor rested his elbows on the table and entwined his fingers under his chin. "You might like to know that I've decided to take your advice."

"My advice?"

"About removing my rival from the picture," Victor said. "Out of the mouth of babes, as the saying goes."

"I'm not no broad. I'm a guy," Paxton said indignantly.

Sighing, Victor nodded at the maid, who had appeared with Paxton's bowl of cereal. After she had placed it on the table and departed, Victor went on. "I've decided to treat myself to a Christmas present. I'm going to give myself Nadine."

"Want me to gift wrap her for you?" Paxton asked and started to laugh. He cut his mirth short when his uncle's features became as hard as granite.

"I will say this only once," Victor said. "Never put your hands on her again or you will live to regret it. I've always tolerated your antics because you remind me so much of myself when I was your age. But there are limits, Pax. Nadine is special to me. Offend her and you offend me. Do you understand?"

Those last words reminded Paxton of a file scraping metal. "Sure, Unc. No problem." Once again he had glimpsed the inferno smoldering under his uncle's surface, and he was glad he wasn't Ben Shields. He lifted a spoon and began eating.

162

Victor slowly softened, then sat back. "If all goes well, Nadine will be living here by year's end. I won her once. I can do it again."

"She'd have to be nuts to keep on giving you the cold shoulder treatment," Paxton said. He failed to see why his uncle was so intent on reclaiming her love when there were so many other fish in the sea, but he wasn't about to criticize.

Victor rose. "I won't be home until late. Ms. Lander will have your supper ready at five. If you go roaming the streets with your friends, be sure to stay out of trouble."

"I will," Paxton said. And he meant it. He wouldn't risk spoiling the fun he had planned for Halloween.

The golden sun rimmed the pink horizon when Victor sank behind the wheel of his car. He rolled down the window so he could breath in the crisp morning air; then he drove along the circle driveway to the street. Glancing back, he admired his mansion, the home for four generations of his family, the single most expensive residence in all of Cemetery Ridge and Jackson County.

The streets were nearly deserted but the town was stirring to life. Victor saw men in bathrobes collecting morning papers from their sidewalks. He saw women shooing small children off to catch a bus. And briefly, he heard a police siren wail to the north.

A terrier ran yapping across the street as Victor pulled onto Edison. Years had gone by since last he had been in that neighborhood but he remembered the house well. Small, quaint, and tidy, as were most on that block. The homes of the little people, as Victor liked to think of them. The homes of the nobodies who would go nowhere in life. They were born without a penny to their names and most of them would pass on with hardly a penny in the bank. What did they have to show for their years of hard work and struggle? It never ceased to amaze him that more of them didn't blow their own brains out before old age hit.

Victor was partway up the walk when the door opened and out strode the man he wanted to see.

Ben wasn't anticipating company at so early an hour. He was smiling, thinking of the night gone by. His flannel shirt hung loosely over his jeans, and he wore slippers instead of shoes. He cast about for the paper, but halted in surprise on seeing his visitor. "Victor!"

"It's been a long time, old buddy," Victor said heartily and held out his hand. "I heard you were back and thought I'd stop by."

Ben shook hands and felt his fingers squeezed so tightly they hurt. He responded in kind and Victor grinned, then let go.

"That's quite a grip for a man who makes his living pounding a typewriter."

"I pound a computer keyboard," Ben said and stood so as to block Victor from going into the house. "What are you up to these days?"

"Compounding interest, as always," Victor said. He expected to be invited in but his old friend showed no inclination to do so. "How's your mother?"

"Doing well," Ben said, glad she was asleep so she wouldn't see fit to invite the man in. "Maybe we should get together later on when I have more time."

Victor was confused but he didn't let on. He had counted on Ben welcoming him warmly, on sitting down over a cup of coffee and sharing tales of their high school years when they had been the best of friends, not on Ben being aloof, almost cold.

"I was hoping we could talk now," Victor said, determined to see his plan through. If nothing else, he could rely on Ben's old-fashioned sense of integrity to influence him to do the right thing.

"About what?" Ben asked. As if he couldn't guess, he thought to himself.

"About my ex, Nadine," Victor said. "I've heard that the two of you ran into each other, and I know how highly you thought of her at one time."

"What does it have to do with you?" Ben asked.

Victor didn't like being quizzed but he offered no complaint because he wanted to stay in his old friend's good graces. "It's like this, Ben," he said confidentially. "I don't know if she mentioned it, but we're in the process of getting back together. Our divorce was a mistake, and it's been sheer hell for both of us." Victor smiled his most charming smile. "It would be terrible if you were to interfere with our reconciliation."

"How could I?" Ben asked.

"Simply by being here," Victor said. "She liked you once, remember? Seeing you again might ignite old sparks, give her second thoughts about us."

Ben said nothing.

"So I figured I'd drive on by and ask you for old times's sake to stay out of the picture," Victor said glibly. "I mean, what do you care, right? You've been away damn near ten years. Nadine can't mean anything to you after all this time." He put a hand on Ben's shoulder. "So what do you say, buddy? Once you think it over you'll see I'm right. Nadine is better off with me."

From the doorway came a scoffing retort. "That'll be the day, Victor. I'd be better off locked in a cage with a rabid wolf than I would living in that throwback to plantation days with you."

Victor glanced over Ben's shoulder and went numb from head to toe. There stood his ex-wife in a bathrobe. Involuntarily Victor glanced at an upstairs window as the horrible truth dawned on him that she had spent the night. All of a sudden Ben's aloof attitude made sense, and a rock-hard knot of sheer hatred formed in Victor's gut.

Nadine came to the edge of the porch. "What was that you were saying? Something about a reconciliation? It's news to me." She stood shoulder to shoulder with Ben and crossed her arms. "I've told him, Victor. Everything. He knows about the other women, about the times you slapped me around, about why I finally called it quits."

Victor was at a loss for words. His clever scheme had backfired, and instead of duping Shields into giving him a free field, he had tied a verbal noose around his own neck.

"I can't believe you did this," Nadine said. "It's a new low, even for you." She shook her head in reproach. "When will you get it through your thick head that I want nothing more to do with you? When will you accept that it's over between us?"

"It—" Victor began, but he had no idea how to finish the sentence.

He looked at Ben, longing for him to smirk or make a smart-ass remark. Then Victor would have an excuse to belt his former friend in the mouth, but there was only pity in Ben's eyes. It made him furious. Turning on his heel, he made for his car. Neither Ben nor Nadine said another word to him, which fueled his rage. He started his vehicle and screeched into the street. As he zipped past the driveway he spied Nadine's compact parked beside a van.

For the better part of an hour Victor drove aimlessly through the streets and alleys of Cemetery Ridge. He had no destination in mind, no desire to stop. All he could think of was Nadine and Ben. He had lost her for good.

Victor slowly came to his senses and looked around. He was startled to find he had driven out of town and was approaching the cemetery. Anxious to be alone, he pulled into the small lot bordering the fence. He was surprised to see the gate had been smashed and a yellow police ribbon had been stretched between the pillars to keep the public out.

Parking, Victor walked to the ribbon. He scanned the cemetery from east to west, but saw no one. Checking toward town, he saw no vehicles. So with no regard for the legality of violating a crime scene, he slipped under the ribbon, shoved his hands in his trench coat, and strolled in among the mausoleums.

The Richards tomb was the largest by far. Made from solid polished marble, it resembled the Parthenon. An early Richards ancestor had built the mausoleum at a cost that equalled the collective yearly incomes of everyone else in town at the time.

Victor frequently paid the tomb a visit, particularly when he was upset and needed to sort out his thoughts. Several times he had brought Paxton and tried to impress upon the youth the importance of the revered bones that lay within, but he doubted the teen would ever fully appreciate their family history.

For as long as there had been a Cemetery Ridge, the Richards had run the town. During its heyday, they had owned the bank, half-a-dozen businesses, the cemetery, and assorted pieces of valuable real estate. In recent years the family's fortunes had declined as the town waned, but Victor wasn't unduly disturbed. He had inherited millions, enough to last him and all his heirs for countless generations—provided he ever settled down and had children.

Victor placed a palm on the cool marble and smiled. Thinking about his illustrious ancestors lying within the tomb's walls always inspired him. He needed that inspiration now in order to think of a means of paying Nadine back for deserting him and of punishing Ben for stealing her.

Touching his brow to his hand, Victor absently gazed between the ornate columns to his left. He could scarcely believe his eyes when he discovered the mausoleum had been opened.

"What the hell?" Victor said and walked to the entrance. From within came a cool breeze, as if from the bowels of the earth. "Is anyone in here?" he asked, but received no response.

The smashed gate pointed at vandalism. Concerned that the tomb had fallen prey to malicious vandals Victor took a lighter he used to light the cigarettes of his women friends from his coat pocket. He flicked the striker wheel and held the flickering flame aloft. Warily, he entered.

The crypt was as it should be. Victor moved along the line of caskets, reverently touching each one. There was his father's; he had bled the bank dry by lending to phony corporations he set up and then had closed the bank down before the feds could investigate, using the logging bust as an excuse. There was his grandfather's; he had coerced the town council into approving massive construction projects and then had them award the contracts to construction businesses he owned. And there was his great-grandfather's; he had used Chinese, Mexicans, and blacks as cheap labor to cut down entire tracts of wilderness. Victor stroked each and every one of the caskets, grateful they were intact; then he turned to leave.

Someone stood near the doorway.

Victor blinked and said, "Who the hell are you? What are you doing in here?"

The shadowy figure didn't answer.

Angered, Victor held the lighter toward the trespasser but its feeble flame failed to reveal details. He took a step, fixing to throw the bastard out, but halted when the figure's size became apparent. The intruder was immense, towering halfway to the ceiling, which couldn't be. No one was that huge. "Who are you?" Victor asked again. "What do you want?"

A strange thing happened. Victor jerked, his spine tingling sharply as within his mind a peculiar sensation erupted, a sensation unlike any other he had ever experienced. It was as if a cat was purring inside his head. And to his consternation, the feeling gave him intense pleasure. The tingling spread into his groin, his thighs, his belly. He felt himself grow hard, and he was too astounded to move or speak.

"The nectar is the life. One day you will see."

"What did you say?" Victor said and realized he had heard the words inside his head, not with his ears. He saw the creature take a step toward him; then a long arm reached out to touch his cheek. He flinched, drawing back, and the sensual tickling inside his head abruptly ceased. A slight dizziness engulfed him, making him queasy. He put a hand on a casket to keep from falling and looked up.

The figure was gone.

Victor searched high and low, then ran from the tomb, blinking in the glare of sunlight. He scoured the cemetery, but saw no one else. "Who are you?" he cried. "Where did you go?"

No one responded.

Bewildered, Victor gazed westward, seeking signs of Old Man Stoner. The shack door hung open, but the old caretaker was not around. "Damned drunk," Victor grumbled. "Never around when I need him."

Pivoting, he stormed to his car and headed into Cemetery Ridge. He hadn't gone half a mile when it occurred to him that he had thought of a way of ridding himself of Ben Shields—permanently.

Chapter Eleven

Ben and Nadine left Cemetery Ridge for Medford shortly after nine that morning in Ben's van. Ben was slowing to turn onto the entry ramp to the interstate when the sight of the overpass jogged his memory. Instead of driving onto I-5, he pulled onto the gravel at the side of the road.

"What's wrong?" Nadine asked. "Why did you stop?"

"If someone was hitchhiking on the interstate and decided to spend the night here, where would he go?"

"To the Cemetery Ridge Motel," Nadine said.

"That takes money," Ben said. "I'm talking about a pair of tramps who probably didn't have five dollars to their name. Where could they find shelter nearby?"

"Don't you remember Marsten Park?"

It had been so long since Ben had been in the area, he had forgotten. He checked to be sure there was no oncoming traffic, then pulled out, drove under the overpass, and on another 50 yards to a narrow paved road that looped down to a small park flanking the Rogue River. A single car was in the parking lot. Over at a picnic table a mother and two small girls sat, feeding bread to ducks and geese.

A maintenance shack stood close to the lot. Ben tried the knob and wasn't surprised to find it locked. "I doubt they stayed in here," he said.

"Who were these men? Why are they important?" Nadine asked.

Ben explained about Travis's comments at the cemetery while bending his steps toward a cluster of boulders near the water's edge. All he found scattered among them were candy wrappers, crushed beer cans, discarded cigarette packs, and empty whiskey bottles.

"Civilization strikes again," he said and sighed. He should have known that finding clues would be hopeless. There was no telling exactly where Travis had found the bodies, if indeed it had been at the park.

Nadine noted his disappointment and could sense how much finding something meant to him. She longed to be of help. Seeing the sun highlight his hair and the square set of his jaw, she was more in love with him than she had ever been.

"Let's go," Ben said, taking her hand. He

started toward the lot, but stopped when his gaze drifted to the play area reserved for small children. There were four sculpted animals: a slide shaped like a giraffe, a set of monkey bars shaped like a gorilla, a seesaw shaped like a hippo, and a large hollow turtle the kids could crawl over, under, and through. "I wonder," he said.

"Wonder what, handsome?"

Ben pulled her toward the playground and walked up to the turtle. The lower edge of the shell was only two feet off the ground. "This would keep out the wind and the rain," he said, "and it's safe from prying eyes." Kneeling, he peered underneath. The dirt was littered with candy and gum wrappers, and in one spot lay a broken toy gun.

"Anything?" Nadine asked hopefully.

"No luck," Ben said and began to rise. That was when he spied a large round object beside one of the four legs that served to support the shell. He walked around, squatted, and felt behind the leg until his fingers closed on it.

"What did you find?"

Ben pulled out a withered wreath. The wire frame was intact but the roses and other flowers had long since died. Several bright ribbons were attached to the frame. On one were the words: *In Loving Memory Of Susan Parker.*

"Why, that's a gravestone memorial," Nadine said.

"Isn't it, though," Ben said.

"How did it get here?"

Ben was wondering the same thing. He stood

and made for the van, his find in hand. There were two possibilities that he could see. Either some kids had stolen the wreath from a grave at the cemetery and brought it all the way to the park, which seemed highly unlikely, or the tramps had gone through town, perhaps seeking handouts, and wound up out at the graveyard, where one had taken a fancy to the flowers and brought the wreath with him. The thing responsible for killing Horace and Stoner must have jumped the tramps while they slept. On the way into Medford Ben divulged his theory.

"It's possible," Nadine said, "but I don't see what good it does us. We know four people have died, but we still have no idea what killed them."

"We know it wasn't a bear," Ben said and shuddered, thinking of Isaiah Stoner. How many more poor souls would suffer the same horrid fate before the creature was stopped? he mused.

The rest of the ride passed in silence. Ben was preoccupied with ideas for solving the mystery. Nadine dwelled on sweet memories of the tender moments Ben and she had shared the night before. It amazed her that they had taken up where they left off almost ten years earlier without missing a beat. It was as if the past decade had never happened, as if they hadn't been separated a day. But that wasn't true, as she had to keep reminding herself. And Victor Richards wasn't the kind of man to graciously accept the change in the status quo. The look on his face as he left Ben's house that morning forewarned her of trouble looming on the horizon, and she prayed that she would see it coming so she could avert it.

At the local library Ben had the librarian pull up microfilm copies of the only newspaper published in the area 70 years earlier, *The Jackson County Courier*. Ben sat at one machine, Nadine at another, and between them they reviewed the entire year without finding anything of interest. Undaunted, Ben reviewed the *Courier* files for 69 years earlier, but again found nothing.

Over the next several hours they checked a ten-year span without results. The two of them developed cramps in their backs from sitting on small stools for so long. Ben became discouraged. Either Jacob Metz had lied or else the old hunter's memory was faulty. Ben acted on the latter assumption and asked the librarian for the film records prior to seven decades earlier.

Another hour went by. Ben was about ready to call it quits. He picked up another roll, checked the date of the newspaper, which was 73 years old, and threaded the film onto the spool. He smiled at Nadine, who had paused to glance at him; then he gazed at the screen.

Trapper Found Dead At Cemetery, the headline read. Ben leaned forward, scanning the page, learning about a man named Ezekiel Thompson who had been found sprawled across the grave of his beloved wife. The sheriff had blamed the death on a bear but the reporter mentioned there were strange circumstances surrounding the trapper's demise.

"Bingo," Ben said.

Nadine slipped off her stool to stand beside him, her hand on his shoulder. She read the account and grinned. "I think you're on to something, Sherlock."

"Stick with me, Watson," Ben said. "We'll solve this bloody case yet." He kept feeding the film, seeking accounts of other mysterious deaths. He didn't have far to go. The headline for the very next day said it all: *Woman Slain By Brain Eater*.

"Brain eater?" Nadine asked.

"Hush," Ben said and read the story.

Thirty-one-year-old Martha Pitt, the wife of Clarence Pitt, Cemetery Ridge undertaker, was found dead early this morning by her husband.

The cause of her death is still under investigation and few details have been released.

It is known that her body was in the same grisly state as that of Ezekiel Thompson's, with her face and hair white from fright and a sizable hole in the middle of her forehead made by the teeth of her attacker.

Word has spread like wildfire through the community. The sheriff has no answers but has vowed to bring the beast many are calling the Brain Eater to bay.

*   *   *

"Why, that's interesting," Nadine said.

"What is?" Ben asked idly while rereading the account.

"The date of that newspaper."

"October thirtieth. So?"

"So today is October thirtieth, silly. Tomorrow is Halloween, remember?"

Ben's interest intensified. He quickly went through the roll and changed to the next. Nadine gasped when the headline for Halloween appeared: *Five More Slain Overnight.*

"Dear God! What does all this mean?"

"I wish I knew," Ben said, taking a pad and pen from a pocket. He scribbled notes, sorting facts as he did, sifting the important from the unimportant. The account had taken up two full pages of print and from the tone it was clear the countryside had been in a panic.

Two bodies, a pair of woodcutters, had been found on the road between town and the cemetery. The third new victim, a man out fishing, turned up near Gardner Creek. Another dead woman was discovered in an alley in Cemetery Ridge. And the fifth corpse turned up in a ditch behind the church.

The sheriff had deputized 20 men and they were scouring the area. Smaller armed bands were also out looking. Everyone was advised to stay indoors until the animal was slain. Those who had to go out were urged to do so in groups.

"That makes seven so far," Nadine said. "I

wonder if there were any more?"

"Let's find out," Ben said.

Night Of Terror! Six Lose Lives! read the head-line for the next day. The Brain Eater, as the newspaper called the creature, had killed three more people in town and then been cornered at the cemetery by the sheriff's posse. The sheriff and two deputies had perished in the ensuing battle, which was interrupted by a thunder-storm. Under cover of a downpour the wily creature had escaped.

"Maybe they caught it the next day," Nadine said hopefully.

Ben quickly fed in the next spool. The first page was devoted to the hunt for the Brain Eater. Over 100 men, some from as far away as California, had joined in the search. No new deaths had been reported but everyone felt it was just a matter of time.

And so it went for the next week. The crea-ture never showed itself again. Despite diligent efforts by the best trackers in the territory, no trace of it was ever found. The dead were formally buried. Gradually life went on in Cemetery Ridge.

"That's it?" Nadine said.

"It can't be," Ben said. "Let's keep digging."

It was past six in the evening when they called it quits without having uncovered another clue. Nadine found two articles dealing with the Night of the Brain Eater, as the locals had dubbed that horrible Halloween, but both merely rehashed events and speculated on the

179

identity and fate of the mystery beast.

"I guess we didn't learn very much," Nadine said as they walked down the library steps hand in hand.

"I learned that Jacob Metz is a few years older than he claims to be," Ben said, grinning. Then he turned serious. "And we found out enough facts to take a look at the total picture and see if there's a pattern."

"What kind of pattern?"

"Any kind," Ben said.

"Well, what do we have so far?" Nadine said. "Two series of brutal attacks, both around Halloween, but over seventy years apart. I don't think that tells us much."

"Not in and of itself. But it can't be coincidence that the two incidents take place over the same short period." Ben drew up in midstride, realizing an oversight on his part. Swinging around, he headed for the library. "Come on. We forgot something."

"What?"

Nadine had half of the answer in her arms when they emerged a second time. "Fourteen books on Halloween," she said in amazement. "What good will they do us other than build up our biceps?"

"We won't know until we've gone through them," Ben said.

"But why the two books on graveyards?" Nadine asked.

"Doesn't it strike you as odd how many times the cemetery figures in the attacks?" Ben said.

"Of those that took place seventy-three years ago, four took place at the cemetery, two occurred near it, and one just over the ridge at Gardner Creek. The wife of the undertaker, who probably visited the cemetery more than most, was also one of the victims. Old Man Stoner was killed at the cemetery. Horace lived on the north side of the ridge. And the two tramps might have paid the graveyard a visit shortly before they were slain."

Nadine tried to make light of the connection. "Keep this up and you'll have me thinking that we're dealing with the supernatural."

"I wonder," Ben said softly.

He recalled Travis's questions about vampires, werewolves, and the like, and he wondered whether the lawman believed they were up against something similar. Ben had never believed in such nonsense himself, and he refused to accept the possibility just yet although he had to admit the facts strained logic to the breaking point.

On the ride to Cemetery Ridge they compared thoughts but came to no conclusions. Ben turned onto Simmons Boulevard and saw Gertie's Diner on the right. "Care for a bite to eat? My treat."

"You're on," Nadine said, glad she would have Ben to herself a little while longer. Even though they had spent most of the day in a musty old library, she hadn't had so fine a time in ages.

Ben took a corner booth. They had no sooner

sat down than they overheard two men talking at the counter.

"I'm locking the doors and oiling my shotgun. If that damn bear shows up in my yard it won't kill any more dogs," said the taller one.

"Who are you trying to kid? The way you shoot, the safest place for the bear to be will be right in front of you," said his companion.

Ben cleared his throat. "Excuse me. What's this about that bear killing a dog?"

"Where have you been all day, mister?" the tall one said. "Everyone in town is talking about it. Last night the damn thing killed the caretaker out at the cemetery and then had the gall to wander into town and rip a kid's Doberman to pieces."

"A Doberman!" his friend said. "They're supposed to be the toughest dogs around."

The tall one lifted his coffee cup, then glanced at Ben. "That's not the scariest part, if you ask me."

"What is?" Ben asked.

"The newspaper said the police found claw marks on the side of the kid's house," the man said and paused for effect. "The highest marks were ten feet above the ground. Ten feet! Can you imagine the size of the thing?"

Just then the tiny bell suspended above the door tinkled and in walked Travis Sinclair. Features drawn, shoulders drooping, he shuffled to the counter and started to ease his bulk onto a stool when he caught sight of Ben and Nadine.

He mustered a friendly grin and came over. "Mind if I join you?"

"Be our guest," Nadine said, sliding out so she could sit next to Ben.

Travis sank down with a weary sigh. "This is the first time I've been off my feet all day. We've been combing the town for the bear."

The tall man on the stool swung around and drew the interest of every other customer by declaring loudly, "So what about it, Chief? Can we sleep safe tonight? Or do we have to bring in all the pets and bar the doors and windows?"

"Give me a break, Samuels," Travis said testily. "It's just one bear."

"That's killed two people and a Doberman," Samuels said, holding his ground. "What's taking you so long in tracking it down? The old chief would have had the sucker skinned and mounted by this time."

"Get off my back," Travis said. He'd had the worst day of his entire career and was in no mood to tolerate criticism from an armchair expert who had no appreciation for the complexities of the case. "I'm doing the best I can."

"Well, maybe that's not good enough for some of us," Samuels said, rising. He paid his bill, then got in a last dig. "Just remember that you're a servant of the people, and if enough people get fed up and let the town council know, you'll be out of a job faster than you can say black bear." To the chuckles of several patrons, he went out.

"Bastard," Travis said under his breath and

looked glumly at his friends. "That's a perfect example of how my day has gone. I was out at the cemetery until four in the morning, scouring the area for clues. Then this morning at six I got a call from a frantic man who claimed his boy's dog had been torn apart." Travis stifled a yawn. "The damn bear took the dog's head right off."

"We heard there were claw marks on the house," Ben said.

"Were there ever," Travis said. "Judging by the height, it's the opinion of the fish-and-game people that the bear we're after is a monster."

"I seem to recall you were of that opinion once," Ben said. "Quite literally, as I recall."

"Yeah, well, who can say?" Travis said. He motioned at Gertie, who brought his usual cup of black coffee. "I'd also like the special and three glazed donuts for desert." Travis patted his bulging gut. "I have to eat light until this case is over with."

The owner giggled and waddled off. Ben leaned an elbow on the table and regarded the lawman critically. "So you definitely think it's a bear?"

"What else could it be?" Travis asked. Secretly he still had grave doubts, but in an early morning closed session with the town's top officials it had been decided to stick to the bear story for the time being in order to keep the populace calm. They were stalling for time while awaiting the coroner's report, which they fervently hoped would shed new light on the deaths and give them something to go on.

As far as Ben was concerned, his intuition told him there was more going on than Travis admitted. Rather than waste his breath in useless argument, he opted to drop the subject.

Nadine, however, was annoyed by the chief's attitude. Knowing about the tramps as she did, she branded Travis as incompetent if not worse and she was not at all bashful about speaking her mind. "When will the media be given the full story?"

"They've been told all the pertinent facts," Travis said, pressing the hot cup of coffee to his lips. He sipped noisily and nearly choked at Nadine's next query.

"Have you told them about the two hobos found in Marsten Park yet?"

Travis stared into his coffee cup to buy precious seconds to collect his thoughts. So far he had been able to keep knowledge of the two tramps a secret, except for his lapse with Ben. He'd entertained the hope that Ben would forget his comments. Then he could go on as if he'd never failed in his duty by not reporting the two deaths. Yet here he was, having his nose rubbed in his negligence. And if Ben had told the redhead, odds were that others knew. But Travis refused to admit defeat yet. There might still be a way of preventing Jackson County Sheriff Bo Seaver from finding out. All he needed was some time to think things through.

"No," he finally said. "We've been keeping that information under wraps."

"Why, in God's name? Don't you think the people have a right to know that this creature is more dangerous than anyone even suspects?"

"I'd say that the two bodies in the morgue and the butchered dog are enough to get the message across," Travis said.

"It's awful strange," Nadine said. "I never realized law enforcement agencies were supposed to keep secrets from those they're sworn to protect."

"The CIA does it all the time," Travis said and forced a low laugh. "What is this, Ben? I thought you were the reporter. How come she's giving me the third degree?"

Ben could read the underlying tension in the lawman's face. Travis was scared, and Ben had no idea why. Pressing the issue would get them nowhere, so he said good-naturedly, "Ease up on the man, sweetheart. He's had a rough day and deserves to eat his meal in peace."

Nadine glanced at him. He had called her sweetheart. It was the first endearment he had used since they'd gotten back together, and he had said it as naturally as he drew breath. Pleased beyond words, she clasped his hand in hers and kissed him on the cheek.

Travis swallowed more coffee, glad the heat had been taken off him for the moment. Then Ben addressed him again.

"There's a bit of information I need to pass on first, though, old friend. Nadine and I spent the whole day at the library, doing research.

We learned that over seventy years ago, several residents of Cemetery Ridge died the same way as Walker and Stoner. We're afraid there might be a connection."

"Oh, come now," Travis said, for lack of anything better to say. He refused to believe Ben's claim, because if true it rendered his worst fear a reality.

"There's more," Ben said. "All the victims died during the days preceding Halloween or on Halloween itself. And they were all killed at night."

"Coincidence," Travis said. "It has to be."

"You sure as hell better hope so." Ben pointed at the plate-glass window. "The sun just went down."

Chapter Twelve

Paxton Booth tilted a can of pop to his lips and drank, slurping loudly just for the hell of it. He polished off the contents, crushed the can, and tossed it into the street.

"Hey, dude!" Bill Paine quipped with a grin. "Don't you know it's against the law to be a litterbug?"

"Screw the law," Paxton said. "Especially the lousy excuse for a police department this town has. That fat scumbag is as worthless as tits on a turnip."

Cindy Drew, who stood next to the wall of the market with Manda Joyce, pulled her coat closer around her lush body and asked impatiently, "How much longer are we going to wait? It's turning cold. And he's not going to show up."

"Brainiac will show," Paxton said.

"After what happened to his dog this morning?" Cindy said. "I don't think so."

"Jimmy liked that Doberman," Manda said sadly. "He trained it to fetch and sit up and everything."

"Let's break out the violins," Paxton said and chuckled. He knew that as fond as the nerd had been of the mutt, Howell was even more fond of Manda. None of the hicks appeared to have caught on yet, but Paxton had. He'd noticed how Howell liked to admire her form on the sly and how Howell always hung close to her whenever there was trouble, like out at the cemetery the night before. So Paxton knew that the dork would show before too long. Not a minute later he was proven right.

It had taken all the courage Jimmy possessed for him to venture outdoors after sunset. He'd spent the entire day in his room, lying in bed and moping, frequently fighting back tears over the loss of his faithful friend Boomer. When not bemoaning the Doberman, he'd shivered in fear, seeing in his mind's eye the thing that had clung to the side of the house, seeing its arm reaching for him and those terrible claws tapping the glass.

Jimmy had told his parents and the police that the creature responsible for slaying Boomer wasn't a bear, but to his consternation none of them believed him. His father had replied that it had to have been a bear because no other predator living in southwest Oregon grew that big. His mother had merely smiled and hugged him. And the police chief had patted him on the shoulder and gone on about how people imagined all kinds of weird things under stress and emphasized that there were no such things as monsters.

It had only made Jimmy's anguish worse. He'd wanted to scream at them, to try to get it through their thick heads that Cemetery Ridge had become the private hunting preserve of a creature straight out of a horror movie, but he'd been able to keep his frustration in check.

As the sun sank, Jimmy's spirits dipped even farther. He desperately wanted to see Manda but he was afraid to venture outside. The creature was still out there somewhere. It had tried to kill him once for some reason, and for all he knew it might try again. He didn't want to make the chore any easier by leaving the protection of the house.

About the time that the sun vanished below the horizon, Jimmy realized that he was making a mistake that might cost him his life. It really didn't matter whether he stayed home or not, since the creature knew where he lived. He was being stupid if he believed the house offered any protection whatsoever. Indeed, since the thing had already tried to break into the bedroom, his safest bet was to stay anywhere but his room. The more Jimmy thought about it, the more convinced he became that he should leave. If he kept on the go all night, the thing would have a hard time finding him. He hoped.

So it was that Jimmy Howell appeared under the bright lights bathing Clane's Market about half an hour after sunset. He had overheard Paxton's crack about violins and had half a mind to tear into the bigger teen. But the moment he stepped into the light, he was shocked to his core by Manda, who gave a squeal of delight and threw her arms around him.

"Oh, Jimmy! Thank goodness you're all right! We've all been so worried about you!"

Jimmy blushed and heard Paxton roar with mirth. He clung to Manda so long that she drew her head back and studied him quizzically. Bowing his head, he let go and mumbled, "I missed you, too, Manda."

Jess Weaver came over and gave the skinny boy a hard clap on the back. "Glad to see you could make it. I didn't think your folks would let you out of the house."

"I snuck out," Jimmy said.

"Tell us about the bear," Paxton urged.

"I'd rather not," Jimmy said defensively and received a second shock when Manda took his hands in hers.

"Oh, please do! We're dying to hear what happened! The paper didn't say all that much." Manda giggled with excitement. "All the kids have been talking about it."

Reluctantly, Jimmy gave in and related the details. The others hung on every word, even Paxton. He almost broke down when he described Boomer lying in the pool of blood, but he bit his lip and plowed on.

"The police and my parents think a bear was to blame. I know better. And now you do. I hope that you'll believe me." He was staring at Manda but his statement applied to all his friends.

The other teens exchanged looks. Jess whistled long and loud, then said, "That's some story, pal. I'd like to believe you, but I'd have to see this thing with my own eyes first."

"Yeah," Bill said. "Don't get me wrong, but you were probably half asleep and only thought you saw a monster."

Paxton nodded. "That's what happens when you read too many books. Your imagination gets the better of you."

Profoundly disappointed, Jimmy looked at Cindy, who gave him the same sort of sickly smile his mother had all day, and then at Manda. She was his last hope. Surely she would believe.

Manda opened her mouth to laugh. The story was so preposterous that she didn't understand why Jimmy was so upset. No one in his right mind would believe Jimmy. But just as she was about to burst into mirth, she noticed a peculiar look in his eyes, a haunted, pleading look, the likes of which she had never seen before. It gave her pause and made her realize that her answer meant a lot to him. And it brought to mind the constant attention he had been lavishing on her for months on end. He always stayed close to her when the gang was out and about. He was always quick to buy her a pop if she was thirsty or candy if she was hungry. He never refused her when she asked for help with her homework. And just now, he had hugged her as if trying to squeeze her in half.

Manda's laughter died in her throat. She was stunned beyond words to realize that the thin boy in front of her cared for her as more than a friend. Doubly stunned because such a thing had never happened to her before. Cindy was the one who always got the boys. Not her. Not ever.

"I believe you, Jimmy," Manda said, hoping he wouldn't see through her lie.

Jimmy brightened for the first time all day. "Thank you," he said softly and made bold to squeeze her hand in gratitude. He wanted to stand there holding her hand forever but the magic moment lasted mere seconds, until Jess spoke and Manda self-consciously lowered her arm.

"So what's on tap for tonight, Pax? Maybe we can puncture a few car tires. Or how about if we catch a cat and set it on fire?"

"Not tonight," Paxton said. "Tonight we're being good little kids."

"We are?" Jess said.

"Why?" Bill asked.

"Because if I get into trouble tonight, my damn uncle will ground me tomorrow," Paxton said. "I don't want anything to screw up the night I have planned. "We're all set, aren't we,

Jess? I don't want any hitches at the last minute."

"We've got a green light," Jess said. "My buddy will cover for me. But you'd better be right about getting the stuff back before morning or my butt will be in a sling."

"No problem," Paxton said.

Jimmy had been listening with half an ear. He had seen a drastic change come over Manda's expression and was aware of a subtle change in her attitude toward him. She had stayed by his side instead of returning to Cindy's; she was even casting shy sidelong glances at him. On hearing the comments made by Paxton and Jess, he tore his gaze from her to ask, "What stuff are you talking about? Have the two of you been making plans behind our backs?"

"I came up with the plan," Paxton said. "And you'll find out what it is tomorrow night, along with everyone else."

Bill acted hurt. "Don't you trust me, Pax? After all the time we've been hanging out together?"

"Sure I do, Bill," Paxton said. "I just want to surprise you. Trust me. You'll like what I have planned."

Bill grinned. But Jimmy was far from happy. He wouldn't put it past Paxton to get all of them into a lot of hot water, maybe even thrown into jail. Jimmy wasn't about to let that happen to him or to Mandy.

"I just hope that, whatever you have up your sleeve, you don't go overboard," he said.

"Hell," Paxton said. "What's the use of being alive if a person doesn't push life to the limit now and then?" He gestured at the tranquil town. "I don't want to end up like the rest of these losers, doing the same boring things day in and day out. Where's the fun in that?" He shook a fist at the sky as if challenging an unseen deity. "I want excitement. I want adventure. So when I die, I can look back on my life and say that I lived to the max!"

"Right on," Jess said.

"I'm with you," Cindy said. "When I kick the bucket, I want to do it in style, not sitting on a couch watching the boob tube."

Jimmy turned away. They were hopeless, a mindless bunch of overgrown kids who couldn't see reality because of their own selfishness. Manda, he noticed, didn't join in their banter, which made him proud of her. She, he assumed, had the brains to foresee the trouble they could get into. Without being obvious, he enfolded her hand in his and was thrilled when she made no move to break contact. For the time being he forgot all about Boomer—and the creature.

Several miles to the north stood a man who hadn't been able to put the monstrosity from his mind for a moment since it nearly killed him. Fred Larkin stood near the front of his mobile home, staring thoughtfully at the ridge to the south.

Larkin wanted to nail the creature that had attacked him. He wanted to pay it back for his pain and suffering, but even more crucial was his yearning to get even for the shame of having been beaten at his own game and in his own element.

The poacher had never been one to take being beaten gracefully. Every animal he poached was a challenge to his skill. Never, in all the years he had plied his illegal trade, had a beast bested him before. He had confronted bears, mountain lions, wolverines, and coyotes on their own terms time and time again and proven himself the victor.

Since his return home, Larkin had spent every waking moment plotting and scheming. He had reviewed every moment of the encounter, from the initial sighting high on the ridge to the clash in the pool. Over and over he had relived each instant, concentrating on the creature's behavior, on its actions and reactions.

Therein, Larkin knew, lay the key to beating the thing. Every wild creature had certain habits, certain weaknesses. All a skilled hunter had to do was identify his quarry's Achilles' heel and use it to prevail. He'd applied the same technique countless times on lesser beasts and it had always worked.

Of the creature's habits, Larkin mentally noted that it was nocturnal, it hunted humans for prey, and it somehow paralyzed its victims right before striking. Of its weaknesses he isolated only one, and then he wasn't completely certain it qualified as a weakness. Time would prove him right one way or another because he was determined to confront the creature again.

Fred Larkin wasn't a fool. He knew that the creature was no ordinary animal; if he went up against it a second time he might pay with his life. But he could no more pass up the challenge than he could stop breathing.

In a quirky twist of logic, Larkin was almost grateful the creature had appeared when it had. Poaching had lost a lot of its luster. Real challenges rarely presented themselves anymore, Larkin's skill being such that the craftiest of animals were no match for him.

This thing was different. It was almost as if it had been sent on purpose by a higher power to test Larkin's ability. Or if not by a higher power, then from somewhere very like the alien realms and dimensions he had seen on *The Twilight Zone* so many years ago. It was a dream made real, an answer to his innermost longing, the challenge to end all challenges.

Suddenly Larkin's reflection was cut short by the distant growl of a car engine. He glanced toward Knob Road and was surprised to see headlights sweep onto his dirt drive. Figuring it had to be the nosy chief of police, he dashed into the mobile home, grabbed his rifle, and hastened out into the strip of brush bordering the overgrown yard. He loaded a round into the chamber and left the hammer cocked.

The vehicle came on slowly. When it was still a quarter of a mile away Larkin could tell it was too big to be a police car. At 300 yards he pegged it for a van and tried to think of anyone he knew who drove one. None of his few freinds did, nor any of his customers.

The van braked near the mobile home. A big man climbed out and spoke to someone in the passenger seat before facing the house and calling out, "Fred Larkin! It's Ben Shields! I met you at Metz's last night. I'd like to talk."

The name was unfamiliar but Larkin remembered the voice of the stranger who had made him out to be an idiot. Rising, he stalked soundlessly forward until he was so close he could have hit the man with the rifle. "Looking for Martians, mister?"

Ben whirled, his heart in his throat. He took a moment to control his nerves, then plastered a smile on his face. "I shouldn't have poked fun at you, Fred. That was uncalled for and I'll apologize right off."

Larkin glanced at the van and saw a woman staring back at him. He shifted so he could keep both of them in sight. "What do you want, Shields? I'm a man who likes his privacy."

"I need your help," Ben said. "Or perhaps I should say the entire town needs your help."

"You're not making any sense," Larkin said. "Most of the people in that rotten town can't stand my guts. They see me coming down the street and they cross to the other side just so they won't have to give me the time of day."

"That may be," Ben said, his gaze on the rifle. "But is that any reason not to help them when they need it most?"

"Are you sure that you're talking to the right person? What could I possibly do for them?"

"Help me track down the thing that nearly killed you before it claims more victims."

Larkin snorted. "What do I care? Those people don't mean squat to me."

"Women and children included?"

Deciding his visitors were harmless, the poacher lowered the hammer and set the stock on the ground. "Mister, you have your nerve. Last night you accused me of seeing little green men. Tonight you want me to risk my hide for people who would just as soon spit on my grave." He gestured toward Knob Road. "Get off my property before I laugh myself to death."

Larkin went to go by but Ben stepped into his path. "Hear me out, please."

"Give me one good reason why I should?"

Ben paused, seeking the right words. Back at the diner, the idea had occurred to him to ask for the poacher's help. He'd waited until Travis had left and then grabbed Nadine and jumped in the van. He hadn't really thought out how to present his pitch and he could see it was going to be a lot harder than he'd anticipated. Humanitarian instincts weren't Larkin's strong suit.

"Did you know that over seventy years ago several people were killed by the same creature or another just like it?"

"So? I wasn't alive then."

"Jacob Metz was. And he claims you're the one man who might stand a chance against the thing."

"Metz said that?" Larkin asked, tickled. The old hunter was one of the few people he truly respected.

"He was surprised it got you," Ben said. "He said he didn't think anything could get the better of you in the woods."

Larkin grinned like a little kid. "I'll be damned. I didn't know the cagey fart thought that highly of me." He studied Ben a moment. "But buttering me up won't make me change my mind. I have as little use for the good people of Cemetery Ridge as they have for me." The poacher chuckled. "Except for my customers, of course."

Ben wouldn't accept that the man could be so callous. "You don't understand. Based on our research, I believe there's a pattern at work here. Why, I don't know. But if I'm right, it will strike again tonight and tomorrow night unless someone stops it, And you're the only one who can."

"If I do, I'll stop it when and how I see fit."

"We can't delay, Larkin," Ben said. "I'm not talking about one or two more deaths. This thing will kill lots of people before it's done. Men, women, kids—it doesn't care."

"Just so I'm not one of them."

Growing peeved at the man's stubbornness, Ben gestured at the rifle. "Damn it, you have a better chance than Chief Sinclair and his deputies. You're a skilled woodsman. They're next to worthless."

Larkin winked. "At last we agree on something, mister." He raised the .45-70 and propped it on his right shoulder. "But that's all we agree on. So you and the lady go pester someone else. Or maybe try Metz. He might lend a hand."

"We need you," Ben said plaintively.

Laughing, Larkin started toward his mobile home. He had taken several strides when the van door slammed and the woman rushed over.

"What's the matter?" Nadine asked Ben. "Won't he help?"

"No," Ben said, wondering how many more deaths he would read about in the next day's newspaper.

Nadine swung toward the poacher. The odor he gave off nearly gagged her but she was too mad to care. "Why won't you? Are you scared?"

Larkin cocked his head. He was of half a mind to slap her for the insult. "I'm not afraid of anything that lives, lady."

"Then why?" Nadine said. "Ben tells me that you faced this thing once and lived to tell of it, which makes you unique."

"No fooling," Larkin said, admiring her perky features and red hair. It wasn't often he got so close to a woman. He'd almost forgotten how pretty they could be, and he found himself envying Ben.

"You're a human being, aren't you?" Nadine said, trying another tack. "So there must be a shred of human decency somewhere inside you. Last night that creature almost broke into a teenager's bedroom. Tonight it might be a baby. Or maybe a young girl."

"Your boyfriend already tried the women and kids approach," Larkin said. "It didn't work none too well, so I wouldn't waste my breath if I were you."

Nadine stiffened. "Oh, I get it now. You don't give a damn about anybody but yourself."

"Smart lady." Larkin grinned at Ben. "Stick with her, mister. You'll go places."

"Then I was wrong," Nadine said stiffly. "You don't have a shred of human decency."

"Another home run," Larkin said.

Ben had tolerated all of the poacher's smug retorts he was going to. Taking Nadine's wrist, he said, "Let's go. We're wasting our time here. We'll go pay Jacob Metz a visit. He'll help. Let Metz get all the glory."

"What was that?" Larkin said.

Ben answered while guiding Nadine to the door. "Whoever kills this thing will be in all the papers. On TV and radio, too, I should think. He'll be famous." Ben grabbed the handle. "But fame doesn't interest you, I know. Travis told me how you make a living. A poacher has to keep a low profile. It wouldn't do for you to get all that publicity. Sorry to have bothered you. I should have thought of it sooner."

Larkin didn't give a damn about glory. He saw right through Ben's attempt at manipulation. But it abruptly struck him that, if he killed the creature, everyone in Cemetery Ridge would be in his debt. Better yet, he could rub their noses in it by going on television and telling the whole world.

"Hold on a second, mister."

Ben had the door half open. "What's on your mind?"

"How do you propose we work this out? The creature isn't about to come running when we whistle."

"I have a police scanner in my van," Ben said. "We'll spend all night combing the streets and hope we get a break. If we do, killing the creature will be up to you."

"If you can," Nadine said.

Fred Larkin strolled over to the van and leaned on the fender. "Lady, there isn't an animal born I can't lick, whether from this world or another."

"What?" Nadine said.

"Never mind," Larkin said. "Just slide on in and wait while I fetch a few things. It never hurts to have an ace up your sleeve." Chortling, he dashed off.

"We did it!" Nadine said, thrilled by their success.

"Yeah," Ben said. "I just hope we don't live to regret it."

Chapter Thirteen

Travis walked into his spartan office and plopped his rotund frame down in his swivel chair with a sigh of relief. It felt great to have some time to himself after the nerve-racking day he'd just gone through. The meal at Gertie's had hit the proverbial spot and made him drowsy enough to consider taking a nap. He pushed his hat back on his head and began to stretch, then froze.

The front door had swung open and a lean figure in a neatly ironed uniform stood framed in the doorway. Jackson County Sheriff Bo Seaver looked right and left before sauntering in and flipping the door shut with a deft backward toss of his left hand. He came over to one of the chairs and took a seat without being bid to enter or sit.

"We need to talk, fat boy," he said harshly.

Travis slowly lowered his arms and struggled to control his temper and his fear. He licked his lips, rested his elbows on the desk, and said casually, "Hello to you, too, Bo. To what do I owe this honor?"

"Cut the crap, Sinclair," Seaver said with disdain. "We both know that I can't stand the sight of you. So don't bother acting friendly to me when I'm not about to return the favor."

"As pleasant as ever, I see," Travis said dryly.

"What else do you expect?" Seaver said, his flinty features hardening. "Hell, boy, we've been all through this a dozen times. I don't think you're qualified to wear that badge. It's that simple."

"You have yet to give me a valid reason," Travis said. "I know I barely squeaked through the academy, and I don't run my department with the same spit and polish that you do yours. But that's no excuse for your hating me the way you do." Travis sniffed in indignation. "You told me years ago I'd never amount to much in law enforcement, so you must have been pretty jealous when I was picked as chief of Cemetery Ridge."

Seaver drummed his fingers on the chair arm a moment. "How long before you get it through your head, fat boy? Nearly failing the academy doesn't matter all that much. I've seen others do the same and go on to be outstanding officers." He glanced around the unkempt office.

"And being a pig doesn't matter either. If you don't have any pride in yourself, that's your business."

"Then—"

"You know the bottom line," Seaver said, "and it has nothing to do with jealousy. How many times must I keep rubbing your nose in it? You don't deserve to wear a badge because you're the laziest son of a bitch on the face of the earth, and you have been since you were knee high to a grasshopper."

"Even if that's true, and I'm not admitting it is, since when has laziness been a crime?"

"You just refuse to get the point, don't you?" Seaver said. "In most any profession a man can be a little lazy and get away with it. Who cares if a garbageman slacks off a few minutes a day, or if a sales clerk hides out in the stock room for a half hour or so? No one else is affected. But when a cop slacks off, other people pay the price." Seaver sat forward. "If a traffic cop is catching forty winks in the back of his cruiser when he shouldn't be, he might miss spotting a drunk driver who later causes an accident and kills someone. Or if an officer sees a drug deal going down, but doesn't bother to collar the suspects because he can't stand the thought of all the aggravation and paperwork he has to go through, he could be responsible for making a lot of people suffer."

"You're blowing my past out of all proportion," Travis said. "A man can change. I do a good job."

"Do you?" Seaver started ticking off incidents on his fingers. "Who sat in his patrol car at the south end of Simmons one night with his radar on and let four speeders go by without stopping one of them? Who let those bikers trash Hagan's Bar and didn't bother going in to arrest them until they were so drunk they couldn't see straight? Why is it that arrests in all categories dropped like a rock in Cemetery Ridge after you took over? Thefts, down forty percent. Controlled substance abuse, down sixty percent. Assaults and disturbing the peace, down seventy percent."

"I can explain. There are extenuating circumstances you have to take into account," Travis said. He regretted not letting the matter drop when Seaver had brought it up. Practically every time they saw one another, Travis ended up with a major headache.

"Bull," Seaver said. "There's never any excuse for a cop not doing his job. A good cop, anyway." He scowled. "I wish to hell that this town was in someone else's county, so I wouldn't have to put up with your incompetence. Which brings me to the purpose for my visit."

Travis stayed silent, his fear flaring.

"I've been doing some checking on this bear business," Seaver said. "It's bad enough you didn't notify me when the first victim was brought in—"

"Horace Walker died in my jurisdiction," Travis said.

"True. But it would have been common courtesy to let me know that a killer bear was roaming the county, which is my jurisdiction," Seaver said. "Of course, now we know it isn't a bear. But I'm straying off the point." The sheriff's dark eyes bored into Travis. "I talked to Doc Rutledge. I suppose there were extenuating circumstances why you didn't handle Walker's death by the book?"

"I thought it was a bear. I didn't see any need for an in-depth investigation."

"Uh-huh. Or were you just being your lazy self again?"

Travis let himself unwind a bit. Apparently the sheriff hadn't uncovered his gross negligence. Or so he thought until Seaver opened his mouth again.

"And what the hell is going on in Marsten Park?"

"What are you referring to?"

"Today the wife of one of my deputies was there with her kids. She told him that she saw a man and a woman hunting all over the park, as if they'd lost something. They finally went over to those sculptures at the playground and pulled a dried-up wreath from under the turtle. What do you make of it?"

"Beats me," Travis said. But he could feel his ulcer kick in and he opened his top drawer to find his medicine.

"Really? That's strange. Because about a week or so ago the same deputy was coming home after a swing shift and he saw your patrol car parked at the park. He drove down to see if you were all right. But there was no sign of you."

Travis's mouth went dry. Deputy Steve Miller lived on the outskirts of Cemetery Ridge and had long been relaying information to Seaver. He'd often wished the man would move to another town.

"What were you doing there?" Seaver asked.

"Probably just making a security sweep," Travis said truthfully. "A lot of transients like to camp out there, as you well know." He didn't mention finding the two bodies under the turtle or detail how he'd dragged them to the river, weighted them down with rocks, and let them sink so he wouldn't have to stay up all night making out paperwork and dealing with the county boys. He'd been at the end of his shift and eager to get home. At the time he hadn't thought that dumping two bums in the Rogue River was any big deal. He'd counted on no one ever missing them. Sure, they had looked downright bizarre, with their faces and hair all white and those holes in their foreheads. But he'd figured that whatever had killed them was long gone. How was he to know the damn thing would decide to haunt his town?

"Hmm," Seaver said. "Well, I guess I'll be going. But don't think I'm letting you off the hook. You violated procedure with this bear business." The steely lawman rose. "I'll be keeping my eye on you, Sinclair. Sooner or later you'll screw up royally and I'll be there to put you out of the county's misery."

"Thanks for the warning," Travis said.

The next instant the radio crackled and the dispatcher came on the line. Sinclair swung his chair to the console and stabbed the send button. "Talk to me," he said.

Sheriff Seaver hissed. "Is that the proper way to use an official channel? Or have you forgotten the codes they taught you at the academy?"

The dispatcher answered before Travis could. "A woman just called in to report that a large animal had broken into her house. The address is 1423 Trammel Drive. She was cut off before I could get her name or other details."

Seaver was already halfway to the door. "Come on. We'll handle this one together."

Travis had no such desire, but he didn't want to antagonize the sheriff further by refusing. He lumbered out briskly and slid into the county cruiser. Seaver shot from the curb as if from a cannon, forcing Travis to hold on tight as the car whipped in a tight U-turn.

They hadn't gone two blocks when the sheriff was on the horn for backup. Two of his boys responded. "Now you'll see how law enforcement should be conducted."

Trammel Drive was north of town, about halfway between Cemetery Ridge and the graveyard. Sheriff Seaver roared down Simmons doing 80, weaving in and out of traffic with polished skill. Once past the town he buried the pedal. "The damn thing isn't getting away this time. With any luck we can be on the scene before it gets away."

The prospect made Travis's brow break out in a sweat. He put a hand on his service revolver, trying to recall the last time he had checked to see if it was loaded.

"Forget that peashooter," Seaver said. He handed over a key and nodded at a shotgun mounted on the dash. "We'll need heavy artillery. Check in the glove compartment and you'll find a box of buckshot and a box of slugs. Take your pick."

Travis fumbled with the lock, then dropped the key. He had to rummage around the floor for a minute before finding it. The patrol car had swerved onto Trammel by the time he had the shotgun in his hands and was opening the glove compartment.

"Hurry it up, fat boy," Seaver said in disgust. "We'll be there in thirty seconds."

Travis tried his best but he spilled shells all over the seat as he took the buckshot from the glove compartment. It had been so long since he handled a shotgun that he bruised his thumb inserting the first shell.

"You're pathetic, you know that?" Seaver said. He was reading house numbers, and when he came to a mailbox marked 1423 he veered onto the lawn and braked so sharply that the patrol car slid sideways to a stop, narrowly missing an oak tree. In a twinkling he was out, his nine-millimeter SIG/SAUER cocked and in the ready position. "Come on, lard butt," he said. "Bring that cannon."

Travis threw his door wide open and jumped out. He had one shell in the shotgun and worked feverishly to add more. Seaver dashed ahead, then halted at the front porch. Moments later Travis saw why.

The door had been ripped off its hinges and lay on the porch, split down the middle. Part of the frame had also been torn off, leaving jagged wooden daggers from ceiling to floor. The interior of the house was as black as pitch.

Sheriff Seaver moved to the left of the door and motioned for Travis to take the other side. Travis remembered to feed a shell into the chamber as he did, which drew another glance of disapproval for making noise. Seaver then ducked low and scooted inside, turning from right to left, his body as well as his automatic on a hair trigger.

Travis imitated his peer, keeping his broad back to the wall. He stopped to orient himself and observed a hallway to his right, another room to his left. From somewhere at the back of the house came a dripping sound, as if a faucet leaked.

Suddenly the living room blazed with light. Seaver had switched on the overheads. Bent at the waist, he dashed to the room. He shook his head, then gestured for Travis to join him in converging on the hall.

Tucking the shotgun against his side, Travis complied. He was sweating profusely and his knees felt wobbly but he wasn't about to show any weakness with Seaver right there.

The hallway led to an empty bedroom, then beyond to a kitchen. Seaver looped an arm around the corner and flicked the switch several times but the light failed to come on. He glanced at Travis, crouched, and plunged into the darkness.

Travis swallowed hard and did likewise. The silhouettes of a stove, a sink, and a table were unmistakable. The fridge stood to his left, hanging open. He assumed the drips he heard were from ice melting until he saw something hanging from the top of the refrigerator door. Seaver had seen the same object, and they warily advanced.

It was a dog, a big brown mongrel, its neck broken, its throat ripped in half. Whatever killed it had smashed it down on top of the door with such force that its spine had snapped and the head caught fast.

Travis tried to imagine the kind of creature capable of doing that to such a powerful pet, easily twice the size the Doberman had been. He glanced at the back door, which also hung wide open, and took a step, stopping upon hearing a low drone that issued from a corner of the counter.

Seaver found the receiver, upside down on a towel. He reached out to replace it on the phone, then recoiled and sucked in his breath.

Travis had to squint to distinguish the severed hand attached to the receiver. There were dark stains on the towel and counter, more on the floor. He fought back an urge to bring up Gertie's doughnuts.

Just then, in the backyard, there was a loud thud.

Seaver reached the door in three strides, peered out, and sprinted into the night. Left alone, Travis quaked. He had never been so scared, and it took all his willpower to keep from bolting. Holding a finger lightly on the trigger, he followed the sheriff, grateful for the brisk breeze that fanned his florid face. He scoured the wide yard dotted with trees and shrubs, but saw no trace of Seaver.

Travis had a horrible thought. What would happen if the sheriff should be killed? Seaver's men were fanatically loyal. They'd blame Travis, accuse him of incompetence, and do all in their considerable power to make his life miserable. He hurried across the clipped lawn, his concern for his well-being eclipsing his terror.

East of the lawn reared a thin strip of trees. Travis glimpsed a flash of movement among them and raised the shotgun to fire but the figure disappeared in the foliage. He had no inkling of the figure's size or shape. His cheek against the cool metal of the shotgun, he took measured strides toward the spot.

A loud crunch signified a creature was definitely in there. Travis sidled nearer, focused on a point about eight feet above ground level since the creature was supposed to be enormous. If he saw a bestial face staring back at him, he intended to shoot at its head, confident there wasn't a creature on God's green earth able to withstand a load of buckshot at short range.

Travis came to the tree line without spotting the nightmare. He dashed to an oak tree and leaned against the trunk. Deeper in the trees a vague figure moved. Travis took deliberate aim and was on the verge of firing when a shout rang out.

"Sinclair? Where the hell are you? Get over here!"

The figure turned out to be Sheriff Bo Seaver, standing over a body.

The owner of the house had been a heavyset woman in her fifties. She lay on her back, her legs drawn up as if she had been trying to kick at her savage assailant, her hands hooked into claws that she must have used to rake the creature's face. In the middle of her forehead was the same neat hole Travis had seen four times before. The woman's face and hair were the color of paper, her skin shrunken, her nose a malformed blob hanging to one side.

"What in God's name could have done this?" Seaver said, aghast. "What the hell are we dealing with here?"

"If I knew that, I'd know how to kill the thing," Travis said.

The sheriff made a 360-degree turn. "My guess is that it's long gone. I'll call for a meat wagon and notify the coroner. You stay put until I get back."

Travis wasn't fond of the idea of remaining there in the dark all alone. "I should place a call to Jacob Metz and ask him if he'll bring his bloodhounds. They wouldn't track the thing at Walker's but maybe this time will be different."

"I can call Metz. I know him," Seaver said, hastening away. "If you need me, give a holler."

Annoyed that the sheriff had seen fit to take charge, Travis almost defied him and went back to the house. Only the knowledge that it was bound to give Seaver added incentive for causing him trouble kept Travis rooted to the spot.

A gust of wind hit the nape of Travis's neck, sending a shiver down his spine. He looked every which way, alert for footsteps or other sounds. In order not to be so visible, he squatted and shifted, tucking the shotgun to his waist. His elbow accidentally brushed the dead woman's leg.

Travis glanced at her face again. Up close, her features appeared familiar even though he was certain they hadn't been personally acquainted. He stared, imagining how she would look with her cheeks full of life and vitality. The truth hit him with the impact of a hammer blow between the eyes. He had seen her earlier that very day!

There had been a funeral that afternoon. A retired postal employee had passed on a few days earlier. The man had been active in his church and generally liked, so his funeral had been well attended. Naturally, a police officer had to escort the procession to the graveyard. Travis had taken the job because it was a lot easier to do than wearing out shoe leather scouring the town for the creature.

The dead woman lying beside him had been one of the mourners. Travis remembered her clearly. She had stood near the dead man's widow, offering comfort. And now she was dead herself and would soon be in the back of the same hearse, bound for a hole in the ground not all that far from the postal employee's. How ironic, Travis mused.

A rustling sound snapped Travis's gaze to a thicket 20 feet to his left. He snapped the shotgun around, his thick finger curling on the trigger, but not quite tightly enough to fire. What if Seaver was wrong? he asked himself. What if the creature hadn't left? What if it was hidden in the bushes, watching him at that very moment?

Fear gnawed at Travis's insides, and he came close to fleeing. He never had handled potential violence well. That was why in all his years on the force he had never let himself be caught in a violent situation.

Whenever Travis answered a domestic dispute, he always waited outside until the shouting and screaming died down, then knocked. On drunk-and-disorderly calls, he contrived to arrive five or ten minutes after the calls came in to give offenders time to come to their senses and run off. And since he seldom went out of his way to collar drunk drivers, shoplifters, or speeders, he rarely found himself confronting anyone inclined to do him harm. So far his system had worked like a charm.

But not now. Systems didn't work on wild beasts. The creature that had turned Cemetery Ridge into its private hunting ground would rip him apart without hesitation. If the beast spotted him, he wouldn't be able to stall it or reason with it or flee from it. The creature would suck his brain dry, as it had all the others unless he shot it first.

Travis saw part of the thicket shake and heard a low crunch. There could be no doubt. Something was in there and it was coming closer. He considered yelling to try to scare it off, but discarded the idea as stupid. A yell would only enable the creature to pinpoint his position, if it hadn't already.

Sinking onto his elbows and knees, Travis sank flat beside the corpse. He hoped the creature wouldn't notice him lying there. He also hoped Seaver would shout or make enough noise to draw the creature toward the house.

Since he was close to the body, Travis noticed a peculiar odor. It reminded him of one he had smelled previously but he couldn't remember where. It wasn't a nauseating odor by any means. Rather it was sickly sweet, like sour vinegar.

The thicket shook again as whatever lurked in its depths moved northward a few yards.

Travis propped the barrel of the shotgun on the deceased's chest to steady his aim. A drop of sweat trickled down his brow and into his left eye. It set the eye to watering, so he brushed his closed eyelid with a finger.

The moment of distraction proved costly. The thing in the thicket crept into an adjoining patch of high weeds without Travis noticing and was now less than 15 feet away.

In the grip of choking fright, Travis tensed and trained the shotgun on the weeds. He wasn't going to let the damn creature get any closer. Slowly bending stems gave the creature's location away. It was on its belly, slinking toward him. Travis tried to fix a bead, but in the dark he couldn't see the tiny metal dot at the end of the barrel. More sweat rolled into his eyes, stinging them, and for a few moments the world was a blur. Just then the weeds rustled loudly. Travis hastily swiped at both eyes, glimpsed a low-slung shape creeping toward him, and without waiting to verify it was the creature, he jerked the trigger.

At the thunderous blast a piercing, feral screech rent the night.

Chapter Fourteen

Ben, Nadine, and Fred Larkin were driving west on Knob Road when the scanner blared to life. They heard the Jackson County sheriff request backup on an unknown animal call at 1423 Trammel Drive.

"Trammel is quite a ways north of town," Ben said. "We'll have to swing clear around the ridge and go up Simmons, which will take us half an hour. If it's the creature, we'll miss all the action."

"It's just as well," Larkin said from the back. Beside him lay the rifle and spare ammo. "I'm not going anywhere near Bo Seaver. He's one mean son of a bitch, and he's been after my butt for years. Trust me. We don't want anything to do with the man."

Fifteen minutes later they heard the sheriff

on the horn again, asking for an ambulance and calling in deputies from all over the county to help hunt for the creature. In the background a gunshot boomed. Seaver announced he was going to investigate and signed off. Several minutes later he was back on the channel, saying to one of his lieutenants, "You won't believe what the tub of lard just did. Over."

"Don't tell me that he shot himself in the foot? Over."

"No." Seaver laughed into the mike. "He blew a cat to kingdom come."

Larkin snickered at the news. "Sounds like the chief is performing true to form. Travis is a waste of public payroll. The town would be better served if they pinned the badge on a clump of dirt."

Ben glanced around. Just a few short days ago he would have leaped to his friend's defense, but now he let the slur ride. The poacher had a point. Travis Sinclair's performance as a lawman was suspect. The more Ben learned, the more convinced he became that the best interests of Cemetery Ridge would be better served by someone else.

Nadine was uninterested in the chief of police. To her way of thinking all that mattered in their time of crisis was the cause. So she turned to the poacher and asked, "Do you really think you can kill this thing?"

"I don't see why not," Larkin said. "I never got a good shot the night before. Maybe tonight I'll be luckier. And my rifle can bring down a bull moose."

"We'll circle the area awhile and see if anything develops," Ben said.

He felt as if they were tilting at windmills but he couldn't bring himself to sit home and do nothing while more people lost their lives. He held high hopes for his scheme, yet now that they were on the prowl he realized it would take a miracle for them to be in the right place at the right time. Cemetery Ridge was small by most standards but it still covered several square miles and was lush with trees and brush. Finding the creature might prove akin to finding the vaunted needle in a haystack. He would give anything for a clue to its movements.

"If only there was a way of predicting the creature's attacks," Nadine said, as if reading his mind. "We might have some idea where it will strike next."

"I've been thinking about that all day," Ben said, "and the only item I came up with that ties some of the killings together is the cemetery."

"The cemetery, you say?" Larkin said.

"Yeah. A number of its victims have been killed there. And another was an undertaker's wife."

"That's not much of a link," Nadine said. "The thing has killed more people outside the cemetery than in it."

Larkin sat forward and rubbed his pointed chin. "Maybe it's more of a link than you think, pretty lady. I was at the cemetery the night before the thing came after me."

"What were you doing there?" Ben asked.

The poacher took his time replying. "I suppose it can't do any harm to tell you since Stoner is dead. He was one of my best customers. Bought venison from me every week, regular as clockwork."

"No wonder he hardly ever went into town for anything except liquor," Ben said.

The germ of an idea had been planted but before it could sprout the squall of the scanner filled the van. "Twelve-thirteen. This is unit seventeen. I have the animal in sight and am in pursuit. Repeat. I have the animal in sight. It is heading south on Johnson Street at fifty-two miles an hour. We've just crossed Morrison. Request backups ASAP. Unit seventeen, out."

"Morrison?" Nadine said. "That's just ahead, maybe two blocks."

Ben jammed the accelerator to the floor. He shot through one intersection and approached the second. To the south, Morrison was quiet. To the north a row of oak trees prevented him from seeing oncoming traffic but he could hear the wail of a siren. At the last moment he slammed on the brakes to keep from shooting out past the crosswalk.

Nadine screamed because their quarry had streaked into the intersection. The creature had been about to turn onto the street they were on, but it drew up short yards shy of the van. For a few seconds it reared into the night in front of them, bathed in the glow from their headlights.

"My God!" Nadine cried.

The creature had a reptilian build, yet did not appear completely reptilian. It was covered with big scales that were in a constant state of flux. The scales rippled and flexed as if each and every one was alive. There were three bony fingers on its hands, each capped with ebony claws. On its feet were more claws and on the heel of each a curved spike that appeared capable of ripping through solid steel. Its color brought to mind sparkling obsidian.

Ben took all this in at a glance. Then he saw the creature's face and couldn't look away. The head was like that of a dragon, but a dragon of unbelievable ugliness and bestial ferocity. Eyes as black as night shimmered with volcanic intensity. Piranha teeth rimmed a mouth able to swallow half a man in a single bite. And on the sides of the creature's head, where its ears should be, were a pair of short, curved horns.

. "I knew it!" Larkin exclaimed. "It's an alien!"

Before Ben could ask him what he meant by that, the creature twisted its head and drew back its lips to hiss like an enraged serpent. Then it whirled and sped off down Morrison, its form a blur. Not a second later the sheriff's car roared past, lights flashing and siren caterwauling.

"Follow them!" Larkin said.

Ben started to turn the wheel, but had to slam on the brakes again when another county car flashed past in the wake of the first. He looked to be sure there were no more, then zoomed onto Morrison in pursuit. Already the creature was four blocks away and moving much faster than the sheriff's men.

"How can it run like that?" Nadine said.

"It's an overgrown lizard," Larkin said, thinking of the tracks he had found.

Suddenly a third patrol car shot onto the scene, almost directly in front of the creature. The deputy brought his vehicle to a lurching stop in the beast's path, trapping it between his car and the other two.

"They'll get it now!" Nadine said.

But she was wrong. The creature never slowed, never broke stride. It raced up to the third sheriff's car, leaped high into the air, and cleared the cruiser in a smooth hurtle. On landing, it raced on, never once looking back. The two pursuing cars had to slow while their fellow officer got his unit turned around, and soon all three were in heated pursuit once more.

Ben wished he'd had the presence of mind to bring a video camera along. A whim of fate had put him in Cemetery Ridge just as a major news story unfolded, perhaps one of the top ten stories of the year, and he wasn't recording the events for posterity.

"After it! After it!" Larkin said.

The van was doing sixty. Ben pushed it faster, grateful there was little traffic at that time of night. All along Morrison lights had blinked on and curious residents were stepping outside.

"Behind us!" Nadine cried.

Ben glanced into the rearview mirror and saw yet another sheriff's car bearing down on them at what seemed the speed of light. He'd been so engrossed in the scene ahead that he'd neglected to watch his back. He cut to the left just in time. The patrol car flew by at well over 100 miles an hour, the officer at the wheel giving them an angry look as it did.

"Oh, Lord," Larkin said. "That's the man himself, Sheriff Bo Seaver. We're lucky he's in a hurry or he'd pull us over and cite us for obstructing justice or some such crap."

Ben wasn't about to let himself be intimidated. He was a newspaperman. He had every right to be following the story as it unfolded. Hands glued to the steering wheel, he did his best to stay on Seaver's tail. The cruiser soon outdistanced him, though, and they had to rely on the scanner to stay abreast of the chase, which didn't last much longer.

The creature traveled another quarter of a mile down Morrison, then turned into a vacant lot choked with weeds and trees. The deputies promptly lost sight of it. They ringed the lot with their patrol cars and went in on foot, each man armed with a shotgun. Sheriff Seaver arrived and joined them, directing the hunt.

From a block away, Ben, Nadine, and Larkin sat and watched. The combined headlights of the four cruisers made the lot as bright as day. They saw the officers poking into every possible hiding place.

"They're wasting their time," Larkin said. "It's not there."

"How do you know?" Nadine asked.

"I know." Larkin tapped Ben on the shoulder. "Head east. Maybe we can catch sight of it again."

Ben delayed long enough to witness a deputy fling the door to a dilapidated shed open and then shake his head. Switching on the turn signal, Ben pulled into the traffic lane, turned onto a side street, and drove at the speed limit. His head constantly swiveled as he sought the nocturnal terror.

"It could be anywhere," Larkin grumbled. "Finding it will be like finding a needle in a haystack."

"Except that it's an awfully big needle," Nadine said. "Did you see that thing's face? And those horns? I'd like to know what it is and where it came from."

Larkin looked at her, amazed she couldn't see the truth when it had stared her right in the face less than a minute earlier. No animal on earth resembled that thing. Therefore, it had to be from somewhere other than earth. The conclusion was so obvious that a child could figure it out.

"I'm more interested in knowing where it went," Ben said absently while scouring a branch street.

The poacher shifted to read a sign. "We're at the junction of Hardesty and Boone," he said. "Wait a minute!"

"What is it?" Ben asked.

"You mentioned that the thing once killed the wife of an undertaker," Larkin said, pointing along Boone. "Well, this is probably a long shot, but about six blocks from here is the Ferguson Funeral Chapel."

Ben remembered the funeral home from his early years. He accelerated, saying, "If we do spot the thing, don't start blasting away unless you have a definite target. I don't want any innocent bystanders hit or we'll all face prison terms."

Larkin sat back and picked up the rifle. "You don't know me very well. No hunter worthy of the name wants an animal to suffer. Sure, I take a few illegally now and then. But my kills are always quick and clean. One shot is usually all it takes."

"The animals must be very grateful to be blown away by someone so compassionate," Nadine said.

"Ouch," Larkin said. "You're tongue is sharper than my knife, lady." He patted his rifle. "Make fun all you want to. But if you were a deer, would you rather be shot once between the eyes and die on the spot? Or would you rather be shot five or six times and suffer for hours before you kick the bucket?"

"If I were a deer," Nadine said, "I'd want to live to a ripe old age."

"Just great. A Bambi lover," Larkin muttered. "The truth is, lady, that few animals of any kind ever see old age. In the wild it's survival of the fittest, not survival of the cutest. More deer die every year from mountain lions and other natural causes than from all the hunters combined."

"I know all about nature's checks and balances, Mr. Larkin," Nadine said stiffly. "And since I went hunting quite a lot with my dad when I was younger, I don't qualify as a Bambi lover. But I do hold what you do against you. You're not an ordinary hunter, mister. You're a poacher."

"So some people claim. Where's your proof?"

"Don't bandy words with me. You've all but admitted it to us," Nadine said. "And any man who will go around killing game out of season is vermin in my book."

Larkin sighed. "That's what I get for being born a hundred years too late. If I'd been living in the last century, I'd be respected as a great provider. But now look!"

Ben intruded on their spat. "We're here."

The van's beams had caught the large black sign outside the funeral home in their glare. Also visible in front of the establishment was a shiny hearse.

"Looks quiet to me," Nadine said.

She spoke too soon. Ben slowed and turned into the small paved lot. The headlights danced over the front of the building, revealing a ragged, gaping hole where the front window had been. Ben immediately applied the brakes. He didn't care to get too close and have the creature leap out at them.

David Robbins

"Party time, boys and girls," Larkin said glee-fully, hefting his hardware. He opened the side door and hopped out. "Are the two of you coming?"

"I am," Ben said.

"So am I," Nadine said, reaching for the handle.

Ben put a hand on her arm. "One of us should go find a phone and notify the police."

"I'm sure there's a phone inside," Nadine said, knowing full well he was sending her away to spare her from harm. It bothered Nadine that he would treat her like a little girl instead of a grown woman.

"So is the creature," Ben said. "And there might be people inside who are hurt or dying. If all three of us go in and the thing gets us, who will help those people?"

"I don't like leaving you," Nadine said.

"You don't need to go far." Ben indicated the nearest house, 40 yards away. "Ask to use their phone."

Nadine still hesitated, unwilling to abandon him. For the first time in years she felt truly happy, and Ben was the reason. She didn't want to ever let him out of her sight ever again. But she also felt guilty thinking of the poor souls who might be suffering inside the funeral home.

"If you want, come back as soon as you make the call," Ben said. "Larkin and I will go slow so—" He had turned to look at the poacher as he spoke and saw with a start that Larkin was

230

gone. "What the hell! Where did he go?"

The answer was inside. Larkin had been too keyed up to stand there listening to the pair squabble while the challenge of his lifetime awaited within. And he knew rank amateurs would only be a hindrance. Either they would make too much noise and scare the beast off, or they would get in the way when the creature attacked. He'd rather confront the monster alone.

Larkin had thumbed back the hammer of his rifle as he stepped through the hole in the window. His feet crunched on fallen glass although he tried to tread lightly. He stopped and crouched to let his eyes adjust to the gloom.

Years earlier Larkin had been in that very room. It was where Ferguson laid out the dead for viewings and such. On a polished pedestal near the far wall stood an empty coffin. There were a dozen rows of chairs, many of which had been knocked over in a clear path between the window and a wide hallway leading into the recesses of the long, low building.

Larkin glided stealthily to the hall. Ferguson lived at the rear in a spacious apartment. Larkin recalled hearing somewhere that Ferguson's wife had passed on a while back. The only one home should be the undertaker himself since his kids had long since flown the nest.

As Larkin entered the tiled corridor, a faint clicking noise reached his ears. It sounded as if someone were tapping one of the tiles—or as if the creature were clacking its claws together. Breathless with excitement, Larkin padded deeper into the darkness. He held the rifle level at his hip, his finger on the trigger.

An open door gave Larkin pause. Ducking low, he probed the dark interior, but could distinguish nothing. His nose registered a strong odor reminiscent of chemicals, leading him to surmise he was looking in the embalming room. He listened for evidence of the creature's presence.

From down the hall rose a dull thud attended by the sounds of a struggle. Larkin heard a distinct grunt and a mouselike squeal. Discarding caution in his eagerness to slay the creature, he jogged to the door leading into the apartment. The door hung open wide enough to permit him entry.

The squeal was repeated, coming from a room to the right. Larkin moved forward cautiously, slanting to the middle of the carpet so he would have room to maneuver if the creature came at him. The angle enabled him to see into a plush bedroom, where two figures struggled on the floor.

The creature was astride Olaf Ferguson, its knees resting on the thin man's sparrow shoulders, its head tilting from side to side as it studied Ferguson's features. The undertaker was trying to break free, but feebly, which was understandable since one of the creature's hands rested on Ferguson's throat. Whenever

Ferguson tried to push the creature off and rise, it squeezed, eliciting a squeal.

Larkin stopped in case the creature glanced in his direction. He lacked a clear shot, but a few more careful strides would do the trick. As he lifted his right leg, the creature on Ferguson suddenly bent low. It gripped the undertaker's chin and jerked it back and forth as if curious how far the neck could swivel. Ferguson whined in abject terror.

The next second the creature's lips parted, revealing its deadly saber teeth. It opened them wide, as if to bite down. Larkin took another step and aimed, centering the bead on the creature's temple. He only had to squeeze the trigger but he delayed an instant to be certain. In that instant of time a long, circular tube shot out of the creature's mouth and into Ferguson's forehead. There was a sickening crunch as the tube seared through flesh and bone, much like a drill bit biting into wood. The undertaker's body arched and he tried to call out but the claws around his throat stifled his outcry. Then the creature commenced making sucking noises.

Larkin was transfixed by the horrid sight. He could see the creature's cheeks expand and contract with every slurp. A shimmering glint shined in its black eyes. A pale bluish glow enveloped the tube. Ferguson had gone rigid, his mouth agape.

The creature was sucking the man dry, or so it seemed to Larkin, who was horrified and fascinated at the same time. And more determined than ever to put an end to the abomination, to do what no one else had been able to do.

Larkin steadied his arms and fired. In the confined space the blast of the heavy-caliber rifle was like the blast of a howitzer, the recoil like the kick of a mule.

As he had bragged he would, Larkin shot the creature in its head. The slug ripped into its temple, snapping the great head to one side, but not far enough to dislodge the tube. At the point of impact a scintillating aura of sparkling multicolored lights erupted, flitting in the air like a swarm of fireflies. The bright pinpoints were dazzling to look upon. They flew wildly about the creature's head for about ten seconds, then formed into a column of light and flowed back into the monster's head through the wound!

Larkin had never witnessed the like. It was the first and only time in all his years as a poacher that something he shot didn't keel over dead. He worked the rifle's lever, ejecting the spent shell and inserting another. As he raised the .45-70 a second time, the creature turned its head enough for it to stare at him while it continued feeding.

Larkin sighted and steeled his body. As he went to fire, words blared in his brain, words not of his own mental making, words that rasped with a life of their own.

"Sweet nectar!"

They were words Larkin had heard the other night at Gardner Creek when he'd nearly died. They had the same disorienting effect. He fought the sensation, gritted his teeth, and went to shoot, too stubborn to admit his rifle was having no effect. Suddenly a white light filled his mind and he went numb all over. He was held immobile by a force he could neither see nor comprehend.

The creature slurped a few more times, its eyes never leaving the poacher. Silently the tube retracted into its maw and it smacked its lips like someone who had eaten a hearty meal.

Larkin realized he must escape before he suffered the same fate as the undertaker. He willed his legs to flee but they wouldn't obey. He willed his trigger finger to squeeze but it wouldn't curl.

And then the monster rose.

Chapter Fifteen

Paxton Booth had endured a boring night—
boring because he had behaved himself, for
one thing, and because Cindy had to go home
early, which kept him from giving his hormones
a workout. Yet another dull evening in the
sticks, Paxton reflected as he bent his steps
homeward.

There was one consolation. By denying himself his kicks, Paxton had ensured he would be
allowed out on Halloween and he could hardly
wait for prank night to begin so he could make
up for lost time in a big way.

Anticipation made Paxton chuckle. He'd
worked out a timetable with Jess and Bill, and
everything was all set. At sundown the next day
they would put his scheme into operation. By
the morning after Halloween they would be the

talk of the town, maybe of the whole state.

Paxton had a secret agenda at work. He hoped that by embarrassing his uncle he would be sent packing back to Denver, where he longed to be. He couldn't wait to see his old gang again and to cuddle with his main babes.

The plan was not without risks. Paxton knew he might end up behind bars for a while or sent to a juvenile detention center, but he rated the potential gain as well worth the possible pitfalls.

There was one wild card in the deck, namely Paxton's uncle. Victor had been unpredictable of late and shown he had a temper that wouldn't quit. Paxton had no idea whether his uncle would take his high jinks in stride or go ballistic. It was his only worry. If Victor decided to press charges, Paxton wouldn't see Denver for a long time.

Mulling over the prospects, Paxton entered the mansion and slammed the door behind him. He made for the kitchen, hungry for a late snack before turning in. Ordinarily he had the house all to himself at that time of the night. The maid was gone for the day and his uncle was off partying with one fox or another.

This night was different. Paxton walked into the kitchen, flicked on the light switch, and tensed on seeing his uncle seated in a kitchen chair.

"Come on in, nephew," Victor said suavely. "I've been waiting for you."

"In the dark?" Paxton asked nervously. His uncle had never done such a thing before and he didn't know how to take it. Was he in trouble and didn't know it?

"It's important," Victor said, but did not yet reveal his reason. He had to sound out the teenager first and confirm Paxton would support him 100 percent. "I know you always feed your face about this time of night."

"I'm still a growing stud, Unc," Paxton said, trying to sound more carefree than he felt. "I need mass quantities to fuel the furnace, if you get my drift."

"I hear through the grapevine that you consume mass quantities of a lot of things," Victor said. "Beer, wine, whiskey, even drugs."

Paxton had been about to open the fridge. His smirk died and he turned, putting on an indignant act. "Where did you hear such garbage? Sure, I drink a little now and then. Hey, who doesn't? But I'm not a wino or an alcoholic or anything, so what's the big deal?"

Victor reached into the pocket of his trench coat and pulled out a small plastic bag. "I found this in your room, Pax. In my day we called it grass. Dope. Pot."

"You searched my room?" Pax said, genuinely shocked. "Man, how could you? That's cold. It's an invasion of my privacy, too. I don't think you have the right."

"So long as you live in my house, and so long as your mother has appointed me your temporary guardian, I can do as I damn well please," Victor said. He dropped the bag on the table. "What else do you use?"

Paxton thought fast. It was plain his uncle had been checking up on him. Given his uncle's wealth and contacts, it was a safe bet that Victor knew all there was to know about his dabbling on the illicit market. In that event he would be smarter to admit the truth straight out and play on his uncle's sympathy if Victor hit the roof.

"A little coke, some cartwheels and yellow-jackets now and then. It's no big deal. I'm not addicted."

"Who do you buy your cocaine from?" Victor said.

"You want me to snitch on my source?" Pax asked, stalling for time. "That's a no-no, Unc, in case you haven't heard. They don't take kindly to being ratted out."

"Your source, nephew, or you're off to the military academy by noon tomorrow."

Paxton gazed into his uncle's eyes and was convinced Victor wasn't bluffing. "His name is Jim Roth. He's in the same grade I am."

"Roth? I know his father. Interesting," Victor said. He rose and stepped to the sink, where he poured himself a glass of cold water. "What's the most coke you've ever bought from him at one time?"

"A bullet here, a bullet there," Paxton said while wondering why the amount was important.

"How much do you think he could sell you on short notice?"

Puzzled, Paxton studied the older man. He couldn't see where their conversation was leading and suspected his uncle of having an ulterior motive for interrogating him. "I really don't know. I've never asked him. Why?"

"Do you think he might have a pound or so on hand that we could buy?"

"We?" Paxton said, flabbergasted. "What the hell! Are you going into the drug business?"

"Not quite. Sit down." After the teen obeyed, Victor swirled the water in the glass and said, "I've decided to take your advice and eliminate the competition, as it were. I intend to put Ben Shields where he won't be able to meddle in my life ever again."

"Awesome, Unc. But what's that have to do with all the questions you've been asking me?"

Victor leaned back against the sink and swallowed several mouthfuls of water. "I want Shields out of the picture, but I can't just up and kill him. No, I have to be subtle. I have to do it in such a way that no one will ever suspect my involvement, especially my ex-wife. It defeats my whole purpose if she blames me."

"Blames you for what?"

"For having Shields thrown into prison."

"What are you going to do?" Paxton asked in jest. "Plant drugs on him?"

"Yes."

The teenager was speechless.

"I want you to buy a pound of cocaine from Roth. I, in turn, will plant it in Shields's van, then tip our illustrious chief of the police to the fact a pusher is prowling the streets of our fair town." Victor snickered. "Shields will deny it, of course, but he won't be able to refute the evidence. And since there is a big drive on in our judicial system to crack down on pushers, I would imagine that Ben Shields will be a very old man before he gets out from behind bars."

"Uncle, you're one def dude. I never would have thought you had it in you."

"A Richards always gets what he wants, nephew. Always. And I want Nadine back in this house, where she belongs." Victor set the glass down. "Now why don't you get on the phone and find out if your pusher can accommodate us?"

Paxton grinned in appreciation of his uncle's devious nature. He regarded the older man in a whole new light and meant it when he said, "There's more to you than I ever figured, Unc. You're my kind of guy." He stood and walked toward the wall phone. "That wimp of a writer should have known better than to mess with a Richards. He'd have been better off if he'd never shown his ugly puss back in Cemetery Ridge."

Fred Larkin knew he was going to die. The creature had straightened and swung toward him, its wolfish maw curled in a wicked sneer. It held its arms out and clicked its claws together as if taunting him with the fate it had in store for him.

The poacher stared at its head, at the spot where the slug had torn through its temple.

There should be a gaping wound, but there wasn't. There should be blood and gore pouring out, but the reptilian skin was unbroken. A gun—not even a .45-70—had no effect on the creature.

The beast took a small step toward Larkin, who inwardly recoiled. His sole regret was that he would die without knowing where it came from or what it was.

Suddenly a pair of strong hands fell on Larkin from behind. The contact broke the paralysis and Larkin turned to find Ben beside him, gawking at the fiend.

"Run!" Larkin barked and gave Ben a shove. Then, he lunged, caught hold of the knob on the bedroom door, and yanked the door shut just as the creature sprang. A resounding crash shook the wall so hard it cracked.

Larkin ran into the hallway and slammed the front door to the apartment. Ben had slowed to wait for him, so Larkin gave him another push. "Damn it, run! The doors won't stop it for long!"

As if to accent the point, from within the undertaker's came a tremendous crash as wood and plaster were smashed to smithereens.

Ben needed no further urging. Whirling, he ran for his life, with the poacher hard on his heels. He'd seen how fast the creature could move and had no doubt of the outcome should the beast get through the second door before they escaped from the building and found a place to hide. Arms and legs pumping, Ben flew across the smooth tile.

Larkin could have passed the journalist. He had always been fleet of foot, more so than the average man, and he was much faster than Ben. But he kept pace a few steps behind, ready to do what little he could to slow the monster down if it gained the corridor and came after them.

A second later the creature did just that. The apartment door and part of the wall virtually exploded outward in a swirling cloud of broken wood, shattered masonry, and dust. From out of the cloud strode the creature, stooping to get through the ragged opening. It looked down the hall and spied the fleeing men.

Ben was almost to the front room. He glanced over his shoulder and saw the creature lumbering toward them. Dashing around the corner, he headed for the broken window. In his haste he forgot about the overturned chairs. His left ankle struck one, throwing him off balance, and before he could recover he hit the floor hard on his chest and slid several feet.

Larkin nearly blundered into a chair, too, but his wilderness—honed reflexes enabled him to jump over it unhurt. Darting to Ben's aid, he hooked a hand under the other man's shoulder and hoisted him erect.

Ben skirted another chair and had a clear field to the window. He paused as he was about to step over the shard-covered sill, and when he looked back, the monster strode into view.

A long leap carried Ben outside. Larkin was a heartbeat behind him. They whirled to face their pursuer at the very moment the creature filled the hole in the front window. Simultaneously bright light splashed over them, catching the nightmare in its harsh glare, causing the monstrosity to raise a hand over its eyes.

The van screamed to a stop behind them and Nadine shouted, "Get in! Hurry!"

Ben darted to the passenger door, held it open for the poacher to slip past, and vaulted onto the passenger seat. The van surged to the rear before he settled himself, throwing him against the dashboard. He had to clutch it to keep from being pitched out the swinging door.

Nadine had only one thought on her mind: to get out of there before the creature caught them. She had never driven a van before and found it awkward to navigate backward. A glance into the side mirror showed only darkness behind her. Afraid she would collide with a telephone pole she knew was back there, she slowed and twisted to locate the pole.

"Look out!" Larkin cried.

Nadine faced front and let out a screech. The creature was inches from the van, matching their speed as it studied her through the glass. Without thinking, she leaned on the horn. At the strident blast the thing halted and cocked its grotesque head from side to side.

Nadine twisted again and realized she was too close to the road at the wrong spot. She tried to brake but the van ran into a ditch with such force she was tossed into the air and smacked her head on the roof. The van bounced a second time and then lurched to a stop in the middle of the street.

The creature still stood there. It swung an arm in their direction and coiled to charge.

"I need a clear shot!" Larkin declared, desperately trying to roll down his window.

From out of the night thundered two patrol cars, their sirens wailing to life. They careened into the parking lot, separating to catch the nightmare between them. From one leaped a deputy, from the other slid Sheriff Bo Seaver. Both officers trained shotguns on the creature and cut loose with murderous vengeance, the reports of their shots rocking the air itself.

Ben's gaze was riveted to the tableau as the beast absorbed enough lead to sink a battleship. Blast after blast rocked it on its heels, yet the creature stood there without flinching or uttering a sound. The impact of each round created a shower of tiny cascading lights that whizzed about as if endowed with a life of their own.

The officers used up the rounds in their weapons at the same time and stood staring at the creature in transparent disbelief. Ben could understand their shock. Nothing should be able to take such punishment and live. The creature was supposed to be lying on the ground in bloody pieces, not standing there regarding the officers with cold contempt.

The thing took a few steps toward them and Sheriff Seaver went for his pistol. Before he could fire, two more sirens added to the tumult, and the other deputies arrived to help their fellows.

Apparently the noise or the flashing lights weren't to the creature's liking because it suddenly spun and streaked to the road. Turning west, it made for Morrison, moving at such speed its body was almost invisible.

Sheriff Seaver bellowed orders. In seconds the patrol cars were racing in the nightmare's wake.

The abrupt quiet that descended seemed unnatural. Ben watched the red lights recede and slowly let out the breath he hadn't realized he was holding. "My God," he said.

"Let's get out of here before the sheriff comes back," Larkin said. "He'll want to question us, otherwise, and we'll be tied up at the sheriff's office for hours."

"Where should we go?" Nadine asked, sounding as dazed as Ben felt.

"Gertie's is open twenty-four hours," Larkin said. "We can have us a cup of coffee and decide our next move."

Ben nodded in agreement and switched places with Nadine. The diner was as good a place as any to collect their wits. He expected it to be deserted at that time of night and was bewildered to find nearly every booth and stool taken.

"Bowling league night?" he said to Gertie as she deposited three menus on their table.

"Not hardly," the big woman said and jabbed a pudgy thumb at a police scanner mounted on a shelf above the counter. "We've been listening in to the big chase. Have you heard about it?"

"No," Larkin said with a straight face. "What's happening?"

Gertie's jowls positively shook with glee. She loved to gossip almost as much as she loved to eat, which was saying a lot. "Old Bo and his boys are trying to catch the thing that's been going around killing people."

"I thought it was a bear," Ben said to gauge her reaction.

"Bear, hell," Gertie said. "That's the official line. But everyone in town knows better. The story making the rounds is that the creature's victims have the tops of their heads bitten off and their brains eaten out. Ever hear of a bear doing that?"

"Can't say as I have," Ben said. "So if it's not a bear, what is it?"

"No one rightly knows," Gertie said. "Some of the old-timers call it the Brain Eater, which is accurate enough, I guess, but a damn silly name, if you ask me." She bobbed her double chin at the scanner. "Whatever it is, the creature has run the sheriff's men near ragged. They chased it down Morrison a while ago, then had it cornered at the undertaker's but it got away." She paused. "Poor Mr. Ferguson. It killed him just like it killed Mabel Criswell earlier tonight."

Ben's insides churned with impotent anger. Two victims and the night was still young.

How many more would fall prey to the fiend before it was made to pay? Would anyone be able to kill the thing? Or would it simply fade away as it had over 70 years earlier? And if so, then what? Would it lie dormant for another 73 years? There were so many questions that needed to be answered but Ben had no idea where to start looking for the answers.

"Give me a holler when you're ready to order," Gertie said, leaving them to wait on a man at the counter.

"Brain Eater," Larkin said softly. "It's as good a name as any. I saw that thing sucking a man's brains out with my own two eyes."

"Not the brain," Ben said. "Something else."

"I saw it, I tell you."

"And I've seen one of the creature's victims not long after it got through," Ben said, referring to Stoner. "The brain was all shriveled and white, but it was still in the skull."

"Then what the hell does the creature suck out? Brain fluid or something?"

"I don't know," Ben said.

Nadine had been studying the menu. She set it down and said, "So much for the snack I was thinking of having. A glass of water should do me fine, provided I can keep it down."

"Squeamish sort, are you?" Larkin said, grinning.

"Too squeamish to be a poacher," Nadine said.

Larkin glanced at the nearest customers to see if any had overheard, then touched a finger to his lips. "Hold it down, will you, lady? In a crowd this size there are always a few self-righteous types who wouldn't think twice about pounding me to a pulp if they heard you say that."

"Scared, Mr. Larkin?" Nadine asked.

"I just don't care to be hospitalized, thank you."

The argument was nipped in the bud by the squawking of the scanner. All eyes swung toward the counter as a deputy came on to report that he had made a thorough sweep of his assigned sector and seen no trace of the animal, as he called it.

"Animal, my ass," Larking grumbled. "I know animals better than any man in these parts, and that's not one. It's an alien, I tell you."

Ben had been about to order. He glanced at the poacher and said, "So you mentioned once before. What do you mean by that?"

"You're a writer and you don't know the meaning of the word alien?" Larkin chuckled. "It means that the sucker is from another world off in space somewheres. Say, maybe that's why it disappeared for so long. Maybe it flew on back to its home planet and just now got around to paying us a visit again."

Nadine laughed. "I guess it's fitting that you believe in life on other planets."

"Meaning what, lady?" Larkin said. "If you have a better idea, I'm ready to listen. But you

249

saw those cops shoot the hell out of it, same as me, and saw it run off without a scratch. Tell me what kind of earthly animal can survive ten shotguns blasts and take a slug from a big rifle without being phased? I'd really like to know."

"There is none," Nadine said, "but there has to be another explanation."

She had never been a big believer in UFOs or in the current notion that little gray men were coming down from the stars to abduct earthlings for the express purpose of performing genetic experiments in order to rear a hybrid species. That all fell under the realm of make believe, as far as she was concerned. But, she mused, if she discounted the alien idea, what did that leave her with? Was the thing from another dimension? The idea was as ridiculous as saying it was an alien.

"Whatever the creature is," Ben said, "we'd be wasting our time going out after it again now that we know guns can't kill it. Which reminds me, Nadine. I thought you were going to the next house to call the police. How was it that you showed up when you did?"

"I was halfway there when I heard a gunshot and got so worried I turned around," Nadine said.

"I, for one, am glad you did, lady," Larkin said. "You saved our bacon for sure."

"And the sheriff and his boys saved all three of us," Ben said. "I'm surprised Seaver hasn't called in the National Guard by now."

"Bo Seaver ask someone else for help?" Larkin shook his head. "Never happen. He'd rather die than admit there was a job he couldn't handle."

"No one can handle that thing," Ben said.

"Then what's our next step?" Nadine asked. "How do we fight something that can't be killed?"

Ben had no answer. As he stared out into the darkness and listened to the distant howl of sirens, Nadine's words echoing in his mind. He'd seen the creature with his own two eyes—a real, honest-to-goodness monster like those he'd written about. Yet he'd never actually believed such creatures existed.

How fitting, Ben reflected ruefully. The horror writer who didn't believe in monsters being confronted by a living, breathing specimen. It made him wonder. If monsters were real, what else was?

Chapter Sixteen

Halloween day dawned overcast and chilly. A delayed cold front was due in later, bringing with it a promise of rain and perhaps snow.

Those residents of Cemetery Ridge who didn't own a police scanner or hadn't stopped by Gertie's awoke to learn that the so-called bear had killed the undertaker and a middle-aged woman. No other deaths had been reported.

Rumors spread like wildlife. One claimed the governor had been contacted and promised the aid of the guard. Another claimed that the creature was actually a huge man running around in a bizarre costume and using a power drill to attack people. And a third was to the effect that the chief of police had decided to impose a curfew and cancel trick or treating.

Thanks to the latter, by the middle of the

morning Chief Travis Sinclair had fielded over 90 phone calls from irate parents who demanded that Halloween be celebrated as usual. A measely bear, so the common argument went, was no reason to deny the town's youngsters their traditional fine time. Many of the fathers calling in informed Travis in no uncertain terms that they planned to escort their children around, armed with guns. It was suggested that all Travis need do was take a take a few additional steps to protect the young trick or treaters and Halloween would go off smoothly.

For once a rumor had some basis in fact. Travis had considered canceling all festivities and had mentioned as much to his good friend Gertie while eating breakfast. But the outpouring of angry public sentiment convinced him to change his mind. He was already on shaky enough ground with the town council. It wouldn't do for him to antagonize the public, too. Enough complaints might be just the thing to compel the council to give him a vote of no confidence and send him packing.

One person, however, didn't agree with his decision. On being told, Sheriff Bo Seaver looked at him as if he were insane and smacked a hand down on Travis's desk. "Damn it all, if I had jurisdiction I'd sure as hell impose a curfew. You weren't at Ferguson's. You didn't see this thing."

"I've seen its handiwork." Travis refused to be ruffled. "But I don't think the trick or treaters are in any real danger. Most of the kids are home by eight or nine and the creature doesn't show itself until later."

"You're cutting it awfully close," Seaver said. "If that monster should come on a street full of children, you'll have more bodies on your hands than you can count."

"Which is why I'm hoping you'll lend me a half-dozen men for patrol duty between dusk and dawn," Travis said. He was prepared to debate the point, but received a surprise.

"You'll have them."

"Just like that?"

"I wasn't finished," Seaver said. "You'll have them, all right. And another six besides. I'm assigning every deputy I can spare to Cemetery Ridge. But I'm not doing it for you, lard butt. I'm doing it for the people of this town and because I'm going to nail the son of a bitch that made a fool out of me last night if it's the last thing I do." Wheeling, he stalked from the office.

Travis leaned back and grinned. As much aggravation as the situation had caused him, he had one thing to be thankful for; in all the excitement over the creature, Seaver had forgotten about Marsten Park.

There had been another bonus, of sorts. Travis opened the top desk drawer and stared at the two thick stacks of crisp 100-dollar bills he had found by accident while at the Criswell house. Apparently the woman hadn't believed in banks or she wouldn't have kept 9,000 dollars stashed in a cookie tin in the kitchen.

Travis laughed out loud. He'd only wanted a snack and wound up with more money than he'd ever had at one time in his whole life. It would tide him over for a while in case he was fired. And if he wasn't, who knew? Maybe he'd put some of it down on a new car or treat the wife to a vacation in Hawaii or just salt it away for a rainy day. There were so many wonderful options.

Travis had never stolen anything before and he marveled at the ease with which the deed had been done. No one had seen him. None of the woman's relatives had shown up to report the money missing. He doubted that anyone knew she'd had it. He wondered how many more there were like her in Cemetery Ridge. It was food for a lot of thought.

The front door opened again and Travis quickly closed the drawer and glanced up. He figured that Seaver had forgotten something, but coming toward him was Ben Shields. The sight of the writer ruined his morning. Because while the sheriff had forgotten about Marsten Park, Ben most certainly had not.

Travis plastered a phony smile on his face and called out, "Good morning, Ben. You're up early."

"I haven't been to bed," Ben said, taking a seat. He was so tired he had nearly fallen asleep on the ride over. "I was up all night, studying books I picked up at the library."

"Doing research for another novel?" Travis

asked just to make small talk.

"No." Ben looked closely at his former friend. His opinion of Travis had dropped dramatically in recent days but he still believed the man was doing all in his power to put an end to the menace that had the town in turmoil. "Have you figured out what you're up against yet?"

"If this is on the record, then we've got us a man-eating bear on our hands," Travis said, not quite sure why Ben was asking.

"How about off the record? Just between us?"

"Then we don't have the slightest idea," Travis said. "The autopsies were inconclusive. Death due to wild animal attack, all the certificates state. But the coroner has no idea what kind of animal."

"What do you personally think?"

Travis twined his fingers behind his neck. "To tell you the truth, old buddy, I'm at a complete loss. What kind of animal can shrug off buckshot, run faster than a speeding patrol car, and disappear without a trace? Not to mention how it kills its victims." He shook his head. "For a while I toyed with the idea it was an honest-to-goodness monster, maybe not even of this earth. But you pointed out that such things are figments of the imagination."

"I was wrong, terribly wrong." Ben sighed. "Larkin thinks it's an alien, too."

Travis grew wary. "Since when have you been spending time with that damned poacher?"

"I looked him up to help track down the

creature," Ben said. "But all we succeeded in doing was almost getting ourselves killed."

"Leave this business to the professionals," Travis said. "Bo Seaver and I will kill this mother one way or another."

"Maybe. Maybe not." Ben stretched out his legs and got to the subject that had brought him to the station. "Do you remember my telling you about a similar string of deaths that took place over seventy years ago?"

"And you still think there's a connection?"

"I do. You can see the newspaper accounts for yourself at the public library." Ben choose his next words carefully in order not to come across as a raving lunatic. "As I said, I've been up all night studying, trying to make sense of this ordeal. And I came across a few pertinent facts."

Travis could see the earnest look on Ben's face. He almost laughed at the role reversal that had taken place. The man who had convinced him that the creature couldn't be a monster was trying hard to persuade him it was one.

"Let's hear them," Travis said.

"What do you know about Halloween?"

"What's to know? Kids dress up in stupid costumes and go around collecting enough sweets to rot all their teeth out. St. Halloween is the patron saint of dentists and candymakers alike."

"Be serious," Ben said. "Have you ever read about Halloween's history, how it got started, what it means?"

Travis shrugged. "I suppose a candymaker started it way back when. What's the difference?"

"The difference could explain our nocturnal prowler," Ben said and recited some of the information he had gleaned from long hours of study. "Halloween itself didn't start out as a special holiday. The name means hallowed evening or All Hallows' Eve because it falls on the day before All Saints' Day."

"So?"

"So follow me on this," Ben said. "Back in ancient times, the druids and others believed that All Hallows' Eve was the night that evil reigned, a night when spirits, ghosts, fairies, demons, and elves came out to harm people."

"Who were the druids?" Travis asked.

"A priestly cult that flourished in England, Ireland, and France hundreds of years ago. The Romans destroyed most of them, and later Christianity displaced the rest. But the Druids aren't important here. It's their beliefs that have a bearing on our problem."

"How so?" Travis said.

"Don't you see? Halloween is the one night of the year when evil flourishes, when evil beings roam the world at will."

"Oh, I get it," Travis said, the implications troubling him. "You think that the creature we're up against is some sort of incarnate evil?"

"Well, it's sure as hell not an elf on steroids," Ben said, trying to inject some levity. He had worked hard overnight in an effort to uncover the truth and it pleased him that Travis was taking him seriously.

Travis felt all his old worries return. When he'd first suspected that he was dealing with something far out of the ordinary, he'd lost sleep fretting over how he was going to put a stop to it. Now here he was back at square one, with a longer list of victims and still no concrete answers.

"Let's say you're right. What good does it do me?"

Ben wearily rubbed his chin. "Point taken. It's not as if you can broadcast my ideas from the rooftops. I just wanted you to know."

"I appreciate that," Travis said.

"I'm surprised Seaver hasn't figured it out, too," Ben said. "He knows how the victims died. And he and his men poured enough buckshot into that thing last night to drop an elephant, yet it ran off unhurt."

"Seaver would never accept the monster idea."

"Why not?"

"He doesn't believe in them."

"Wonderful."

Travis gnawed on his lower lip a few seconds. "Back up a bit. Do you know exactly what this creature is? And more importantly, do you know exactly how we can kill it?"

"No on both counts," Ben said glumly.

"One more thing. According to the research you've done, these evil beings are supposed to roam the world on Halloween, right? So how come our creature has been active for several nights now?"

"I wish I knew," Ben said. "I don't have all the answers yet. Maybe this thing is stronger than most evil beings and can come to life early. Or maybe its hunger brought it to life sooner."

"Well, let me know if you find the answers," Travis said, consulting his watch. "I have an appointment in ten minutes or I'd stay and talk some more. If you do come up with anything new, I'm willing to listen." He patted Ben on the shoulder as he went out the door.

Ben sat in the chair a while longer, too tired to leave right away. He'd hardly slept a wink in two nights and the lack of rest was beginning to take its toll. He was glad he hadn't gone to Seaver first, as he had considered doing. He might have punched Seaver if he'd laughed at the Halloween angle.

Ben wanted to go back to the library for more books, but figured he should get some sleep first. He was having a hard time thinking straight.

A lucid thought did occur to him. He couldn't very well work with Sheriff Seaver since the man would brand him a crackpot. And Travis would be busy enough attending to his regular duties. So if Ben truly desired to stop the creature before it slaughtered more innocents, he must hunt the thing himself.

Slowly, Ben rose. He didn't have much time to find the solution. The sun would set in less than ten hours. And then, based on the events of 70 years earlier, all hell would break loose in Cemetery Ridge.

Victor Richards was on the phone to his investment counselor in Grants Pass when the door to his study banged open and Paxton strode in, a parcel under his arm.

"I got it, Unc!" Paxton said, waving the cocaine in the air. His uncle glared, so Paxton promptly shut up and waited while the conversation concluded. "Sorry," he said as soon as the receiver touched the cradle. "I didn't realize you were busy."

"Did you ever think to knock first?" Victor said testily. He had about had his fill of his nephew's rudeness and stupidity. Were it not for needing the boy to procure the drug, he would have been tempted to ship Paxton back to Denver. Victor could have bought the coke from his own source, but he deemed it smarter not to leave a money trail that could be traced directly back to him.

"I said I was sorry. What more to do you want?" Paxton said, resenting the treatment. The way he saw it, he had done his uncle a major favor and deserved to be treated with more respect. He plopped the package on the desk. "A pound and a half, just like you wanted."

Victor placed a hand on the plain brown wrapper. "You didn't mention my name to Roth, did you?"

"What do you take me for?" Paxton said. "I

David Robbins

know how to keep a secret."

"I hope so," Victor said. Because if it turned out that Roth knew he was behind the buy, he'd need to insure that both his nephew and the pusher were unable to pass on the information to anyone else. "Did Roth ask a lot of questions?"

"Hell, no. Jimbo is cool. I told him my birthday is coming up and my folks sent me a wad of bread to use as I saw fit." Paxton laughed. "He said I could have a real blowout with all this coke. Get it?"

"I get it," Victor said, unimpressed by the juvenile humor. "Go into the kitchen and look under the sink. There should be a pile of grocery bags. Bring one back."

"What for?" Paxton asked.

Victor indicated the package. "Your fingerprints are all over the wrapping. Unless you want the police to find them, we'd better put the coke in something else."

"Now why didn't I think of that?" Paxton said. "It's a good thing you have my best interests at heart."

And my own, Victor almost said, but didn't. He opened a drawer and took out a letter opener. After cutting the tape that bound the wrapper, he peeled the folded layers back, exposing the clear plastic bag that contained the cocaine. Next he went to a closet and rummaged inside until he found a pair of leather gloves. He donned them as his nephew showed up bearing a brown bag.

262

"Here it is, Unc. And look. I carried it back using a napkin so my prints wouldn't be on it."

"Smart boy," Victor said. From another drawer he removed a pair of scissors and cut the bag from top to bottom and across the bottom so that he could spread it out flat. Taking a handkerchief from a pocket, he wiped off both sides. Then he placed the cocaine in the center, trimmed off the excess, and taped up the package. "We're all set."

"Too bad you didn't think to keep a little out for us," Paxton said. "I wouldn't mind a little snow right about now."

"You need both feet on solid ground for the work we have to do," Victor said. He put away the tape and scissors, but left on the gloves. "Come on."

The sports car turned over the first time. Victor slid the bundle under his seat and peeled out, cranking the stereo so he wouldn't have to listen to his nephew's brainless chatter. He took a roundabout course and came up on the Shields residence through an alley near the driveway. The van was nowhere in sight.

"Damn," Victor groused. "I was afraid of this. The bastard will probably be out with Nadine most of the day."

"We can wait," Paxton said, although his heart wasn't in it. His uncle had let him stay home from school to make the buy and he wanted to catch some shut-eye before evening. He had a long night ahead of him.

Several small children ran past the drive, giggling and laughing as they tossed a ball back and forth.

"Maybe it's just as well," Victor said. "There are too many people around. We'll wait until after dark and then plant the coke."

"Hold the phone, Unc," Paxton said. "You promised me that I could go out with my buds tonight, remember? We have a bitchin' prank night planned and I don't want to miss it."

"Go play your games," Victor said. "I'll handle this job myself."

"Then what? You get right on the horn to the fuzz?"

"You've got it," Victor said and grinned. "By tomorrow morning Ben Shields will be behind bars and I'll have a clear playing field."

Paxton rapped the dashboard and cackled. "Yes, sir! There's going to be a hot time in the old town tonight!"

Unknown to the two schemers, miles away another party was making plans for Halloween, plans that would have a bearing on the outcome of their respective schemes.

In his mobile home north of town, Fred Larkin sat hunched over a table. He had an allen wrench in hand and was tightening the last of several screws on his crossbow.

The poacher had spent most of the night reviewing his clash with the creature. Over and over again he had seen his slug strike the thing in the temple and do no more than make a batch of colorful sparks. Since his prized .45-70 had let him down, he had gone into the storage room and found the bow.

Many times before Larkin had relied on the weapon, usually when he needed to make a kill and silence was in order. The crossbow had a 150-pound draw, powerful enough to kill any animal that lived. He stroked the black metal, recalling the mountain lion he had once downed at 50 yards with an arrow through the head.

Larkin had no particular reason for relying on the crossbow in this instance. He had no cause to think a wooden shaft would have any more effect than a lead slug. He was simply adapting to the situation by relying on the second-best weapon in his small arsenal.

The poacher went to the fridge for a beer. If he had half a brain, as the saying went, he'd stay home and let the writer and the redhead deal with the monster on their own. But he couldn't. There was more involved than avenging that attack in the woods. There was his pride to think of.

Larkin was extremely proud of the fact that in all the years he'd been poaching, no animal had ever eluded him. He'd never failed to bag his quarry, which was why he had the reputation of being the best damn poacher in all of Oregon. Only now his record had a blemish. And the damned alien was to blame.

No matter how silly the others thought his idea, Larkin was firmly persuaded they were dealing with a creature from another world. He'd tried to convince Ben and Nadine and seen the laughter in their eyes. So be it.

To Larkin's way of reckoning, aliens were no different from humans or wild beasts. They must have weaknesses. So all he had to do was identify the creature's and he would have the grandest trophy any man ever owned—provided the alien didn't disappear in a puff of smoke when it died, like some of those he had seen on television.

Larkin went into the closet and brought out a small quiver containing 20 shafts. He checked the fletching, made certain the points were screwed on tight, and placed the quiver beside the bow. All was in readiness.

Beer in hand, the poacher strolled outdoors and noted the position of the sun. It would be hours yet before the van showed up. He wasn't tired but he figured he should get some rest. He needed to be as sharp as a bowie if he hoped to stand a prayer against the creature.

The ridge drew Larkin's attention. He remembered Ben claiming there might be a connection between the cemetery and the alien. The brainstorm had merit. He should have seen the connection himself.

Larkin took a swallow, pondering. The alien, like any other animal, must have a lair, somewhere it hid out during the day. And the lair had to be somewhere near Cemetery Ridge. If the creature didn't have a spaceship handy, and if it wasn't living in the forest, the next best place would be the graveyard. Few people went there, except for funerals and the like. It was an ideal spot to lie low. Adding credence to the writer's claim, one of the victims had died there, the man who had known the cemetery the best.

Larkin polished off the brew, crushed the can, and went back into the mobile home. When Ben and the woman showed up, he'd suggest that they pay the cemetery a visit. It couldn't hurt. With that in mind, the poacher stretched out on his sagging sofa and was soon snoring loud enough to wake the dead.

Chapter Seventeen

At four o'clock that afternoon Ben awoke to the persistent buzzing of his alarm. He shuffled downstairs and found a note from his mother saying that she had gone shopping with Nadine. Using the microwave, he heated a cup of instant black coffee and carried it to the kitchen table, where the library books were stacked.

Ben had the nagging feeling that he had overlooked a crucial fact or two. He scanned the titles of the volumes again, trying to decide which ones deserved a second look and which should be set aside and forgotten.

Seating himself, Ben sipped the scalding coffee. He opened a book on ghosts first, but shortly discarded it as useless. His second choice was a volume on vampires and werewolves, which soon ended up on the kitchen floor. The third book was entitled *Legions Of The Dead*. He had merely flipped through it the day before and had been turned off by its grisly depictions of zombies eating human flesh. This time he paid more attention.

Toward the back of the book Ben found a chapter dealing with assorted reports of strange creatures seen at or near cemeteries. Some were traditional vampires, a few pale ogres observed eating corpses. Others were spectral wraiths. At the end of the chapter were four reports of lizardlike beings.

Ben found those the most interesting. All four had allegedly taken place many years ago; the first had been recorded in the tenth century and the last only 200 years earlier. In each case the creature had gone on a spree of wanton slaughter, then faded into oblivion without being found or slain.

The book had no name for these evil beings. The author went on about them being demonic archetypes projected by the human subconscious, which Ben equated to so much nonsense.

An hour had gone by and the coffee cup was drained. Ben went out onto the porch for fresh air and leaned against a post. In two hours the sun would set. The vicious cycle of carnage would begin anew. Only this time there would be scores of young children abroad.

Would the creature prey on the children? Ben asked himself. Or had he been right about the cemetery connection? He wished he had the time to check into the recent activities of those killed to determine whether or not most or all of them had visited the graveyard within the past few days. He was willing to bet a year's wages that they had.

The knowledge, though, did Ben little good. Its significance eluded him, as did how he could use it against the creature.

To the west a bank of gray clouds had appeared. For once the weatherman had been right. A storm was on the way, and Ben was glad to see it. Heavy rain would keep some of the trick or treaters home and give the monster fewer victims to prey upon.

Going indoors, Ben went upstairs and started the shower running. He stripped and was about to step under the hot spray when he thought he heard a car pull up in front of the house. He listened a minute for the slam of doors that would tell him his mother and Nadine had returned, but there were none. So he stepped into the stall and broke into a sour rendition of *Hey Jude*.

If Ben had bothered to look out a front window he would have learned why no doors had slammed.

Victor Richards had spent a restless afternoon pacing the rooms of his mansion. He couldn't bear to think of Nadine and Ben out together, of the tender moments they might be sharing. The longer he dwelled on the subject, the more incensed he became. Accordingly, about five o'clock, he hopped into his car and drove over to see if they were back.

Victor was in luck. Ben's van was there, but not his mother's car or Nadine's. Acting on the spur of the moment, Victor pulled into the driveway, slipped the bundle of cocaine out from under his seat, and eased through the open window rather than make noise opening and closing the door.

A hedge sheltered the yard, affording Victor all the cover he needed. He scoured the street, which was empty of passersby since most were in eating supper, then he dashed to the van and quickly yet quietly opened the sliding door. The interior was plush, with carpeting on the floor and the walls and a pair of large, expensive speakers mounted at the rear.

Victor moved to the nearest speaker. It hung on brackets mounted on the wall of the van. Jiggling the speaker he discovered that it could be removed and did so with a violent twist. There was more than enough room inside for the package. He wedged the cocaine between the woofer and the side of the speaker, then froze on hearing voices.

Peeking out a back window, Victor saw a young couple walking down the street. They showed no interest in the van or in his sports car and were soon halfway down the block.

Working swiftly, Victor carefully mounted the speaker and gave it a solid shake to be certain it wouldn't fall off when the van hit a bump. Satisfied, he backed out, closed the door as silently as he could, and slid into his car.

Victor shifted into neutral, let the vehicle coast back down the incline that lead to the garage, and popped the clutch the moment all four tires were in the street. Like a bat out of hell he took off, reaching third gear before he came to the corner and taking the turn at 20 miles over the speed limit.

He had done it! Victor whooped for joy and slapped the dashboard. Now he had only to report the presence of a vile pusher in their fair town to the chief of police and Nadine would be his again.

Victor took a right on Simmons, went several blocks, and pulled up beside a phone booth. He shook with glee as he inserted the proper change and dialed the number for the police department.

"Cemetery Ridge Police Department. May I help you?"

The voice was a woman's. Victor hesitated, unsure whether he should try again later in the hope of talking directly to Travis.

"Is anyone there? This is the dispatcher. How may I be of service?"

Victor didn't want to wait. The sooner Ben was in custody, the happier he would be. He pinched his nose, lowered his voice as deep as he could, and said, "I'd like to speak to the chief of police. It's urgent."

"In regards to what, sir?"

"I can't say," Victor said. "I must speak to the chief in person."

"I'm sorry, sir, but it's my job to screen all his calls. Unless this is an emergency I can't put you through."

"It is," Victor lied.

"One moment, please."

Victor impatiently tapped his foot and marked the passing of a full minute before someone came on the other end of the line again.

"This is Chief Sinclair. Who is this?"

"I'd rather not say," Victor said.

"Look, mister, I'm a busy man. You told the dispatcher this is an emergency, so it had better be one. What do you want?"

"I'm calling to do my civic duty, sir. I just want to help you out."

"How so?"

"By letting you know the name and address of a drug pusher. If you hurry, you can arrest him before he disposes of the stuff he's been selling."

"You don't say," Travis said, not sounding at all interested.

"Yes, sir," Victor said. "Do you have a pencil and paper handy? I'll tell you who it is."

"I don't want to know."

It took a few moments for the lawman's reply to sink in. Victor had been all set to blurt out the information, and it threw him off his mental stride. "What did you say?" he asked in surprise, positive he had misheard.

"You can keep your information to yourself, mister," Travis told him. "I'm not interested."

"How can you say that?" Victor said. "You're the chief of police, for crying out loud. You have to be interested. It's your job."

"My job," Travis said sourly, "is to arrest people I see breaking the law or those who have been formally charged with crimes. Note the key word there, mister. Formally. "It's been my policy as long as I've held this post not to accept anonymous tips. Half the time they don't pan out. And the other half usually involve people trying to get back at someone they're mad at by sending the police to his or her doorstep to put a good scare into them."

"This is insane," Victor said. "You have to act on this tip. It's legitimate." He racked his brain for another reason. "The cops on TV do it all the time."

Sinclair chortled. "Television isn't real life, friend. If you care to come down to the station and file a formal complaint, I'll be more than glad to conduct an investigation. And if it's warranted, I'll make an arrest. But I absolutely refuse to act on anonymous tips, especially when it's obvious the caller is disguising his voice. That always puts the motivation in a questionable light."

"I just don't want my identity known," Victor said, astonished by the turn of events. This couldn't be happening, he told himself. What kind of idiot lawman didn't accept anonymous tips? Why, if the idea weren't so ridiculous, he'd suspect Travis of using it as a pretext for getting out of doing work.

"So," Travis said, "are you willing to tell me your name now that you understand department policy?"

"I can't," Victor said.

"Then I can't waste more of my valuable time talking to you. In case you haven't heard, I have a killer bear to catch. Good day to you, sir."

The line went dead. Victor stared at the receiver, then smashed it down on the cradle in a fit of temper. He wished Travis were standing in front of him so he could throttle the dumb bastard's throat! So mad he could hardly see straight, Victor stepped from the booth to the curb. All his scheming had backfired. He'd gone to all that trouble for nothing!

Victor felt his temples begin to throb and worried one of his infrequent migraines was coming on. A loud rumbling drew his gaze to the boulevard, where a large truck hauling a backhoe on a flatbed trailer was going past. He absently glanced at the cab and could have sworn he saw his nephew staring back at him. Blinking, he looked again, but there was no one on the passenger side.

Just great! Victor reflected. Now he was seeing things! He walked to his car and got in. Struggling to control his rare flash of anger, he saw that his first priority was to reclaim the cocaine. He wasn't about to let Ben go riding off to Portland with a small fortune in snow.

Cranking the engine, Victor drove to the next corner and hung a right. He was over a block from the Shields residence when he spotted Nadine and Ben's mother carrying in groceries from Nadine's car. Quickly he turned left at the intersection before either of them spotted him.

Victor slapped the steering wheel with both hands. Some days not a damn thing went right! Now he had to wait until dark and then retrieve the package. He could use Paxton's help, have the kid stand watch while he sneaked into the van, but the teenager had already left the mansion to join his buddies for their prank-night activities.

Victor sighed and headed home, figuring a few stiff drinks were in order. The way his day was going, he'd be lucky to live through the night. The damned bear would probably eat him. Laughing at the thought, the richest man in Cemetery Ridge put the pedal to the metal.

"Do you think he saw us, man?" Jess Weaver asked nervously while staring into the rearview mirror. "Oh, God. If we're caught, my old man will kill me."

"Quit your whining, you big baby," Paxton said. "If Uncle Vic had seen me, he'd have already caught up with us. We're safe, dude. Calm down."

Jess braked for a red light and downshifted. He couldn't stop fidgeting or looking into the three mirrors, one after the other. When the light changed he shifted roughly and the gears made a grinding sound. "I don't know why I let you talk me into this. The more I think about it, the more stupid it seems."

"Chill, damn it," Paxton said. "We'll be out of town in a few minutes and from there on we'll have smooth sailing."

"I don't know why we couldn't have waited until after dark. Driving down the main drag in broad daylight is asking for grief."

Paxton rested a hand on the other boy's arm. "Take a few deep breaths and you'll feel better." He watched a sexy young girl cross in front of them and beamed at her when she glanced their way, but she ignored him. "We've been all through this a dozen times. After sunset there's hardly any traffic. We'd be too obvious. Heavy equipment like this doesn't move around a lot after dark. And you know as well as I do that the cops will be out in force tonight, it being Halloween and all. No, it's best to get the rig there and hide it until nightfall. Then we can get to work."

"I'd like to know where the hell you're going to hide something this big," Jess muttered.

"You'll see, bro. I have it all worked out," Paxton said. He checked his watch and grinned. They were right on schedule.

"Look!" Jess cried, pointing. "It's the chief!"

Sure enough, a patrol car was pulling out of the police station parking lot. It turned onto Simmons and headed south. The chief never bothered to look their way as his patrol car went by in the opposite direction.

"See? You were worried over nothing," Paxton said. "That fat idiot didn't pay any attention to us. He's too busy worrying about the thing that's been killing people right and left."

"Which reminds me," Jess said. "Why the hell are we planning to spend hours out at the cemetery when that bear or whatever it is might show up and decide to make a meal of us?"

"I've got that covered."

"How?"

Paxton slid a hand under his coat and pulled out the Colt Combat Elite .45-caliber automatic he had stolen from his uncle's bedroom. "Check this baby out. The clip is loaded with seven rounds. I'm ready to rock and roll if that thing shows its ugly face."

Jess ogled the shiny pistol. "Man, you think of everything. I wish I had a piece like that."

"Still worried about the boogeyman?" Paxton asked.

"Not if you can shoot worth a damn."

"I've had a lot of practice," Paxton lied. "At fifty yards I can plug a quarter."

"Really? Hot damn!" Jess said.

"I can probably shoot better than that fat-butt excuse for a chief we have," Paxton said. "Trust me. If anything shows up at the cemetery before we're done, it's history."

Travis Sinclair was quite pleased with himself. He had 9,000 dollars stashed in a locked briefcase beside him. He had an hour of spare time to kill and was going to indulge in a few of Gertie's doughnuts. And best of all, most of his workload for Halloween night was being handled by Bo Seaver's boys.

The only blemish on Travis's immediate horizon was the very real threat of the hellish creature striking again. He hoped against hope it wouldn't but he had to be realistic. Odds were it would add to the body count before another dawn, which meant long hours and a ton of extra paperwork for him. Unless, by some miracle, the sheriff and his men managed to kill the thing.

All day Travis had been thinking about his conversation with Ben. It was ironic that Ben had proposed the very idea Travis had entertained before the writer's arrival.

Travis had a thought that made him chuckle. The creature loose in Cemetery Ridge was something otherworldly, an entity so unique it might qualify for the endangered species list. Maybe he should contact the Environmental Protection Agency and request the creature be granted federal protection. Then the feds could put it under their protection and it would be their headache, not his.

The ludicrous idea brought a belly laugh. Travis was still laughing when he saw Victor Richards make a turn off of Simmons, violating the speed limit as he did. Travis reached for the switch to activate the lights and siren, but immediately lowered his arm. He'd have to be crazy to give a ticket to the most influential man in town. Richards only had to snap his fingers and the town council would give Travis the boot.

Not that it mattered much. Travis had the nine grand. He gave the briefcase an affectionate pat and looked forward to hiding it in his cellar, where it would be safe.

Travis drove a few more yards, then glanced over his shoulder, down the side street Richards had taken. Thinking of the look on the other man's face, he realized Victor had appeared mad as hell, which was highly unusual.

Victor Richards was known for always taking whatever life had to offer in stride. It came of having enough money to buy Fort Knox, Travis supposed. Since the wealthy could buy their way out of any trouble, the petty problems that plagued everyone else rarely bothered them. Rich people were able to sneer at life while others had to suffer.

Why, then, had Victor looked mad enough to kill someone? Travis wondered. Curious, he took a left at the next block and prowled eastward on the off chance of spotting the sports car. To his surprise, it sped across the street he was on, several blocks away, heading south.

Travis coasted close to the intersection and leaned forward to peek out the corner of his windshield. He was just in time to see Victor make another hairpin turn. Beyond Richards two women were unloading groceries. Travis looked and recognized Nadine Somersby. Then he gazed at the house and felt a tingle of excitement. It was the Shields place.

Going straight, Travis came to the next intersection and saw Richards racing southward. Had it been coincidence that Victor was driving in the vicinity? Or did it have something to do with his ex-wife seeing Ben?

Travis gave a toss of his head and went around the block and back to Simmons. It was none of his business. He had more important issues weighing on his mind. His mouth watering, he hurried to fill his belly with doughnuts.

Ben was toweling himself off when he heard merry voices. Throwing on a robe, he walked downstairs and paused in the kitchen doorway, watching his mother and Nadine put groceries in the cupboards. The two of them got along so well together that he couldn't help thinking Nadine would fit right into the family if he ever decided to pop the big question.

"How was the ride to Grants Pass?" he asked.

"Same as ever," his mother answered. "They haven't changed the course of the interstate since the last time we went."

"Smart aleck," Ben said.

"We listened to as many radio stations as we could," Nadine said. "All the news reports kept referring to the creature as a black bear. Why won't the authorities admit the truth?"

"For the same reason they never give out all the gory details when a serial killer is on the loose," Ben said. "They don't want to stir up the local populace and have hordes of vigilantes on their hands."

"They'll have some tonight," Nadine said. "I saw one man escorting a pair of small trick or treaters around early. He was armed with a rifle."

Ben stepped to the window and stared at the western sky. Sunset would take place within the hour. "It won't be long now," he said. "Tonight will be a night Cemetery Ridge will long remember."

"I wish you wouldn't talk like that, son," Elizabeth Shields said. "It scares me a little."

"Sorry, Mom. Don't worry. We'll be all right." Ben pecked her on the cheek and went upstairs to dress.

He was buttoning his shirt when he sensed another presence and turned to find Nadine giving him the sort of look a condemned man might get as he walked to the electric chair. "Something on your mind?"

"We don't have to go out again tonight, you know," Nadine said. The second full day spent with Ben and his mother had made her more keenly aware than ever how much he meant to her. She wouldn't risk losing him or their future together. "Killing that monster is a job for the police."

"You saw them last night. They can't handle it and you know it."

"And we can?" Nadine said. "We know little more than they do. What makes you think we can succeed where they've failed?"

"I don't know we can, but we have to try. I know it sounds corny to say, but this is our town. We grew up here. My mom lives here, so do your folks. We have an obligation to do whatever we can to protect them and everyone else." Ben walked over and took Nadine into his arms. "You can stay here with my mother if you'd like."

"And leave you to face that thing alone? No way. I carry my own weight, Ben Shields. Where you go, I go." Nadine wanted to say more but Ben silenced her by smothering her lips with passionate kisses.

Outside, the sun sank steadily lower.

Chapter Eighteen

The veil of night shrouded southwest Oregon when the three who were one stirred. For a long while it simply lay there, savoring the sweet thrill of being alive. Then it slowly uncoiled and floated in the dank darkness of the mausoleum, attuning its senses to the nocturnal rhythms. It could hear, but not with ears, because it had none. It could relish scents, but not with a nose, because at the moment it lacked nostrils. And it could see, but not as men or animals saw, since it had no eyes.

The cemetery was quiet. Its cocoon was quiet. All seemed well. So it willed itself to take shape, coalescing from an intangible entity into a creature that existed on the same electromagnetic plane as its prey.

The transformation complete, it crouched beside the coffins, regaining its strength. The change always tired it greatly. At any other time of the year it would be impossible to perform, but this was the special time, the time allotted its kind in the scheme of things, the time when the energy focus made the feasting possible, the time when it could gather unto itself the sweet nectar that would preserve its existence over the long cold span that extended from one feeding time to the next. Such were the cycles of its life.

The creature effortlessly opened the heavy door to the crypt and stepped out. Right away it knew something was wrong. A taste of moisture in the air warned it of rain on the way. Water was the bane of its kind, the one element that could disrupt its continuity.

The three who were one raised its head and sniffed. There was time yet. The atmospheric conditions would not be conducive to rainfall for hours. It could feed. It could store up the energy it needed. But it must hurry.

The creature scanned the cemetery, seeking aura trails left by those who had been there during its rest. To its chagrin, there were none. Not a single one. Without them, it could not track its prey.

Suddenly the creature felt a shift in the energy patterns surrounding the cemetery. It strained its heightened senses to the utmost and perceived the convergence of six humans on its domain. Six were more than enough to supply sufficient nectar to ensure its survival until the next cycle was complete.

Retreating into the cocoon, the creature closed the door and waited silently with a patience few beings could match. The six must come much nearer before it would feast.

It must be cautious this time, since under no circumstances could it allow the humans to suspect the importance of the cocoon. Without the cocoon, the nectar would serve no purpose. Without the cocoon the creature would cease to exist, and that must never be.

Like an imposing statue of a gray gargoyle perched high on the ramparts of a medieval building, the inwardly pulsating creature stood motionless next to the door. Waiting. Simply waiting.

A quarter of a mile from the cemetery, Paxton turned to Jess and grinned. "See? I told you it would work. I'm so brilliant it's scary."

Jess Weaver had to agree. "I didn't even know this old dirt road was here," he said while slowly taking a turn. Vegetation hemmed them in so closely on either side that limbs brushed against the truck and the trailer.

"That's what you get for not being observant," Paxton said. "I noticed it the other night when we were out here."

Years earlier, evidently, it had been a logging access road into the forest on the west slope of the ridge. Long since abandoned, the dirt road was rarely used except by an occasional hunter. The nearest house was a goodly distance to the south, much too far for the occupants to hear the diesel truck.

Paxton stared straight ahead at the taillights in front of them. Bill Paine had come through and taken his folks's car without their permission. Riding with Paine were Cindy, Manda, and Jimmy. The gang was all there. It was time to teach the hicks how boys in the big city got their kicks.

"Say, I had a thought," Jess said.

"Uh-oh."

"I'm serious, Pax," Jess said. "What if the gate is locked like it was the last time?"

"Duh," Paxton said and gave the roof of the cab a whack. "This mother weighs tons. We can bust through any gate ever made with no problem."

Jess looked at him. "No way, Jose. I told you that we can't damage the merchandise or my dad will have a fit. You're not the one who will be grounded until the next ice age if the equipment has so much as a dent in it tomorrow."

Paxton came close to cuffing Jess for daring to defy him. He needed the heavy equipment, though, so he merely clenched his fists and said, "Relax, I'll think of something. Don't I always?"

"Yeah, you do," Jess said. "I don't know how you do it. I wish I was as smart as you."

"Never wish for the impossible," Paxton said, gazing at the sedan. Cindy had her nose pressed to the back window and was grinning and waving. "Now what the hell does she think she's doing?"

"Having a bitchin' time, I expect," Jess said.

And he was right. Cindy Drew was giddy with the thrill of adventure. She had never been involved in anything so exciting in her whole life, and she owed it all to the handsome hunk who didn't seem to notice that she was trying to get his attention. She waved a final time, then turned around and said, "Must be the glare on the window. Pax can't see me."

Bill Paine, who had both hands glued to the wheel and was steering carefully to avoid putting nicks and scratches in the car's finish, said, "Maybe he has his eyes on this bear of a road. It's got more twists and bends than a figure eight." One of those turns forced him to spin the wheel madly. "I'll be glad when we reach the street."

"Well, I don't know about you, but I'm having a swell time," Cindy said, then poked Manda with her right elbow. "How about you, girl?"

"I'm with you all the way," Manda said.

"And you?" Cindy asked, bending to see Jimmy Howell, who sat with one arm on the door rest and the other draped around Manda's slim shoulders.

"It's a night I'll never forget," Jimmy said, which was true to a point. He would never be able to look at himself in the mirror again without thinking of the time he was stupid enough to get arrested for trespassing, destroying private property, disinterring the dead, and possibly abusing a corpse if Paxton and the others got carried away.

"Another minute and we'll be in the clear," Bill said.

"I can't wait to get there," Cindy said.

Jimmy could. He'd have been overjoyed if the car had broken down at that very spot, or if the diesel had sputtered and died. Were it not for Manda, he wouldn't have shown up. He gave her a gentle squeeze and received in return a smile that would melt gold.

"Stay close to me tonight," she whispered.

"I will," Jimmy said. "I won't let anything happen to you." Not after the night before, not after he had gotten to walk her home and been treated to a kiss that had set his head to spinning. Manda had mashed against him so hard that he had felt her breasts rub his chest. And most marvelous of all, she had glided her silken tongue into his mouth and swirled his own tongue as if it were a piece of candy. It had been an experience to die for.

The thought made Jimmy somber. He and the others were idiots to go back to the graveyard after the incident the other night. And he was the biggest idiot of all since he'd had a good look at the thing when it had come after him at his house. He alone had a fair idea of what they would be up against if the creature showed while they were playing their great prank.

Jimmy knew that none of his friends, except Manda, believed his story. They all bought the official line that a bear was stalking the town. And they figured they could hold their own against a lousy bear. But they were so wrong.

Were it not for Manda, Jimmy wouldn't be there. He would have stayed home and left them to face whatever fate had in store. But he couldn't desert Manda after that kiss. She was the first true girlfriend he had ever had, and he would gladly give his life if need be to safeguard hers.

Of course, Jimmy would never mention his feelings to the others. They'd only laugh at him, especially that damned Paxton. They'd label him as old-fashioned, call him a dork or worse. And all because he cared for someone. Why did his peers get all bent out of shape when one of their own showed genuine feelings for another? Was it because they had so little love in their own miserable lives that they couldn't stand the thought of someone else having the happiness they were denied? He really didn't know.

"There's the street!" Bill called out.

A hard knot formed in the pit of Jimmy's stomach. They would soon be at the cemetery. He must stay alert and hope to hell the creature didn't appear.

Bill turned onto the asphalt and drove slowly until the truck did the same. Then he sped up and presently the wrought-iron gates were illuminated by the headlights.

"Look there," Bill said. "They're wide open."

And so they were. Jimmy saw why as they drove in. Both halves had been damaged somehow, and the lock was twisted out of shape. He scanned the rows of mausoleums and felt an icy finger run down his spine. "I don't like this," he said softly.

"Don't wuss out on us now, Jimbo. We'll only be here a couple of hours. And like Pax says, think of how famous we'll be after this stunt. It will be in all the papers."

"Fame is relative, Billy," Jimmy said. "I'd rather be famous like Albert Einstein than Billy the Kid."

"What's that supposed to mean? Billy the Kid is more famous than that Einstein dude will ever be."

"Never mind," Jimmy said. He twisted to look out the back window as the diesel truck eased through the gate, and he wondered if their fearless leader wasn't the least bit nervous.

Paxton saw Jimmy staring at the truck and frowned. He had never liked the kid and only tolerated Howell's presence because the nerd bought a lot of munchies when the gang was out cruising the town and because the girls might be upset if he kicked Howell's teeth in. But now Jimmy had gone too far. The dork had latched onto Manda.

Paxton never could stick with one girl for any length of time. He'd always had a roving eye. So although he had been seeing Cindy for several months, he'd also been seeing three other girls at the same time. And although Manda was almost too plain for his tastes, he had plans to add her to his long list of conquests later on. Only now she had taken up with the dweeb.

Paxton had felt he had more than enough excuse to bust Jimmy's face, but he'd held off—until now. Before the night was over, he intended to teach the nerd that no one stepped on Paxton Booth's toes and got away with it.

Jess had shifted down into second gear and the diesel truck was crawling along. He gazed out at the tombs, then asked, "Are we going to trash some of them, too, Pax?"

"We might. If there's time."

By prior arrangement, both the truck and Bill's car were driven as far into the cemetery as the road allowed. Bill braked on a gravel strip beside the road and shortly thereafter Jess brought the big rig to a stop alongside the car.

Paxton slid down from the cab, verified that the pistol was securely tucked under his coat where it couldn't be seen, and walked to the rear of the trailer. It required a few minutes to let down the flaps, lower the ramp to the ground, and fire up the backhoe. Since Jess had used the heavy equipment many times, he could expertly back it off the flatbed and over to the closest row of graves.

Paxton grinned and gave the thumb's up sign to Jess. He moved to where he could see the big metal scoop tear neatly into the soft earth and upend the tombstone. The engine revved as Jess angled the bucket deeper into the soil. In no time the heavy machine had dug out a wide trench, exposing a coffin. Weaver hooked the bucket's teeth under the coffin and easily tilted it upward until it stood upright, propped against the side of the trench.

Paxton laughed with glee. He wished he could be there to see the look on the chief of the police's face when he beheld scores of coffins poking up out of the earth as if they were sprouted from seeds. Cackling, Paxton signaled to Jess to go on to the next grave; then he walked over to Bill. He had to yell to make himself heard above the backhoe. "Head on back down the road and keep an eye on the front gate. If you see any cars coming, warn us."

Bill stared into the darkness. "You want me to go all by myself?"

"What's the matter? Don't tell me that you're yellow?" Paxton said. "Here I thought you were the one guy I could count on."

"I am. I just wanted some company." Paine moved off reluctantly, his hands in his pockets. He looked back several times and saw Jimmy and the girls head in another direction. Jimmy did not appear any too happy, and for once Bill couldn't blame him.

The wind increased as Bill hiked slowly down the middle of the road. He spotted a large rock lying at the edge of the grass and picked it up. If he'd known Paxton was going to make him waltz around the graveyard alone, he would have brought his hunting knife.

The growl of the backhoe carried far on the breeze. Paine wondered if the nearest residents would hear and notify the police. He hoped they would think someone was being buried later than usual or else that construction work was being done and not bother.

Clouds floated silently by overhead, there were many more to the west. Bill guessed it would rain before midnight. He hoped they would be done by then. With Paxton, though, there was no telling. The crazy bastard might get it into his head to dig up every grave in the cemetery.

By now Bill had gone 30 yards. He turned and realized that, while he could still see Paxton and the backhoe quite clearly, Paxton could no longer see him. He needn't go any farther since the gate was clearly visible from where he stood.

For minutes on end Bill observed grave after grave being torn open. Presently there were eight coffins upright in a line, some with clumps of earth affixed to them. He snickered at the sight and had to admit that Paxton's brainstorm was outstanding. They'd be the talk of the town.

Rather abruptly a strange feeling came over him. Bill stiffened, his skin pricked by invisible pins. He experienced a sensation of being stared at by unseen eyes. Whirling, he scoured the cemetery, but saw nothing unusual.

Chalking the strange sensation up to raw nerves, Bill resumed watching Jess at work.

The cool breeze and the throaty purr of the motor lulled him into complacency, so he was all the more startled when he distinctly heard the sound of a heavy footstep behind him.

Bill raised the rock and spun. He peered hard into the night, but saw nothing move. Crouching, he studied the length of road winding south. No one was there. He wondered if perhaps a new caretaker had been hired to replace Old Man Stoner or if other kids were there doing pranks of their own.

Gradually Bill relaxed and straightened up. He decided that he had stood guard long enough and someone else should take a turn. Hefting the rock, he retraced his steps toward the backhoe. But he hadn't gone five feet when he heard another loud tread.

Convinced there had to be a logical explanation, Bill slowly pivoted. He should have turned faster, because he wasn't quite all the way around when a vise clamped on his neck, choking off his breath. Another vise closed on his upper arm and he was lifted into the air as if he were weightless.

Terrified, Paine wildly swung the rock and connected. Yet there was no reaction. He struck again as he was carried off among the graves. Sputtering and wheezing, he tried to suck relief into his lungs while continuing to flail away at his attacker. He could breathe, but just barely. The exertion rendered his limbs weaker and weaker. Against his will he blacked out, but only for a few moments. When next he opened his eyes, he was lying flat on his back.

Above Bill reared a living nightmare, a monstrosity that defied description and belief, a creature that shouldn't exist and yet did. In a horrifying flash of insight Bill realized that Jimmy had told the truth. He opened his mouth to give voice to his terror but a white light exploded within his head and he was paralyzed from head to toe.

Bill saw the creature bend toward him and its mouth part wide. The last sight the teenager took with him into eternity was that of a darkly glistening tube shooting from the monster's maw toward his face. Then the world went black. He felt a warm, sticky substance on his face and knew no more.

Above Bill's inert body, the three who were one did not rush the feeding. The creature drank slowly, savoring the sweet nectar, feeling itself grow stronger with every slurp. It was vaguely aware of a slight lowering of the air temperature. Dimly, it sensed three more humans moving in its direction.

Those three were Jimmy and the girls. Cindy had taken a hammer from a toolbox in the sedan and was going around bashing tombstones for the fun of it. She'd haul off and whack a chip of stone from one, then cackle uproariously as if she had committed the funniest act ever.

Manda, Jimmy noticed, stood to one side and seemed downcast. He stayed close to her, now and again brushing his hand against hers.

It would have been nice to cheer her up but he was too upset himself. Jimmy had a bad feeling that they were all in imminent danger. He longed to spirit Manda away from there before it was too late but without wheels it would take them hours to walk back to town.

"Isn't this bitchin'?" Cindy asked, giggling. She took a firm stance next to another headstone, drew the hammer back, and planted a blow that cracked the upper edge. "I bet I can bust every one in the cemetery before we leave."

"What's the point?" Jimmy said.

"Point?" Cindy said. "This is prank night, dummy. Halloween. Trick or treat, remember? There's not supposed to be a point."

"Mindless damage is all it is," Jimmy said. "Damage we'll have to pay for if we're caught."

"Who's going to catch us?" Cindy said. "The cops are all busy keeping the streets safe for munchkins. No one else comes by here at this time of night, so we're in the clear." She regarded him with suspicion. "Unless one of us turns snitch, that is. You're not planning to go angel on us and blab to the law, are you?"

"You know better," Jimmy said.

"Do I?" Cindy resumed smashing headstones but she no longer laughed after each blow. She was mad at Jimmy for being a spoilsport, and she had half a mind to tell Paxton that she suspected the skinny boy of being a snitch.

Jimmy dropped a few yards back. He could see Jess digging up yet another coffin. Paxton stood near the backhoe, directing the excavation. Interesting, Jimmy thought, that Paxton wasn't doing any of the actual digging. Should they be caught, Jess would face the stiffest punishment for working the heavy equipment. Jimmy wondered if Jess was smart enough to figure that out, but doubted it.

Jimmy gazed toward the cemetery drive, where he had last seen Bill. The jock was nowhere in sight. Jimmy scanned every foot of the road to where it disappeared going through the midst of the mausoleums. No Bill.

"Where do you think Bill got to?" he asked.

"Who knows?" Cindy said irritably. "Probably off having a great time since he doesn't have a worrywart to deal with."

"Excuse me for living," Jimmy said. He walked a few yards off before he said a few choice words he might regret. Then he heard Manda come up behind him.

"What's wrong?" she asked.

"This is wrong, all wrong," Jimmy said. "How would you like it if someone came along and trashed your grave?"

"I wouldn't," Manda said and clasped his fingers. "That's why I'm not lending Cindy a hand. But we can't rain on her parade, Jim. She's my best friend, for better or worse. Let her have her fun."

"Some fun," Jimmy said, turning around.

In the pale starlight she was the most beautiful girl he had ever seen, and a lump formed

in his throat, a lump caused by the passionate longing that filled his heart. He yearned
to kiss her but they weren't alone. Impulsively
he gave her a hug instead, then stepped back,
embarrassed.

"What was that for?" Manda asked, grinning.

"Just because," Jimmy said, his voice oddly
strained.

To let his blood cool down, he turned to the
south. There stood the mausoleums. As Jimmy
set eyes on them he was petrified to see a living
thing among the lifeless marble and stone, a
towering figure too far off to identify. But it
could only be one creature. And it was coming
toward them.

Chapter Nineteen

Fred Larkin waited in the thick brush lining Knob Road, a quiver was strapped to his back, a crossbow in his hand. His .44 Magnum rode on one hip, his bowie on the other. He saw the van coming and stepped into the open.

"What in the world is he carrying?" Nadine asked upon spying the poacher.

"I'll be damned," Ben said. "It's a crossbow." He pulled to the edge of the road and waited while Nadine opened the sliding door. "Planning to assault a castle tonight, Fred?"

Larkin chuckled and took a seat. There had been a brief drizzle while he waited and he was soaked. The dampness intensified his normally strong odor so that he smelled like one of the hides he so often skinned off animals. To him, the scent was more aromatic than the most expensive perfume.

"You never know," Larkin said. "The rifle didn't work, so we'll try this puppy."

"Next you'll be shooting spitballs," Nadine said.

"Hey, if I thought they'd work, I would," Larkin said. "Whatever gets the job done." He reached into a pocket, pulled out a white handkerchief bearing so many yellow stains there wasn't a clean spot on it, and commenced wiping the bow off. "Took you long enough to get here. I was expecting you half an hour ago."

"We got a late start," Ben said as he turned back onto the road and wheeled the van in a tight loop. "And the traffic on Simmons was a lot heavier than usual."

"Parents taking their children out trick or treating," Nadine said. "They were everywhere, a lot of them with guns."

Larkin laughed. "Sounds like my kind of holiday."

"The police are everywhere, too," Ben said. "All three patrol cars are cruising the streets and so are a lot of the sheriff's men. We'll have to be extra careful tonight." He saw a pair of headlights swing onto Knob Road from Gardner Road and slowed in case it proved to be a law officer. The headlights promptly swung into a driveway and went out.

"Anything on the scanner yet?" Larkin asked.

"The usual small talk," Ben said. "There have been no reports of the creature. But it has to be out there. If it follows the same pattern as seventy-three years ago, tonight will be the bloodiest of them all."

"Too bad we can't find the damn thing before it starts killing," Larkin said.

"Maybe we can. I have a long shot I want to play," Ben said. "Since the cemetery figures so prominently in the attacks, I'd like to pay it a visit first and look around."

Nadine looked at him. "What better place to be on Halloween than a graveyard?"

The scanner blared to life, but the report turned out to be a deputy reporting a fight between two parents who came to blows when the child of one dropped a piece of candy picked up by the child of the other, who then refused to hand it over.

"My, my," Larkin said. "Tempers are flaring tonight, aren't they? The bear business must have everyone on edge."

Ben slowed as they approached Gardner Road, then made the turn.

No sooner had the van vanished around the corner than Victor Richards twisted the ignition key in his sports car and hastily backed out of the driveway he had pulled into on spotting the van. He had been following Nadine and his old buddy ever since they left the Shields house, waiting for his chance to recover the package of cocaine.

Victor had tried earlier. He'd driven to the alley behind Ben's mother's house about sunset and sneaked through an adjoining yard to a tree near the driveway. But kids and parents had been showing up in a steady stream, bringing Elizabeth Shields to the door to dispense sweets five times every minute. He hadn't dared try sneaking into the van.

Shortly after Victor had crept back to his car, Ben and Nadine walked from the house and drove off. He was not about to let them out of his sight until he had the coke, no matter how long it took, so he had trailed them. Their trip to Knob Road surprised him. He'd stayed far enough behind to prevent them from spotting his car, and as a result he had no idea why they had abruptly turned around and were heading on back toward Cemetery Ridge.

Victor crawled to the intersection and surveyed Gardner. The van was hundreds of yards away, negotiating a bend. He idled the car until the van had disappeared, then took off in pursuit. Since very few homes lined either road, there was no traffic. It worked in Victor's favor that parents who lived on Knob and Gardner invariably took their kids into town to trick or treat.

Over the next several minutes Victor glimpsed the van's taillights and was able to maintain a discreet distance. He was nearing another bend when he gazed through the firs to his left and saw that the van had stopped in the middle of the road. His foot found the brake and he switched off his headlights so he wouldn't be detected.

An old man had appeared. With him were two big dogs. Victor had no idea what Ben was up to, but he found himself growing more curious by the minute.

Jacob Metz had been out walking his bloodhounds when a horn sounded and a van rolled to a stop beside him. He recognized Ben and smiled, showing even more teeth at the sight of the pretty redhead beside him. "Well, I declare. Nice seeing you again, Mr. Shields. Out trick or treating, are you?"

Ben smiled and pointed at the rifle Metz carried. "Are you out hunting at this time of night?"

"Goodness gracious, no," Metz said. "Achilles and Hector need their nightly exercise. And with the Brain Eater running loose, a man can't be too careful."

Fred Larkin slid between the bucket seats so his friend could see him. "How would you and those mutts of yours like to help us put an end to that alien once and for all?"

"Fred?" Metz said, taken aback. "What are you up to?"

Ben responded before the poacher could. He didn't mind having the hunter go along but he drew the line at allowing the bloodhounds into his van. His carpeting would be ruined if they weren't housebroken. "We're after the creature," he said. "You're more than welcome to join us, but I don't know what to do about your dogs."

"Mister, where I go, they go," Metz said.

"Will you come?" Larkin asked.

"This is all kind of sudden," Metz said uncertainly.

Ben nodded. "I understand. Maybe you should stay then. We'll manage just fine by ourselves." He put a hand on the gear lever but the poacher grabbed his wrist.

"Not so fast," Larkin said. "Old Jacob and those dogs of his have held their own against every kind of wild animal in these parts. They could be of help."

Metz put a hand on the door. "Now hold on, Fred. I haven't made up my mind if I'm going to go yet. I've already told you that Achilles and Hector won't track the thing, so what good would I be?"

Larkin looked down at the dogs. "What would those mutts of yours do if they saw it?"

"You reckon you can get that close?" Metz asked.

"We did last night. Maybe lightning will strike twice."

"And maybe it won't," Ben said. "We wouldn't want to waste the man's time."

"What's the matter with you, Shields?" Larkin snapped. "Those dogs have outfought bears. Maybe they can do the same to the alien."

Nadine had listened to the argument in confusion. She realized that Ben didn't want the old man to come along, although why she couldn't guess. By the same token, Larkin was too eager to have the man join them. She stuck her head past the poacher's and said, "Excuse me, Mr. Metz. Neither of these Neanderthals has bothered to introduce me. I'm Nadine Somersby, a close friend of Ben's." She gestured at one of the bloodhounds. "There's something you should know before you decide to let your dogs tackle this creature. Gunfire has no effect on it. And if bullets can't hurt it, what harm could your dogs do?"

"Why, it's awful nice of you to think of their welfare, ma'am," Metz said. "I already know bullets don't work, though. My pa hunted the thing once." He affectionately patted Achilles on the head. "He had him a pair of bear dogs that gave it a good tussle. Maybe mine can do the same or better." He looked at Ben "I'd like to go if you'll have me."

Ben didn't care to delay any longer. He wanted to reach the cemetery before the monster set off on its nightly hunt. "Very well," he said. "Just do me a favor and keep an eye on your bloodhounds. If natures calls, I'll pull over so they can go."

"Don't fret in that regard," Metz said. "My dogs won't do their business unless they're outdoors. And they're used to riding in a vehicle. They go with me in my pickup everywhere I do."

"Hop in, then."

*   *   *

Elsewhere, Chief of Police Travis Sinclair was driving down a side street, keeping his eyes on the trick or treaters and their gun-toting escorts. Halloween had always been one of his favorite holidays because it was one of the few when drunken and rowdy behavior wasn't a problem. This Halloween was drastically different. Everyone, even the kids, seemed to be short-tempered. The strain of the past few days had taken a heavy toll in frayed nerves and those affected were taking it out on anyone who crossed them.

Twice Travis had seen fights. Each time he had stopped and waited until the combatants had beaten themselves half silly before he climbed out and issued citations for disturbing the peace.

Suddenly Travis saw a pair of shouting women who were poking one another and otherwise gave every indication of being about to tear into each other, tooth and nail. He pulled to the curb and got out, thinking this would be an easy dispute to resolve. "What's the matter, ladies?" he asked politely.

The shorter woman, a burly brunette, turned on him. "What makes it any business of yours, pig?"

Travis halted, smiled, and tapped his badge. "This does. Now would you like to tell me why you're so upset?" He glanced at a pair of young girls standing nearby, one dressed as a princess, the other as a ballerina. They held large bags to their chests and glared at him.

"This is personal, buster," said the second woman, who was taller than the first woman, but shared her facial features. "My sister and I were just having a little argument."

"So buzz off, fatso," the short one said.

Travis disliked being treated with contempt and chose to intimidate the women into submission. "Keep it up, you two, and I'll run you in for disorderly conduct."

"I'd like to see you try," the short woman said and marched up to him. "Just because you wear that uniform, you figure you can boss folks around to your heart's content. Well, I've got news for you, pig. Some of us still believe in the Constitution."

"As do I, madam," Travis said, then put his hand on her shoulder. "So why don't you calm—"

The woman hauled off and slugged Travis in the gut with surprising strength. Caught off guard, Travis doubled over as pain lanced through him. "Now hold on, damn you!" he sputtered, but the woman paid no heed and kicked him in the shin. Racked by anguish, Travis sank to one knee. He couldn't believe a runt of a woman was beating up on him and he raised a hand to grab her. Without warning the second woman stepped in close and belted him in the mouth.

Travis felt blood spurt from his split lip. He bent low to ward off other blows but none were forthcoming. High-pitched laughter made him look up. The women and the girls were racing down the street, as happy as a pack of wild dogs that had just feasted on an elk carcass. The tall mother looked back and flipped him the finger, at which the small girls cackled.

Travis was flabbergasted. What was the world coming to when an officer of the law could be rashly assaulted by two mothers whose children thought the attack hilarious? He slowly stood, but made no attempt to give chase. If he caught them, he would have to arrest them, and if he arrested them, there would be an hour of paperwork and the hassle of having to book women and then later release them when their husbands or their lawyers showed up to post bail.

Turning to the car, Travis was shocked to see a county patrol car parked in the street. Bo Seaver wore an expression of total and utter contempt. Travis mustered a wan grin, at which the sheriff shook his head in disgust and drove on.

"Up yours," Travis muttered. He climbed into the cruiser and drove off, aware that a number of residents had witnessed his humiliation. By tomorrow the word would be all over town that he'd had his tush whipped by a couple of women. He would be the laughingstock of Cemetery Ridge. Perhaps, he mused, it was an omen that he should move on. He had the 9,000 dollars, after all. There would never be a better time.

Travis drove into an alley. He pulled a handkerchief from a pocket and dabbed at his mouth until the bleeding stopped. His lip felt puffy already and by morning it would be as big as a pickle.

The thought of food brought Gertie's to mind. Travis drove from the alley and made for Simmons Boulevard. A doughnut or three would suffice to bolster his sagging spirits and put him in a better frame of mind to deal with the ordeal sure to follow; the night was still young and the monster had yet to appear.

The monster. Those words were enough to give Travis the chills. Who would ever have thought that he would live to encounter a living spawn striaght from hell. Such beings were not supposed to exist.

Travis set to wondering about other reports of strange creatures he had read from time to time in newspapers or heard about on newscasts. How many of them had been legitimate? How many had he laughed off just like everyone else because everyone knew monsters didn't exist?

Some years back Travis had read a book on the subject. There had been chapters dealing with phantom cats, demon dogs, things with wings, living phantasms, and more. He'd figured that half of those who reported running into such creatures must be stoned out of their minds and the other half plain crazy. Now he knew better.

The realization placed existence in a whole new light. If there were monsters, then there was a deep, underlying mystery to life that had eluded him.

How could God let such things exist? Travis asked himself. Unless, of course, such things were part of the devil's domain. Buy if that was the case, it meant the Bible was completely true. The idea scared him.

As if to feed Travis's fear, the radio crackled to a noisy furor as the dispatcher reported that the creature had been spotted on the 400 block of McFarland Street, between Allen and Egli. Sheriff Seaver and Deputy Miller responded immediately. Then Travis did, although his heart wasn't in it.

Switching on the lights and siren, Travis roared to the next intersection and took a left. He sped north for ten blocks, avoiding pedestrians and cross traffic. At Liefield Street he turned right and a block later came to McFarland. As he braked and rolled down his window he heard several gunshots.

Bo Seaver roared into view, his deputy on his tail. They passed Travis doing 90 and screeched to a stop about the middle of the block.

Travis made the turn and parked behind the deputy's car. He saw the sheriff and Miller leave their vehicles and dash between two houses. More blasts shattered the night. Rifle fire, by the sound of it.

Taking a breath to steady his nerves, Travis flung open his door and jumped out. He took a few strides on the heels of the other officers, then drew up in midstep when a hair-raising cry rang out. It was part bellow, part wail, part rasped rage. He had never heard the like in all

311

his life and it shook him to his core.

All along the street residents were rushing from homes and shouting to one another, demanding to know the cause of the uproar.

Travis realized he was doing nothing. He broke into a run, heading across the same black patch of lawn that Seaver and Miller had crossed. He didn't expect trouble since they were in front of him and could handle anything thrown at them.

Then something appeared a score of yards away, something large and lumbering and moving toward Travis like a living express train. He looked and almost wet himself.

"Where the hell is it?" someone shouted.

"I don't know," someone else replied. "It gave us the slip."

Travis wasn't conscious of drawing his service revolver but the gun blossomed in his hand. The creature coming his way staggered as if wounded, then threw back its head and gave voice to the same hideous cry he had heard moments ago. It set his heart to pounding like a trip-hammer.

"Cease fire!" Sheriff Seaver called from somewhere off to the left. "No more shooting or you'll answer to me!"

Travis extended his revolver and took aim. It was easy for Seaver to rant about shooting; the monster wasn't bearing down on him. Travis gulped and adopted a two-handed grip as he had been taught at the academy. It occurred to him that he really should have practiced his marksmanship once or twice over the years. Now it was too damn late.

The creature regained its balance, lowered its head, and came on in a rush.

To Travis's shock, his fear abruptly evaporated. A calm, calculating sense of purpose filled him. He felt confident in himself for the first time in his life. And it brought a grim smile to his lips. Apparently the monster could be hurt by gunfire, in which case Travis was about to become the biggest hero in the history of Cemetery Ridge.

Travis's thumb curled back the hammer of its own accord. He held the revolver on the target for a full five seconds, then squeezed off the first shot. At the retort the .357 kicked hard, jerking his hands. He instantly compensated and fired again. The creature cried out, stumbled, then kept on coming.

"Cease firing, damn it!" Sheriff Seaver thundered.

Like hell! Travis thought, and fired twice more. At the fourth shot the monster crashed onto its knees and slid on the slick grass. It tried weakly to rise, couldn't, and collapsed on its side with a loud exhale. Then it lifted its head a final time, waving it in the air as if seeking salvation in the stars. It expired just as figures pounded up out of the darkness.

"Son of a bitch!" Bo Seaver said and shook his fist at Travis. "Congratulations, lard butt. I

313

hope the town council makes you pay for this out of your own pocket."

"Pay for what?" Travis responded, at a loss to explain the sheriff's attitude. Hadn't he just saved countless lives?

"For killing this cow."

"Cow?" Travis asked. He swore he could feel the blood drain from his face. Mortified, he stepped closer, only then did he recognize the bovine silhouette spread out before him.

Deputy Miller snorted. "And it only took him four shots, Sheriff. Maybe we should take him to the next regionals in Eugene. He might win the trophy for us single-handedly."

Some other men Travis didn't know laughed long and loud. He slowly slid the revolver into its holster and turned, his ears burning.

"Hey, where are you going?" Deputy Miller said. "Butcher it for us right here so I can take some tenderloin home to my wife."

Travis strode to his car and got in. Seaver called his name but he ignored the sheriff and burned rubber going down the street. He was so upset he wanted to go home, crawl under the covers, and curl into a ball. His mind went blank, and he drove for minutes without being conscious of where he was or where he was going.

The beep of a horn brought Travis back to reality. In front of him appeared Simmons Boulevard. He braked at a stop sign and sat sadly watching cars go past. His career as police chief was undoubtedly over. Once the town council heard of the cow fiasco, they'd hand him his head on a platter.

Of all the dumb luck! Travis fumed. Now that he had time to think, he remembered that an old man on the west side of town owned six or seven cows, which were always straying through a gap in a fence the old man steadfastly refused to repair. For two cents Travis would have shot the old fart on the spot.

Travis raised his head and saw a familiar van drive by traveling north. He spotted Ben at the wheel. Ben appeared to be pushing against a large dog that was trying to look out the window. "I'm delirious," Travis said to himself. He knew for a fact Ben didn't own a dog.

Those doughnuts sounded more inviting by the minute. Travis had to wait for traffic to pass, then went to turn south. He stopped when he saw Victor Richards speeding northward, intent on the van ahead.

Travis suddenly remembered the anonymous phone call. That voice, he reflected, could have been Victor's. He hadn't talked to Richards in many months, but they had been friends in high school. As if it were yesterday he recalled the bitter rivalry between Ben and Victor over Nadine. Ben had been so shattered at losing her that he'd left town for Portland. And now Nadine was divorced from Victor and seeing Ben again.

Travis couldn't say what made him follow them. Perhaps it was the fact they were both old buddies. Perhaps it was the fact that it gave him a chance to take his mind off the cow and the monster for a while. Or perhaps it was the fact he knew that Victor Richards could never accept being second best at anything and had a violent temper.

Chapter Twenty

In the graveyard, Jimmy Howell blinked and the shape was gone. He blinked again, wondering if he had imagined seeing the monster, then stared intently at the orderly rows of tombs. Overcome by bleak dread, he felt as if his nerves were stretched as tautly as piano wire, and he jumped when a warm hand slipped into his own.

"What's the matter?" Manda Joyce asked. "You act as if you just saw a zombie."

"Nothing," Jimmy said too quickly. He scoured the tombs one more time. "I'm fine."

Manda glanced at Cindy, who had moved off a dozen feet to whack another tombstone; she lowered her voice to a whisper. "Why don't we go off by ourselves for a little bit?"

"Why would you—" Jimmy began and shut up before he made a jerk of himself. There could only be one reason. His heart fluttered and his breath caught in his throat. "Sure. Whatever you want."

Giggling lightly, Manda pulled him off into the darkness. Behind them, unaware she was alone, Cindy Drew slammed the hammer into another grave marker. She had regained her enthusiasm for the job and tittered as stone chips flew in all directions.

Bending close to the chiseled inscription, Cindy read aloud, "In loving memory of my beloved Hazel Washington." She smirked, and said, "Do you believe this crap? Why do people go to all this bother for a decaying pile of bones? When my times comes, I want them to cremate my ass and scatter me on the wind. No grave, no headstone, none of this garbage for this girl."

Cindy hit the tombstone a few more times to show her contempt for those who had to brood over the inevitable, then she walked to the next grave and the next. In short order she had defaced eight more of them and stopped to take a breather.

"Think that's enough or should I keep going?" Cindy asked. She turned to hear Manda's opinion, but Manda wasn't there. And the dork was gone, too. She looked out over the rows of graves, but didn't see them.

"What the hell!" Cindy said angrily. "Where did they get to?"

She knew that Manda had taken a liking to Howell but she hadn't thought her friend would go that far. If word spread at school, Manda would be the butt of every joke told for a week. Worse, since she was Manda's best friend, she would suffer the fallout. She'd be teased for associating with someone brainless enough to fall for a dweeb like Howell.

"You idiot!" Cindy said. Her resentment made her want to hit something, so she dashed to the next tombstone and pounded with fiery vigor. She hit and hit until her arms were heavy. Stepping back, she admired the large chunk she had taken out of the substitute for Jimmy's head.

"I'm going to tell Paxton," Cindy said to herself. "I'll have him make that loser take a hike and never come back." She faced toward the sound of the backhoe and was quite surprised to find it was over 100 yards away. She hadn't realized she had gone quite so far.

Cindy started back. Suddenly she heard the patter of footsteps to the south, followed by a scraping noise like a fingernail on stone. She pivoted. No one was there but she knew who it had been. Manda and Jimmy were trying to scare her.

"It won't work, morons," Cindy said, annoyed by their childish antics. Neither of them answered, which made her madder.

Deep among the ranks of bleak memorials something moved. Cindy caught a flash of someone bent low, darting from marker to marker. Ducking, she ran to the left and crouched behind a tombstone. Two could play at the same game, and she would love to see the looks on Manda's and Jimmy's faces when she leaped out at them.

Cindy waited awhile and faintly heard someone moving around, no doubt searching for her. She bit her lip to keep from laughing. When the sounds faded, she crept to the east, moving from tombstone to tombstone in a wide loop that would bring her up on the two pinheads from the rear. Once she glanced at the backhoe and felt fleeting concern that it was several hundred yards away. She had to remind herself that she had nothing to worry about. She was armed with the hammer. And the racket raised by the backhoe was bound to scare off any animal that wandered near the cemetery.

Cindy noticed she was very near the foremost row of mausoleums. She hadn't heard Manda and Jimmy in a while, and she questioned whether they were still in front of her or if they had worked their way around to where she had been. Confirmation came in the form of the scraping noise sounding from among the tombs.

Tiptoeing to the corner of a mausoleum, Cindy sought some sign of the other two. She had the feeling that she was being watched, but she was still determined to scare Jimmy and Manda before they scared her. Easing downward, she scooted to the next tomb on the right, ran around it to the front corner, and paused.

Off to the south was the biggest mausoleum of all, the one that belonged to the Richards family. Paxton had brought her there once to show her the cool stone carvings that adorned it. As usual he had used their time together as a pretext to get between her legs, which she didn't mind in the least. He was the best lover she had ever had and she'd had plenty.

A smaller tomb stood directly ahead, unique in that it boasted a single sculpture half the size of the tomb itself. Perched on the roof was the crouched form of a wingless gargoyle with a head very similar to a dragon's.

Cindy sprinted to the back wall and pressed her spine to the smooth surface. She looked left and right. No movement betrayed her friend or the geek.

For some time the brisk breeze from the northwest had fanned Cindy's skin. The temperature had dropped a few degrees. It was supposed to be cold, not warm, so she was puzzled when a gust of hot air stirred her hair. Seconds later it was repeated, only more strongly. Mingled with the air was the most putrid odor she had ever smelled, like that of road kill swarming with maggots.

When the hot air struck Cindy a third time, she peered skyward. For a few seconds she was baffled by a dark object that blotted out the patch of sky directly overhead. Then the object moved and she discerned the great dragon head of the stone gargoyle. But that couldn't be, she told herself. Stone wasn't alive.

The terrifying truth hit Cindy at the very instant a blinding white blaze of light filled her mind. She tried to flee, but couldn't. She attempted to scream but her vocal chords wouldn't respond. Every muscle was completely paralyzed.

Above her, the three who were one leaned farther down and seized the frail prey by the shoulder. Leisurely, without any strain whatsoever, the creature picked the human female up and examined her rigid features. It turned her from side to side and sniffed, revolted by a nauseating sweet odor rising from her neck, cheeks, and ears.

Cindy wanted to cry but was unable. She desperately desired to smash the hammer against the creature's face but her arm remained frozen. Inwardly she flinched when the hideous creature raised her face close to its own. And inwardly she screamed when its mouth slowly parted.

Finally tears gushed down Cindy's cheeks. The white light within her skull dimmed a bit and she started trembling uncontrollably. She didn't want to die. She was too young. Death was for others. Death was for old people who were worthless anyway.

The creature tilted the female's head back, aligned its mouth over her forehead, and speared the feeding tube into her brain. It ingested the nectar greedily even though it had fed less than 15 minutes earlier. It could never get enough of the delicious essence. Sitting back on its haunches on top of the tomb, it drank slowly, savoring every drop.

Its senses were as keen as ever. It pinpointed the pair over by the trees and the other two working with the vile mockery of living organisms. They appeared in no hurry to vacate the cemetery, which suited the beast perfectly. It would gorge this night and then sleep through the next cycle.

On the other side of the cemetery, Jimmy sucked on Manda's hard nipple while tweaking her other breast with his hand. He couldn't believe that they were pressed body to body, her warm breath on his neck, his organ as hard as a broom handle and straining for release. Never before had a girl let him do the things Manda was letting him do. He was positively giddy with rampant lust.

Jimmy licked a path to her navel and circled her belly button a few times. Manda cooed, grasped his hair tightly, and said, "Lower. Go lower."

The suggestion caused Jimmy to freeze. He had never been so bold as to touch a girl there. Time and time again his parents and his minister had impressed upon him that good boys didn't do things like that to good girls. He'd had it ingrained into him that having sex was special and should only be done after marriage.

But Jimmy knew that over half the boys in his class had already lost their virginity. The number of girls who had was anyone's guess since few were brazen enough to admit it in public. The few who did were naturally sought after by the top jocks and most popular boys in school, leaving no chance at all for a shunned social outcast like Jimmy.

"Lower," Manda said.

Jimmy's mouth watering as if he were about to eat a buttered ear of corn, he did as his girlfriend wanted and dipped to the junction of her thighs. His face was poised inches from her innermost treasure. A dank, intoxicating scent made his loins twitch. He went to nuzzle against her.

From the direction of the backhoe rose a sharp shout. "Cindy? Manda? Where the hell did you guys get to?"

Manda stiffened. "It's Paxton."

"So?" Jimmy said.

"So we have to go see what he wants," Manda said, pushing him away.

Jimmy rose, crestfallen that his golden opportunity had been ruined. At that moment he disliked Paxton more than he had ever disliked anyone. He watched helplessly as Manda adjusted her clothes.

"All right. Come on," he said.

Paxton stood near Bill's car, sipping from a whiskey bottle. Jess had taken a break and jumped down to share a drink. The backhoe idled near an open grave, puffs of smoke rising from its exhaust.

"There you are!" Paxton said on seeing Manda and Jimmy. He gazed past them, then out over the graveyard. "Where's Cindy?"

"The last we saw, she was smashing tomb-stones like there was no tomorrow," Jimmy said. He had his feelings under control but he was afraid his resentment would show if he stared at Paxton too long.

Paxton took a few steps and cupped his hands to his mouth. "Cindy! Where are you, babe! Come on in!"

The sole reply came in the form of a shriek of wind that shook a stand of trees.

"Maybe she strayed too far and can't hear you," Manda said.

"A deaf person would have heard me," Paxton said. Swinging to the south, he shouted, "Bill, have you seen any sign of Cindy?"

In the silence that followed, the four teen-agers exchanged worried looks.

"It must be the wind," Jimmy said. "That's why they can't hear you."

"They'll hear this," Paxton said, brandishing the Colt. He enjoyed seeing Howell take a timid step back and hearing Manda gasp. Aiming the pistol at the ground, he slipped off the safety and fired once. The report was loud enough to be heard for half a mile. As the echoes rippled across the cemetery, Paxton bellowed with all his might, "Cindy! Bill! Answer me, you dum-mies! Where are you?"

Once more all they heard was the sighing of the wind.

"I don't like this," Manda said, fidgeting. "I don't like this one bit."

"Where could they be?" Jess asked.

David Robbins

"Who knows?" Paxton said, vexed by Bill's and Cindy's disappearance. He couldn't make up his mind whether the pair were in real trouble or whether there was another explanation. Lately Bill had been giving Cindy the eye on the sly, and Paxton had no illusions about her self-control. If the jock came on to her, she'd give Bill a tumble just for the thrill. "I'm going to look for them."

"We'll go with you," Manda said.

"No you won't," Paxton said. "I don't need someone to hold my hand. Stay put or we might lose you, too. Keep digging, Jess. I'll let you know when you can stop."

"Sure thing."

Paxton hurried into the gloom, the Colt in his hand. He was taking no chances in case the killer bear had strayed into the graveyard. "Bill!" he called after going 20 feet. "Cindy?" Behind him, the backhoe roared to mechanical life as Jess resumed working, drowning out his shout. Paxton went farther.

It seemed unlikely that Bill would risk Paxton's wrath by fooling around with Cindy, but Paxton had learned long ago never to take anyone for granted where sex was concerned. When it came to gratifying hormones, people would do just about anything.

Paxton yelled every ten feet or so. He stopped often to look and listen. By the time he had gone hundreds of feet, he was firmly convinced the pair were off humping and couldn't wait to get his hands on Bill. He looked at the pistol, speculating on how much hard time he would have to do if he gave Bill a flesh wound.

Coming to another halt, Paxton felt his right foot bump an object lying on the road. It rolled a few feet to the edge of the grass. He hardly regarded it as important and was about to move on when he noticed its shape. It looked like a tennis shoe. He went over and picked it up.

It was a tennis shoe. Paxton studied the style and realized it was Bill's. The discovery stunned him. Why would Bill leave his sneaker lying there? Paxton envisioned the jock and Cindy going at it fast and heavy, Bill trying to undress and steer her off among the graves at the same time and dropping the shoe by mistake.

Paxton scanned the cemetery and was rewarded by the sight of a slender figure standing among the tombs. The height and build were consistent with Cindy's. Calling her name, Paxton weaved among the tombstones. Oddly, she stood there as limp as a sack of potatoes, just watching him approach.

"What the hell is the matter with you, girl?" he said. "And where have you been? Fooling around with that pooser?

Cindy offered no reply.

"Cat got your tongue, bitch?" Paxton said, believing he had guessed the truth and she was too worried about his temper to speak. "You should know better than to step out on me. Nobody does that to a Richards. Ask my uncle."

Cindy backed up a few feet, closer to a mausoleum, but she did so awkwardly, her legs shuffling stiffly as if she were drunk or on drugs.

"Damn it, answer me!" Paxton said, casting the shoe down. "Tell me where Bill is hiding so I can stomp his sorry butt!"

To Paxton's amazement, Cindy suddenly fell flat on her face like a puppet that had had its strings cut. "Cindy?" he said, thinking she had fainted. He sprinted to her side and bent one knee to roll her over.

From behind the mausoleum reared a huge form, a reptilian deviate straight from a madman's worst nightmare, a living caricature of life that stood over Paxton breathing like a pair of bellows.

Petrified, Paxton gawked. The creature's arm reached for him, its tapered claws wide. Instinctively he swept the Colt up and his finger began to curl on the trigger. At the same split second a brilliant white light detonated within his head, as if someone has switched on a spotlight between his ears. He couldn't move, couldn't even finish squeezing the trigger.

The three who were one lowered its claws to within inches of the human's neck. This male was big and vital; the nectar would be especially zesty. Then the creature noticed the human's aura and it hesitated, baffled by the aura's resemblance to the characteristic aural signature of the human line that produced its kind.

Standing below the creature, Paxton could still think. He expected the thing to tear into him at any moment and frantically tried to work his mouth so he could shout for help. The creature leaned close to him, its face an inch from his own, its eyes boring into his. He had the impression the creature was studying him for some reason, perhaps deciding which part of him to eat first.

The entity was studying the teen, but in an effort to unravel the mystery of an aura so like the rare pattern of the begetter who had visited the cocoon the other day and yet different enough in small respects to be that of another human bloodline. The creature had to be certain. A mistake could break the ancestral string and result in failure to evolve further in the future as more and more of the begetter stock died and that which constituted the sum of their evil was absorbed.

Paxton willed his eyes to close but they wouldn't. The creature opened its mouth and he thought the end had come. Tapered teeth that glistened dully drew within a hairbreadth of his head. Foul breath made him want to retch. Then a miracle occurred. The monster slowly closed its mouth and stepped back, and simultaneously the white light faded out.

Paxton could move again. His finger did, closing the fraction of pressure needed for the Colt to go off. At the blast the creature cocked its head and raised an arm.

Spinning, Paxton fled, speeding pell-mell across the cemetery. A glance showed the creature striding in pursuit. Paxton thought of Cindy and whether she might still be alive; he decided if she was, she was on her own. He had his own skin to save and couldn't be bothered about a sexpot airhead.

To that end he screamed, "Help! Help! Get the car started! We've got to get out of here!"

Jimmy had an arm on Manda's shoulder and was glumly watching Jess tilt another casket on its side. The rumble of the backhoe was so loud that upon hearing a shout he wasn't sure if he had or not. He twisted and saw someone running toward them from the mausoleums. "Who's that?" he said, recognizing Paxton as he did.

"Why's he running like his fanny is on fire?" Manda said.

"I don't know," Jimmy said.

They both saw the massive creature at the same time. Manda screeched and Jimmy grabbed her wrist and darted for the sedan. He threw the door open and shoved her inside. Then he slid behind the wheel, reaching for the ignition.

The keys were gone. Bill had taken them with him.

"We've got to jump start the car but I don't know how," Jimmy said, leaping out again. Paxton was 100 feet off, moving like a track star. The creature was taking its time, as if it knew they couldn't escape or was confident of its ability to stop them.

Jimmy flew toward the backhoe. He waved his arms. "Jess! Jess! The monster!"

Jess was intent on excavating another grave. The engine's racket prevented him from hearing Jimmy until he was right beside the treads. Jess looked down, puzzled. "What did you say?" he shouted.

Jimmy simply pointed, and shock riveted Jess in place. He sat and gaped. His foot slipped off a pedal and the backhoe lurched forward toward the trench he was digging.

"Come on!" Jimmy said. "You have to jump start the car for us!"

Jess heard him, but was not about to vault to the ground when he had a better idea. He ground gears, sending the backhoe shooting backward, then turned the enormous machine on a pin and rattled toward the road. The backhoe was as big as the creature. Jess figured he should be able to hold it at bay with the blade if it came after him.

Jimmy was appalled his friend would abandon them. Manda bawled his name, jarring him into action, and he raced to the car, got in, then slammed, and locked the door. He did the same with the other three.

"What are you doing?" Manda cried. "We should run for it!"

"We wouldn't get five feet," Jimmy said. "I've seen how fast the thing can move when it wants to."

"But I don't want to be cooped up!" Manda argued, growing hysterical. She grabbed for the lock but Jimmy grasped her arm. It took all his strength to prevent her from tearing loose. Suddenly there was a loud thump on the door and they both twisted in terror.

Paxton had his palms pressed to the glass and his fearful gaze on the creature. "Let me in, damn you!" he said. "It's almost here!"

Jimmy lunged, his fingers closing on the latch. He jerked it upward and Paxton began to fling the door open, but unexpectedly changed his mind and fled on foot. "What the—" Jimmy exclaimed, then saw why.

The monster loomed over the car.

Chapter Twenty-one

Ben drove with his window down, not out of choice, but from necessity. Between Fred Larkin's abominable body odor and the awful gas of the two nervous bloodhounds, the smell in the van had been almost enough to make him gag. Metz appeared not to notice, while Nadine kept leaning toward the dash and putting her hand over her nose and mouth for a minute at a time.

Thanks to the open window, Ben heard the distinct crack of a shot not far off. They were close to the cemetery and the shot came from its direction.

"Did anyone hear that?" he asked.

Jacob Metz had been talking to one of his dogs. He shook his his head, saying, "I didn't hear anything, son."

"Hear what?" Nadine asked.

Ben was still certain his ears hadn't deceived him. He glanced at the poacher, who nodded and rested the crossbow in his lap.

"I heard a shot," Larkin said. "Maybe the cops are smarter than we think. Maybe they posted someone at the graveyard. We'd best be ready for anything." He suited his actions to his words by turning the crossbow upside down, extending the stirrup so he could brace his foot on it, and pulling the string back until it caught with an audible click.

"You're not planning to load that thing in here, are you?" Ben asked, dreading the result should the crossbow accidentally release a shaft into one of them.

"You can bet your ass I am," Larkin said, pulling a bolt from the quiver. "Always be prepared; that's my motto."

Ben would have debated the safety of such a move had the shattered wrought-iron cemetery gate not appeared just then. He automatically slowed down, seeking signs of a police car. Instead, he beheld a scene more chilling than he ever could have imagined.

"What the hell is going on?" Larkin said.

At about the middle of the cemetery, the headlights of a sedan and a piece of heavy machinery shined. The latter was heading for the front gate as fast as it could go. The car was parked; outlined against the glare of its beams was the creature Ben and the others sought.

The monster stood stooped over, peering inside the sedan. Suddenly it straightened up, stared at the fleeing backhoe, and took off after it like a greyhound after a rabbit.

"Go! Go!" Larkin said. "This is our chance to pay that ugly son of a bitch back."

For what? Ben wondered as he tramped on the accelerator and sent the van careening through the gate and across the graveyard. As he drew closer he saw that a teenager sat at the controls of the backhoe. The boy looked over a shoulder, discovered the creature was after him, and began rocking forward and back as if trying to will the backhoe to go faster.

"We'll never reach that young man in time!" Metz said.

And they didn't. The van had 200 yards to cover when the creature drew close enough to the backhoe to take a swipe at the driver. Its claws ripped into the roll bar, but didn't slice clean through. Panicked, the young operator did the last thing anyone would expect—he slammed on the brakes.

Larkin came half out of his seat. "What the hell is that idiot doing?"

Only Jess had the answer. He knew he couldn't outrun the beast, so he resolved to turn and fight. As before, he wheeled the backhoe around in its tracks as skillfully as a professional operator would do. He had the heavy blade up; it caught the advancing creature in the shoulder and sent it tumbling.

The three who were one had been taken by surprise by the move. It rolled lightly to its feet and warily regarded the rumbling violation of all that lived. It must be careful, it realized, or the steel machine would crush its physical form to a pulp. Crouching, it closed in and swung.

Jess was ready. He worked the lever flawlessly, spinning the backhoe so that the blade always faced the monster. No matter which way the creature turned, he did the same. The scrape of claws on metal was enough to send shivers down his spine.

In the van, Fred Larkin slapped Ben on the arm and said excitedly, "Look at that! The kid is holding his own! That thing isn't so tough after all."

So it appeared. The creature darted right, then left, and each time was thwarted by the wide blade that held it at bay.

Jess laughed in heartfelt relief. So long as the fuel lasted, he would be safe. Somehow he must carry the fight to the beast before then. Perhaps, he reasoned, he could cripple it, and with that in mind he lowered the blade a few feet and sent the backhoe hurtling forward, trying to break the creature's legs.

The three who were one backpedaled, narrowly evading the heavy steel. It leaped to the left and tensed for another spring, but was bowled over by a sideways sweep of the backhoe. Pain speared its side as it hit the earth. In a twinkling the creature regained its feet but now it was more cautious than ever.

Jess whooped with glee. He had seen the creature's contorted face; he could hurt it if he tried. Now he became the aggressor, driving straight at the beast again and again, parrying with the blade when the thing tried to skip aside. Twice he knocked it down. And all the while he pushed the creature steadily toward the tombstones.

Ben was 40 yards from the battle. He slowed down, not wanting to get too close and inadvertently distract the teenager at the wrong moment.

"That kid doesn't need our help," Larkin said. "He's got the alien on the ropes."

Meanwhile, the three who were one bumped into a headstone and nearly fell. It did not know fatigue as humans did, but it was depleting its reservoir of energy much too fast for its liking. At the same time, it was aware that the rain would soon begin. It must prevail or perish.

Confident of victory, Jess lowered the blade farther, shifted, and drove the backhoe forward. He hoped the creature would be unable to skip backward because of the tombstones, giving him the chance to pin it and finish it off.

But the monster was not so easily dispatched. Instead of retreating, it vaulted high into the air, alighted momentarily on top of the blade, and then sprang at Jess even as it projected the paralyzing mental blast that permitted it to finish off prey at its leisure.

In the van, Nadine watched in horror as the nightmare seized the teen by the neck and literally tore him from his seat. Then the creature jumped off the backhoe, which kept on going, mowing down tombstones in a wide swath. She screamed when the creature raised the boy and opened its mouth.

At that instant the three who were one became aware of the newcomers. It spun and saw the van from the night before. Marveling that the same humans had enough confidence to confront it again, it flung the puny male to the ground and leaped far into the darkness.

"Where did it go?" Larkin shouted as the monster vanished into the gloom.

Ben was more interested in the welfare of the boy. He braked, slid out, and dashed over. The angle at which the teen's neck was bent made feeling for a pulse a moot point. The boy's wide eyes were fixed on the clouds.

The night was abruptly shattered by another piercing scream. Whirling, Ben cried out at the sight of the creature bearing down on the van. Like a living battering ram it smashed into the vehicle's side. The impact of its shoulder lifted two tires clear off the ground, and as they did, the monster hooked its claws under the van's frame. Shoulders bulging, it arced upward.

Ben started forward but there was nothing he could do. The van went up and over. Nadine's shriek wavered on the wind, combined with howls from the bloodhounds and

Larkin's frenzied cursing. All were punctuated by a tremendous crash.

"Nadine!" Ben shouted in despair.

Wearing a sneer of triumph, the three who were one strode to the vanquished van. A door was pushed open from within and it eagerly bent forward to grab one of the humans inside.

Ben heard a fierce snarl and saw the monstrosity recoil, a bloodhound clinging to its forearm. The creature howled louder than the dogs ever could and swatted at Achilles, but the tenacious animal hung on. For some reason the dog was causing it pain whereas bullets had no effect. Bright pinpoints of light danced along the arm the dog held. The monster flailed wildly, smacking Achilles against the hard ground. It placed a foot on the bloodhound and tried to grind the dog into the earth, but another snarl from high on the van caused it to glance up just as Hector leaped onto its back.

For the moment the creature was preoccupied. Ben darted to the van and clambered up onto the side. Larkin and Metz were giving Nadine a boost.

"Grab her!" the poacher yelled. "We've got to get out of this sardine can!"

Nadine had a nasty gash on her forehead. For a few moments there, when the monster had charged the van, she thought that she would die. It had scared her more than anything else. Clinging to Ben as he pulled her up beside him, she realized she must control her fright or perish.

Stepping back, she said, "I'm okay. Help them."

The battle between the bloodhounds and the creature was still going on. All three were on the ground, tumbling, rolling, slashing, and snapping. The creature might be fast but the dog's reflexes were equal to its own, and it was being bitten as often as it scored with its claws. Balls of light the size of quarters swirled in the air around it and clustered where the dogs had bitten.

Nadine had little time to wonder about those lights. Larkin and Metz joined Ben and her, and together they jumped off the far side of the van.

"Now we kill the alien!" Larkin said, taking another bolt from his small quiver to replace the one he had lost when the van had tipped over. He inserted the shaft into the groove. "Take this," he said, handing his gun to Ben. "It's better than nothing." With that, he dashed to the front of the van to get a shot.

Hector lay dead, his side ripped open from ear to tail, his entrails hanging out. Achilles fought on, limping badly though, with one leg nearly slashed in half.

The creature drew back and circled, waiting for an opening so it could finish the dog quickly and feast on the humans. It badly needed to replenish its energy.

Larkin took aim, sighting down the shaft. Before he could squeeze the trigger, the monster pounced, its claws slicing into Achilles's neck and severing the jugular. The bloodhound yipped as it went down, thrashing and snapping at empty air. Larkin saw the alien turn toward him. He had no idea whether the crossbow would work but it was all he had other than the bowie, so he fired.

The bolt flew across the intervening space too swiftly for the human eye to follow, but not too swiftly for the three who were one. Its lightning-fast brain analyzed the molecular structure and identified wood, metal, and tiny pieces of plastic—no threat whatsoever. But to the creature's surprise, coursed through it as the shaft penetrated its chest.

Fred Larkin grinned when the monster threw back its head and voiced a bloodcurdling screech. Working rapidly, he loaded the crossbow again, the tingle of raw excitement invigorating him. This was one of those moments he lived for, when his wits and skill were put to the ultimate test. This was the challenge of a lifetime, and he was determined to prevail.

The creature had clutched its chest and doubled over. It could not understand the pain, not until it felt the dampness on the shaft inside of it. Startled, it suspected that the human who had shot it must know its secret, which made this particular human the most dangerous it had ever faced, one of the very few to offer a challenge. By a perverted twist of logic the creature was pleased. Yes, the human posed a threat, but the challenge was worth the price. For too long the entity had slain its prey with ridiculous ease; it relished a real fight.

Larkin aimed at the monster's head. The creature started to straighten, to lunge toward him. Larkin stroked the trigger, the string twanged, and the shaft imbedded itself in the creature's brow. An eerie, wavering roar rolled across the cemetery.

Ben ran around the other end of the van and saw the creature in its apparent death throes. The thing was on its broad back, both hands pressed to its oversize skull, tossing and pitching in a frenetic, macabre fit.

A hand fell on Ben's arm. Nadine stood at his side, her features mirroring apprehension. "It's over," he said. "Damned if Larkin hasn't killed it."

"I'll believe it when it's breathed its last and not before," Nadine said.

Larkin walked around the front end of the vehicle. He had another bolt ready to release. Grinning like a ten year old at a carnival, he moved toward the convulsing creature. "I nailed your ass, alien! Now everyone will know I'm the best there is at what I do."

Nadine nervously watched the poacher draw within a few yards of the monstrosity. "Fred! Please don't get too close!"

"Not to worry, pretty lady," Larkin said. "This thing from outer space is history." He laughed for joy at the sweetness of his victory.

The three who were one had feigned long enough. Resisting the floodtide of torment, it abruptly ripped the shaft from its head while at the same time it surged onto its knees and rammed a hand into the presumptuous human who had shot the shaft.

Nadine gasped as Fred Larkin was sent flying over 20 feet and rolled to a stop against a tombstone. He made no attempt to rise; he didn't even twitch.

"Oh, no," she said.

Ben had not taken his eyes off the creature. It slowly turned toward them, tearing an arrow from its chest as it did. Ben grabbed Nadine's wrist and fled, keeping the van between them and the living nightmare. He saw the creature step to the corner of the vehicle and glare at them. Nadine tripped, forcing Ben to turn away long enough to help her right herself. When next he looked, the creature was moving past the van, tiny white dots floating around its chest and head. It was about to race after them and, given its inhuman speed, would be upon them in the blink of an eye.

A distraction presented itself in the form of Jacob Metz. The old hunter came into view near the van's grill, his rifle tucked to his shoulder; he levered off rounds as regular as clockwork, the booming cadence of the rifle cracking in the night like the beat of a drum.

"You killed my babies!" he shouted. "You killed my babies!"

Sparks flew from the creature's head and face. It turned to Metz, then attacked, reaching the old man before he could retreat. It paralyzed Metz and immediately commenced feasting to replenish its depleted strength. There was no hurry in chasing the others. They wouldn't get far.

Ben and Nadine raced for the gate. Off to the west, the backhoe clanked slowly onward, continuing to flatten an avenue of gravestones. By the sputtering of its engine, it was apparent the machine would soon run out of gas. Ben was afraid that the same would presently be said of Nadine and him. He looked once at the sedan and spied two people inside. Whoever they were, he hoped they would get the hell out of there before the creature went hunting for another snack.

In that car, Jimmy had the same idea. He faced Manda and said, "We have to make a run for it now."

"Don't be silly," Manda said. "It hasn't bothered us in here. We're safe as long as we stay put."

"No, we're not," Jimmy said. He was still trying to digest all that had just occurred. His hopes had soared when the man with the crossbow had shot the beast, but he should have known it was too good to be true. Somewhere along the line he had lost sight of Paxton.

Jimmy opened the door quietly and slipped out. Manda yanked on his arm, refusing to budge. "Please," he whispered, so as not to attract the reptilian. "Trust me. If we stay, we're dead."

Manda stared at the creature, which had its head bowed and seemed to be sucking the brains out of the old man through a straw. Her foremost impulse was to cower on the floor until the creature went away. But she had learned that the boy who adored her was smarter than most. If he insisted they should leave, she decided it was best to rely on his judgment. "I'm scared to death, but I'll do it."

Since the creature was between them and the gate, Jimmy swung to the east to make a wide circle that would eventually bring them to the road. From there they would go to the nearest house and phone the police. It was their only hope. He scoured the cemetery for signs of Paxton, but failed to see him.

Unknown to Jimmy, Paxton was already halfway past the mausoleums and could see the welcome silhouette of the gate ahead. He also spotted a small car approaching and stifled a cry of elation. The car turned into the cemetery and came toward him. Paxton halted, but flapped his arms to get the driver's attention. The vehicle sped up, then braked sharply, and it wasn't until then that Paxton recognized it.

"Uncle Vic!" he said.

Victor Richards rolled down his window. "What the hell is going on?" he snapped, unable to comprehend what his nephew was doing there in the middle of the cemetery.

Victor had trailed Ben this far, and for a few seconds he entertained the idea that Ben had come for the express purpose of meeting Paxton. Then he saw the gun in his nephew's hand and became more confused than ever. "What are you doing with my pistol?"

"I'll explain later," Paxton said. He ran to the passenger side and hopped in. "Get us out of here before it's too late."

"Too late how?" Victor said.

"Not now, Unc! Please, burn rubber, dude, or we're done for!"

"You're not making sense," Victor said, holding out his hand. "Give me that automatic before you shoot something."

"I already did," Paxton said.

"What? You shot someone?"

"Not someone, something," Paxton said. He gazed to the north, but was unable to see the creature because of the tombs. "I'll tell you all about it on the way back to town. Just haul ass, will you!"

"Not on your life," Victor said, worried that his nephew had shot a trick or treater in a monster costume. Growing madder by the moment, he seized Paxton's wrist and took the gun. "Are you high? Have you been drinking?"

"What's that got to do with anything?" Paxton said, his voice rising as his desperation mounted. "Why the hell won't you listen to me? The creature is out there, the thing that's been killing people."

"The bear, you mean?"

"It's not a stinking bear!" Paxton said; he was on the verge of hysteria. "Jimmy Howell was right all along. It's a monster, damn it, a living, man-eating monster."

Victor remembered the strange shape in the Richards mausoleum, the figure in the shadows that had acted so friendly toward him and then disappeared. "Did you kill it? Where is it?"

"I don't have any frigging idea," Paxton said.

"I want to see it," Victor said, remembering the pleasant sensation he had experienced. Somehow, he knew that the thing wouldn't hurt him.

"You what?" Paxton said. "Are you crazy? Haven't you been listening to a word I've said? If we don't get out of here, we'll die!"

Victor caught a whiff of whiskey. "You're exaggerating, I'm sure. And it's plain you have been drinking, so don't try to deny it." Placing the gun between his legs, he put the car into motion.

Paxton was nearly beside himself with fear. He grabbed the steering wheel and cried, "Turn this around, damn you!"

It was the last straw for Victor, who rammed his elbow into the teen's gut, doubling Paxton in half. "I've had enough of your bullshit!" he said. When Paxton tried to clutch the wheel again, Victor slugged him on the chin, crumpling his nephew against the door. "When we get home, I'm calling your mother and advising her that I'm sending you to the academy. For real this time, you ungrateful little bastard."

The car had nearly gone off the road. Victor steered back to the center and went around a curve. He was surprised to see three vehicles with their lights on. Almost by the west fence sat a backhoe. A sedan was parked to the north, one door open. Victor focused on the third vehicle and turned pale. The van belonging to Ben lay on its side, partially crumpled. Beside it squatted the creature Paxton had warned him about, and the thing appeared to be eating someone.

"My God!" Victor said, jumping to conclusions. "Nadine!"

He rocketed to her rescue. Paxton looked, saw where the car was headed, and screamed. Victor shut his ears to his nephew's cowardice and closed in for the kill.

Chapter Twenty-two

The three who were one finished feeding on Jacob Metz and flung the worthless husk aside. It slowly rose, savoring the psychic aftertaste. The growl of a car engine from up the cemetery drive alerted it to yet another newcomer and it turned to see a shiny red vehicle zooming toward it. An arm poked out a window and a pistol boomed several times, the slugs doing no more than tickling the creature's exoskeletal skin.

Victor Richards emptied half the clip without apparent effect. Thinking he must get closer for the bullets to penetrate, and confident in his ability to turn the car and escape before the monster could reach him, he buried the pedal. He intended to swerve past the abomination, then swing around Ben's van and have a clear shot to the gate.

Paxton, unable to stop himself, went on screaming. He was terrified at the thought of dying. Tears poured down his cheeks and he shook violently. He nearly emptied his bladder. He wanted to grab for the steering wheel, but was afraid they would crash if they lost control while going so fast.

The car was on the creature so quickly that it had little time to react. Instinctively, it mentally emitted its sting once more, blasting the driver with the numbing psychic venom and freezing the human in place.

A split second later the creature's augmented senses flared with alarm. It recognized the rare aura pattern of the human who had visited the cocoon the other day, the same human who would one day die and add his essence to the creature's wellspring of being, transforming the three who were one into the four who were one. Frantically the creature dampened the sting, but it was too late.

Victor Richards had no idea why his entire body had gone numb with paralysis for those few critical seconds. He abruptly found he could move again, but by then the car was so close to the monster that a collision seemed inevitable. Without thinking, he spun the steering wheel to the right to avoid the monstrosity and headed straight at the van. Victor realized his mistake and tried to compensate but there simply wasn't enough time.

The creature took a step to try to seize the

car before the impact. There was a thunderous crash, attended instantly by a gigantic explosion. A searing cloud of fire spewed in all directions as an invisible wall of force slammed into the creature, hurling it over two dozen feet.

The cloud spiraled upward, the fire spreading. Flames engulfed the car and the van as thick smoke wafted to the heavens.

Stunned beyond measure, the creature stood and watched the destroyed vehicles burning. The donor would be charred to a cinder, his crucial essence lost forever. The creature's very being was in severe turmoil at the devastating setback. It knew this one had been the last of the line. His female sibling lacked the unique genetic trait.

The creature charged into the core of the raging inferno to try to remove the donor's body before it was burned beyond use. Blistering heat struck it in staggering waves so intense they weakened its limbs. While the creature could tolerate heat extremes far beyond human endurance, there were limits. Bowing its head, it tried to bull its way through the flames, but was driven back. Finally it staggered from out of the inferno, smoke pouring from its skin.

Rage coursed through the entity—rage that caused it to throw back its head and vent a primeval roar that set coyotes to howling for miles around. The cycle had been broken. It would always be as it was. Further growth was impossible.

Suddenly the creature wanted to smash, to

destroy, to kill, to vent its rage in the only way it knew. It spun, seeking more humans, and beheld yet another machine speeding toward it, this one with flashing lights on top and a wail like a banshee's. Talons wide, teeth bared, it rushed to meet the vehicle.

Travis Sinclair had arrived on the scene in time to witness Victor Richards's death. Switching on the sirens and overheads, he drove toward the beast in the faint hope the racket would drive the monster off, so he could look for Ben and Nadine. When he saw the creature start toward him, he punched the brakes and brought the patrol car to a sliding stop. He knew he couldn't stop the huge predator on his own, and he had no intention of sacrificing himself in the line of duty.

Travis threw the car into reverse, backed onto a grave, and spun his tires as he headed for the gate. He raised the microphone to call for backup, then glanced into the rearview mirror. The creature was overtaking the cruiser with astonishing speed. Already it was less than 20 feet away.

The car leaped forward, the speedometer climbing. Travis drew his revolver, his eyes flicking between the road and the mirror. He saw the creature rear large against the night and its arm whip out to grab the rear fender. It missed and fell a few yards behind, but not for long.

Travis was aghast when the monster took a few long strides and jumped onto the trunk. Its claws sank into the metal, anchoring it while it edged toward the rear window. Twisting, Travis snapped off a shot. The slug smashed the glass to bits, but didn't slow the nightmare.

His fright rising, Travis gripped the wheel with both hands and worked it back and forth, swinging the car from side to side, deliberately fishtailing in order to dislodge his unwanted passenger. One of the monster's hands came loose and for a moment it hung on by one arm. Travis wrenched the wheel again, expecting to see the creature go flying. Instead, its arm muscles bunched and it dug both feet into the trunk, steadying itself so it could reach with the free hand and rip into the roof.

Shifting, Travis saw those wicked claws shear through the metal above the shattered window. He turned the wheel a few more times without result. Thumps sounded overhead as the monster took roost above him. There was a metallic rending noise and the roof began to peel back like the skin of an orange. A bestial face materialized, radiating raw hatred.

Travis pointed the revolver upward and squeezed the trigger. He heard a click. Quickly he squeezed again, then again. After the third click he remembered that he had neglected to reload after shooting the cow. He had been lazy just once too often.

The three who were one ripped off a large section of the roof and hurled it into the night. It cocked its head, glaring at the obese human who gaped at it in dismay. It needed sustenance but its rage would not be denied. With a hiss, it swooped down, its claws closing on the upturned head and slicing through the skull as sharp knives would slice a melon. The human's strangled wail was cut short and the heavy body went into convulsions.

There was a thump as the patrol car veered from the road. The creature looked and saw it barreling toward a mausoleum. It leaped clear with mere moments to spare. The jarring crash flattened the front end and drove the steering column through the prey's chest.

The three who were one advanced on the car to salvage the human for feasting. It was reaching for the crumpled door when from the front end spewed a spray of scalding green liquid. The creature thought nothing of it since the fluid had a revolting sugary odor. Large drops rained down, and it discovered the hard way that the liquid contained the one substance it dreaded.

Excruciating anguish tore at the creature as the water ate into its body, just as acid would eat through human flesh. Puffs of putrid smoke spurted into the air. Its skin began to deteriorate, shedding small amounts of its essence. Spray landed on its shoulders as it turned to flee. Some struck its face, hitting one eye. Half the world promptly went black. The creature ran, covering its ravaged orb. In its haste, it stumbled and collided with a tomb. Once clear of the spray, it fell to its knees and tried to shut its sentience to the terrible agony.

Unknown to the creature, others eyes were watching. Fred Larkin had the crossbow pressed to his shoulder, a bolt ready to fly. But he didn't fire. He stared at the alien, then at the wrecked patrol car. A crafty grin curled his lips and he shuffled toward the vehicle, limping because of his fractured left leg. The pain was as nothing compared with that caused by his broken ribs. He ignored both.

Larkin was going to slay the alien if it was the last thing he ever did. No animal, even one from another world, was going to get the better of him and go on living. The creature had made a mistake in not making sure Larkin was dead, and it would pay for the oversight.

Puddles of antifreeze lay near Travis's car. Larkin removed the arrow from the groove, grit his teeth so he could stoop without crying out, and rolled the shaft in one of them. He quickly took several others from the quiver and did the same. After replacing all but the first one, he loaded it on the bow.

The monster had risen and was moving off toward the largest mausoleum in the graveyard. It walked stiffly, its movements disjointed, the tiny lights that danced around it resembling a swarm of fireflies.

Larkin had a clear shot, but wanted better. He stalked the creature, availing himself of the cover the mausoleums offered. The thing was in so much distress, it never noticed him. They came to a gap in the tombs and the creature halted. Larkin had waited long enough. He hobbled into the open, elevated the crossbow, and fired.

Never had the three who were one felt such exquisite pain as it did when the bolt pierced the nape of its neck. It stiffened and went into a quaking fit, as would an animal being electrocuted.

"Got you, bastard!" Larkin cried, loading rapidly. He wasn't going to give the shafts time to dry off. At last he knew the creature's weakness, and like any good hunter, he was exploiting it. His next shaft caught the creature low in the back.

A searing, red-hot poker ripped through the creature. The impact made it arch its spine. It turned, seeking the cause of its suffering, and beheld one of the humans it had thought dead. Usually when the creature hit a mortal, that mortal went down and stayed down. This one was different. This one was more of a challenge than it had counted on.

Fred Larkin pulled back the string, lifted the bow, and selected another wet arrow. The creature started in his direction but he wasn't worried. He had plenty of bolts. His sole regret was that no one else was there to witness his triumph.

Actually, others were watching.

To the west, huddled at the base of a crypt wall, were Jimmy and Manda. They had been picking their way back to the street when Jimmy spotted the monster coming toward them and pulled Manda into the darkest patch he could find.

When the man with the bow appeared, Jimmy thought him insane. As the creature took a third arrow in the stomach and toppled to its knees, however, he wanted to yell for the man to keep on shooting until the creature was dead. But he knew better.

Manda saw the monster go down and went to squeal in delight. Jimmy noticed and thrust his hand over her mouth in time to stifle the outcry. "Not yet," he said. "Not until it's dead."

To the east, Ben and Nadine also watched the brutal tableau unfold. They had been wending a course among the headstones when they'd spied Victor's sports car and run to intercept it. After Victor crashed, they had kept on going and soon observed the police car arrive.

Side by side they sprinted toward the car, only to see Travis meet his grisly end. Now they were at the edge of the asphalt, both vibrant with hope as the wounded poacher did battle with the massive beast that shouldn't exist, yet did.

Larkin took several shambling steps. The creature looked as if it were groveling, its claws biting into the ground as it squirmed and trembled. "There was never any doubt which of us would live and which would die," he said, aiming. "But I've got to admit that you're one tough mother. I just hope to hell you don't go up in smoke so I can skin you and mount you in my living room."

The creature heard the words through a shifting veil of crackling distortion. Its vital essence had been depleted almost to the point where it would be unable to maintain its corporeal form. Unless it dispatched the human immediately, it would die.

Fred Larkin had the monster dead in his sights. A tap of the finger was all it would take. He paused, treasuring the moment, and said, "Good-bye, alien."

Like a rattler unwinding, the creature came up off the ground and struck, its blow delivered with all the precision and power it could muster. Its claws caught the poacher flush at the bottom of his throat and decapitated him as neatly as if he were on a guillotine. Larkin's head sailed to the right, spurting blood, while his body did a graceful pirouette and lay limply, the bow resting on his chest.

In a pique of fury, the three who were one stepped to Larkin's body and stomped him to a gory pulp. Stepping back, it looked down at itself and was shocked by the amount of skin that had dissolved. It needed to replenish itself swiftly. To do that, it needed to feast, not once but several times. Straightening, the creature reached out into the darkness with its senses and located four humans close by. Two young ones were much nearer than the other pair, so it whirled and made for them.

Manda screamed. She was yanked to her feet by Jimmy, who pulled her to the south. Her eyes lingered on the monster, which strode after them with long, measured strides. Choking back her terror, she worked at keeping pace with Jimmy.

Over by the road, Nadine rose partway and said softly, "Oh, God! It's after a pair of kids!"

Ben stood and hefted the useless Magnum. He might as well throw it as shoot it for all the good it did them. "There's nothing we can do," he said, thinking of Nadine's safety. "If we try to help them, it might nail us."

"We have to do something," Nadine said. "We can't just stand here while they're torn to pieces."

She was right, and Ben knew it. He squeezed her hand and said, "I have an idea I can try, but only if you give me your word that you'll stay right here. I can't help them and protect you at the same time."

Nadine glanced at the fleeing teens. She would rather be by Ben's side but those kids had to come first. "I promise. Do what you can."

Ben shoved the gun into her hands and jogged off before she changed her mind or caught on to his lie. He had no plan. He was winging it, with no idea how to stop the monster. Then he thought of the crossbow and of the bolts he had seen Larkin dip in the antifreeze. Slanting to corpse, he was upset to find the bow had been twisted into so much scrap. The quiver had also been trod to bits but miraculously two of the shafts were undamaged. He scooped them up and gave chase.

The moment Nadine saw him running southward, she jogged after him. Promise or no promise, she would stick close to him, come what might.

Up ahead, Jimmy heard Manda's breath rasp in her throat and guessed she was becoming winded. Thankfully the monster was not moving as fast as before and hadn't gained on them.

Jimmy estimated there were only 20 or 30 graves between them and the gate. He was at a loss to know what to do once they got there. Out in the open, exposed and vulnerable, they would be slain in no time.

The three who were one was rationing its remaining strength. It calculated that at its rate of travel it would overtake the young humans in under two minutes. Then it would feed on both, and all would be well.

Ben was running as he had never ran before. He was closing swiftly on the monster, which qualified as suicide by any standard. How could he hope to stop it with two small arrows? he asked himself over and over.

Nadine stayed far enough back so that her man wouldn't see her. She was ready to leap to his aid if need be, although she stood as much of a prayer against the creature as a mouse against a mountain lion.

A tense minute elapsed, the five figures moving across the cemetery grounds in somber silence.

It was Ben who felt the initial drops of cold rain. He glanced at the overcast sky and more splattered on his face. Remembering the anti-freeze, he concentrated on the monster.

So intent was the creature on catching its quarry that it did not awaken to the new peril until seconds later when a steady drizzle began. Instantly it halted in baffled outrage. In its thirst for nectar it had forgotten about the oncoming storm. It must find shelter or the acidic scorching of its form would annihilate it.

Turning, the creature flew toward the cocoon. The sanctuary was its only hope. It had not gone far when it sensed another human in front of it, a male whose nectar was critical to its survival. Snatching him would only take a few moments; then it could feed at its leisure in the tomb.

The drizzle prevented Ben from realizing the monster had turned toward him until it was too late to flee. Suddenly it was just there, its body shimmering and emitting pinpoints of light as if it were a huge Fourth of July sparkler. The creature grabbed for him. Ben skipped to the side and stabbed with an arrow. The barbed tip, soaked by the rain, bit deep into the thing's hand.

The creature jerked back, then roared. To be so close to safety and to have this weakling of a human oppose it was more than the creature could stand. It tried to employ its sting, but was too weak. Whipping forward, it lunged and grabbed the human around the waist with both hands. It lifted the struggling male into the air and started toward the Richards mausoleum.

Ben feared he would be torn into pieces at any second. He was being held a few feet from the monster's face and could see a ragged socket where one eye had been. The sight was an inspiration. Ben flung back both arms, then drove the two dripping arrows into the creature's good eye.

It was if a lightning bolt cleaved the monster from head to toe. It went rigid, its mouth agape, but no sound came out. Its essence poured from the new wound, rendering it too weak to hold Ben, who fell to the grass and rolled aside. The creature attempted to walk, took a faltering step, and sank to one knee.

The drizzle turned into a downpour. Ben heard drops smacking loudly onto the tombs, the grass, and the monster. It raised its arms skyward in seeming mute appeal. Or was the gesture an act of final defiance? Ben wondered. The motion was wasted as the rain cascaded down in an unrelenting tempest. The balls of light that swarmed around the creature were being extinguished, one after the other. The creature itself was dissolving, collapsing in upon itself as its skin melted away.

Ben shook his head to clear water from his eyes. He had to move forward to see the creature clearly. Its head was half gone, its chest riddled with blank cavities the size of basketballs. One arm was missing from the elbow out. Its feet were also missing.

Suddenly the creature turned toward Ben, extended its remaining arm, and lurched at him. He threw himself backward and the monster's claws swished past his face. The thing fell flat, twitched, and was still.

How long Ben stood there, he could never say. He watched the rain eat away at the Brain Eater of Cemetery Ridge until there was not so much as a smudge to mark the spot where it had dissolved. When, at length, the creature was gone, he looked up into the sky and gave silent thanks.

A figure moved among the tombs and Ben tensed, dreading another nightmare. Nadine appeared, flung herself into his arms, and whispered in his ear, "I saw it. Oh, God! What was it?"

"We'll probably never know," Ben said. The warm pressure of her body on his and the moist fragrance of her hair were like a tonic for his soul. He inhaled deeply, happy to be alive, happier that she was alive and that the two of them would share the future together.

Ben took her hand and looked about for shelter from the rain. He spotted an open mausoleum and drew her toward it. The interior was pitch-black. Stopping just inside the entrance, he held her close. "I'd like you to come back to Portland with me."

Nadine swung around. "Why, Mr. Shields, is that an official proposal?" she asked impishly.

"I guess it is."

"That's what I like about you. You're always so decisive." Nadine laughed and hugged him again.

"So what's the answer?"

"Yes! Yes! A thousand times, yes!" Nadine was giddy with joy until she thought about the ordeal they had just been through. "But first things first. What about tonight? What do we tell the police when they question us?"

"We know nothing."

"You can't be serious?"

"Never more so." Ben sighed. "Think about it. There's no real proof the monster ever existed. Seaver saw it, but he has no proof. So the state and federal authorities would never believe us, not in a million years. All they'd do is pester us with questions for days on end, pry into every aspect of our personal lives, and treat us like loons the whole time." He kissed her cheek. "Hell, even my own editor wouldn't believe this happened. If we want to get on with our lives as soon as possible, we tell them that we think the animal we ran up against was a bear and let it go at that. If those kids are smart, they'll do the same."

"I suppose you're right," Nadine said, bothered by the thought of lying.

"Let's catch up with those two kids," Ben said. "If we all compare notes we can have our stories down pat for later on." He tugged on her arm. "Can you stand a little more rain?"

"I'm already soaked. So lead on, handsome," Nadine said, chuckling. She started to follow him, then drew up, staring in surprise at the middle of the tomb.

"What is it?" Ben asked.

"Nothing, I guess," Nadine said, shrugging. "My eyes must be playing tricks on me. For a second there I thought I saw one of those balls of light."

Together they ran out into the night.

Don't miss these gripping tales of
HALLOWEEN TERROR

Hell-O-Ween by David Robbins. On Halloween night, two high school buddies decide to play a joke on the class brain, intending only to scare him to death...but their prank goes awry and one of their friends ends up dead, her body ripped to pieces. Soon seven teenagers are frantically fighting to save themselves from unthinkably gruesome ends.
_3335-6 $4.50 US/$5.50 CAN

Pranks by Dennis J. Higman. It is Halloween night and the kids of Puget Sound are dressed to kill. All they want is a little harmless fun—a little revenge against the uptight citizens who look down on them. But as it grows darker, their pranks turn meaner and nastier. Driven by mindless bloodlust, the children go on a rampage of death and destruction. Murder becomes their favorite trick, and their victims' only treat is to die...
_3521-9 $4.50 US/$5.50 CAN

Don't Miss These Novels of Bone-chilling Horror from Leisure Books!

The Lake by R. Karl Largent. From out of the murky depths rises a horror born of a technological disaster—a terrifying force that defies the laws of nature and threatens mankind. To save the environment, it has to be controlled. To save the town, it has to be destroyed.

_3455-7 $4.50 US/$5.50 CAN

Borderland by S. K. Epperson. Not much has changed in remote Denke, Kansas, since the pioneer days. For over one hundred years, the citizens of Denke have worked far outside the laws of man and nature, hunting down strangers, stealing their money and their lives. But the time has come at last when every one of them will pay for their unspeakable crimes....

_3435-2 $4.50 US/$5.50 CAN

Madeleine by Bernard Taylor. To all appearances, Madeleine and Tess are identical in every way. But beneath Madeleine's beauty, her soul is possessed by a dark nature. Slowly, relentlessly, she turns her sister's happy life into a horrifying nightmare, pushing Tess to the very edge of sanity, waiting for the day she can claim Tess's life for her own.

_3404-2 $4.50 US/$5.50 CAN

CHARMED LIFE

By Bernard Taylor

Bestselling Author of *Mother's Boys*

"Move over, Stephen King!" —*New York Daily News*

Time and again, Guy Holman eludes death. No disease or disaster seems capable of killing him; no injury can do him mortal harm. But for all his good fortune, he loses everyone he has ever loved. Then a young woman who bears an eerie resemblance to his dead wife appears, and he thinks his luck has changed. But unknown to Holman, he is the innocent pawn in an age-old battle between the forces of good and evil. Blessed by some miracle or damned by some horror, Holman has the power to change the destiny of the world—the power to decimate or spare the souls of untold millions—the power that can only be realized by saving or destroying his charmed life.

_3561-8 $4.50